Aloha Betrayed

A *Murder, She Wrote* Mystery

Aloha Betrayed

A *Murder, She Wrote* Mystery

A NOVEL BY
JESSICA FLETCHER & DONALD BAIN

Based on the Universal Television series created by
Peter S. Fischer, Richard Levinson & William Link

AN OBSIDIAN MYSTERY

OBSIDIAN
Published by the Penguin Group
Penguin Group (USA) LLC, 375 Hudson Street,
New York, New York 10014

USA | Canada | UK | Ireland | Australia | New Zealand | India | South Africa | China
penguin.com
A Penguin Random House Company

First published by Obsidian, an imprint of New American Library,
a division of Penguin Group (USA) LLC

First Printing, April 2014

LIBRARY OF CONGRESS CATALOGING-IN-PUBLICATION DATA:

Fletcher, Jessica.
Aloha betrayed: a Murder, she wrote mystery: a novel/by Jessica Fletcher, Donald Bain.
pages cm
"Based on the Universal Television series created by Peter S. Fischer,
Richard Levinson & William Link."
ISBN 978-0-451-46654-9 (hardback)
1. Fletcher, Jessica—Fiction. 2. Women novelists—Fiction. I. Bain, Donald, author.
II. Murder, she wrote (Television program) III. Title.
PS3552.A376A68 2014
813'.54—dc23   2013043479

Printed in the United States of America
1 3 5 7 9 10 8 6 4 2

Set in Minion

ACKNOWLEDGMENTS

Many people graciously provided us with insight into the unique and lovely Hawaiian island of Maui while we were researching *Aloha Betrayed*, and we're grateful to all of them. Becoming conversant in the Hawaiian language wasn't easy; thank you to those who patiently guided us through it.

Officer Edith Quintero, the community relations officer for the Maui Police Department, gave us considerable time and shared her expertise about how the Maui PD operates. If we've taken some liberties with her information, we apologize in advance.

Bill Countryman, cluster general manager of the stunning Wailea Beach Marriott Resort and Spa, not only manages a first-rate resort on Maui; he went out of his way to make our research trip there fruitful and pleasant. Thank you, Bill. And thanks to Bill's delightful assistant, Keo.

John Finnegan, former New York City detective, now working loss prevention at the Wailea Beach Marriott Resort and Spa, introduced us to the legendary Mike Casicas, former Maui detective, who inspired us to create Mike Kane and who shared a wealth of information about his policing experience on Maui. As both detectives pointed out, there are virtually no murders on the island—although now that Jessica has visited, a dead body is sure to turn up.

Acknowledgments

And a final shout-out to all the warm and wonderful people we met while on Maui. We thank them all and ask their forbearance for any errors. Just a note: We have taken artistic liberties with parts of Maui geography for the sake of the story, but we promise the island truly is a paradise, and we departed immersed in the "aloha spirit."

Aloha Betrayed

A Murder, She Wrote Mystery

Chapter One

Aloha—Hawaiian Greeting That Can Mean "Hello"

"Look at the enemy. It looks beautiful, doesn't it? But it, like the shiny red apple handed to Snow White, is poisonous. Touch the sap and it will burn you. Ingest it and its cardiac glycosides will impede your heart function. Breathe in the powdery fumes of the dry, dead vine and it will induce a violent cough. Yet some gardeners still insist on planting *Cryptostegia grandiflora* as an ornamental."

Mala Kapule tapped a key on her laptop and the image of the flower projected on the wall disappeared. "So this is your assignment for the weekend. Take your camera, your cell phone, your tablet, and look into your neighbors' yards. Don't tell them I said to."

I laughed along with the rest of class.

"You're looking for *Cryptostegia grandiflora*, also known as the Malay rubber vine. Look for pink buds and white flowers with a pink throat. Look for the glossy leaves set opposite each other on the stem. But do not touch it! Just fill out the report for the Maui Invasive Species Committee, the same as you did for the Madagascan ragwort or fireweed. See the handout for more instructions."

A buzzer sounded and Mala's students gathered their papers and filed out of the room. One tall young man lingered near her desk, perhaps hoping for a moment of private attention. He stooped over so that his head was closer to hers.

"Not now, Dale," I heard her say. "We can discuss it on Monday."

Dale scowled at her. "You're always putting me off."

"Perhaps you should think about why that is," his young professor replied, stuffing her briefcase with the extra handouts left on her desk. "Now, please excuse me."

She aimed a wide smile in my direction and came forward with her right arm extended. "Mrs. Fletcher, I'd know you anywhere. What a surprise to see you here. I heard you were coming, but I didn't expect you to slip into the back of my classroom." She pumped my hand.

"I hope I didn't disturb the lesson," I said, returning her smile.

"Not at all. How is Dr. Hazlitt? Charming as ever?"

"He would blush to hear you say that," I replied.

Mala chuckled. "Uncle Barrett said that Seth Hazlitt was the crabbiest fellow in their class at medical school, but also the best diagnostician."

"I don't doubt it," I said, "about being a superb diagnostician. But Seth really isn't crabby. He just doesn't suffer fools easily."

"Uncle Barrett was the same way."

"I was sorry to hear about your uncle," I said.

Mala's expression turned wistful. "He was a marvelous man. I think I disappointed him in choosing botany over medicine, but he always graciously included me when he boasted about the *scientists* in the family."

"As well he should. I understand that you're in line for chair of the department."

"That was Uncle Barrett's idea, not mine." Mala walked with me down the hallway of the one-story building. "It's never going to happen. Even forgetting my political views— which they won't—there's a lot of competition in the college's horticultural department. The landscaping specialists have an edge. My specialty, invasive species, doesn't have the snob appeal of aquaponics and xeriscaping."

"I'll take your word for it," I said through a laugh, "but you're speaking a different language."

"Aquaponics is a fancy term for a kind of agriculture that grows fish and plants in the same pond, and xeriscaping is simply landscaping with drought-resistant plants," she said, pulling a pair of sunglasses from her handbag and putting them on. "The climate on Maui is variable depending upon where you are on the island. It's a challenge for landscapers to match plants to the conditions, which gives them a chance to show off."

"But such variety must be rewarding for botanists, too." We pushed through the doors to the outside, where I also donned sunglasses.

"There's certainly a lot to keep us busy," she replied. "Do you have time for a cup of coffee? They're featuring Kona at the café today."

"I'd love it."

I had arrived in Hawaii the day before, a guest of the Maui Police Department, to teach a class on community involvement in criminal investigations. My co-teacher was a retired Maui detective and local legend. Since it is the rare government that will pay for a mystery writer's opinion, my expenses had been defrayed by a foundation dedicated to bringing in speakers "to broaden the vision of police recruits and encourage the application of creative thinking to solving crime." At least that's what the invitation letter had stated as its goal.

I was hesitant at first, not certain what I could contribute to the education of future police officers since the field had changed so drastically with the integration of technology into forensics. Besides, it had been a good many years since I'd taught criminology in Manhattan. But Seth Hazlitt, my dear friend and Cabot Cove's favorite physician, had convinced me to accept.

"Anyone wants to give me a free trip to Hawaii, I'd be a fool not to take it," he'd said with the lack of subtlety for which he's renowned.

Since I was between books, and with the added incentive of Seth's insistence that I look up his medical school buddy, I had accepted the challenge to conduct a class on community involvement in police investigations. Unfortunately, Barrett Kapule, Mala's uncle and Seth's old friend, had died the month before my arrival, and Seth had asked me to deliver a condolence letter he'd written to the family. I hadn't done it yet, wanting to wait for the appropriate time.

Mala and I entered the bustling campus café and found an unoccupied table. She insisted on getting the coffee and I gratefully accepted. The ten-and-a-half-hour trip to Honolulu from New York's John F. Kennedy Airport was catching up to me, not counting the travel time it had taken me to get to New York from my home in Cabot Cove, Maine, on one end of the trip and the connecting flight to Maui from the Hawaiian capital on the other. Although I'd slept well the night I arrived, my body wasn't certain what time zone it was in, nor was my brain.

"Is this your first trip to Hawaii?" Mala asked when she'd returned to our table carrying a tray with two mugs.

"Ooh, that smells wonderful," I said, taking one of them. "I've been to Hawaii a couple of times, but not in recent years. The last time, I was returning to the States from a book tour in Japan and stopped off in Honolulu for a vacation. This time, it's a working trip, but I'm looking forward to exploring the island between classes. May I count on you for suggestions of special places to see?"

Mala laughed. "Try to stop me. There are so many beautiful and interesting things to see here. Do you have a car?"

I smiled at her over the rim of my mug. "I'm afraid I don't drive."

"Really?"

"I've never gotten around to it, which never fails to amuse my friends back home. I do have a pilot's license, though, but that won't do me much good."

"Not driving may prove a little tricky, but I'm sure we can fix you up with some form of transportation. I have a cousin who drives a cab."

"I can ride a bike," I said. "In fact, I biked over here from the resort where I'm staying."

She looked me up and down.

"What is it?"

"I don't want to offend you."

"How can you offend me?"

"There is a famous bike excursion, but it's not for the faint of heart."

"I'm listening."

"Tour companies host a sunrise trip up the Haleakala volcano and offer bicycles to those brave enough to ride down. It's pretty harrowing biking on those twisting roads. Think you might be up for that?"

I took a sip of the aromatic coffee and stifled a yawn. "Not today or tomorrow," I said with a wink, "but maybe later in the week."

Mala's silvery laugh had several students turning to see to whom it belonged.

She was a beautiful woman with thick black hair pulled back into a low ponytail and deep brown eyes that tilted up when she smiled, which was often. I estimated her to be in her mid-thirties, but with her smooth skin and delicate build, she could have passed for a student instead of a teacher. It was her manner, however, that gave her age away. She held herself confidently and ignored the appreciative glances sent her way. She assumed that people were interested in her because of what she had to say rather than her looks, which only enhanced her attraction. To be fair to her admirers, perhaps it was a little bit of both.

Seth had shown me some of Barrett's e-mail messages to

him extolling Mala's intelligence and the contributions she made, not only to the college but also to the community, through her activism on the ecological front. While she'd rattled a few commercial cages—nurseries that insisted on selling plants she considered a threat to the native vegetation— her latest project, and the one that raised the most controversy, was her opposition to a new telescope being built atop Haleakala.

With the University of Hawaii firmly in the "pro" column for the telescope, Mala had offended the powers that be by siding with a group of Hawaiians who argued that the construction not only jeopardized the ecological balance of the mountain, but also threatened to have a devastating impact on the dormant volcano, a *wahi pana*, or sacred site, a cultural touchstone for the Hawaiian people. Mala's contrary stance notwithstanding, her uncle Barrett was certain the university would recognize and reward her brilliance.

"Speaking of Haleakala," I said, "is that controversial telescope project still going forward?"

"Unfortunately, yes. I have a meeting next week on what our next steps should be. What do you know about it?"

"Not very much, only what your uncle Barrett passed along to Seth Hazlitt."

"Are you interested? Maybe you'd like to join us," she said eagerly. "We can always use an extra voice, especially one as articulate as yours."

"It's nice of you to say, but I don't see what help I could provide, not being knowledgeable about the topic or its history. You certainly wouldn't want this voice to say the wrong thing."

"No, I wouldn't. But somehow I don't think you would expound about a subject you don't know. You're not opposed to the idea of learning more about it, are you?"

"No, of course not. I'm always interested in new things."

"I hope you won't be sorry you said that," Mala said, laughing as she pulled her briefcase back into her lap. "I get furious e-mails from people who object to what I'm doing. Next thing you know, there'll be death threats."

"Oh, my, is it as bad as that?"

"I'm afraid so. It's an emotional issue." She opened a side pocket and withdrew a large envelope containing a sheaf of papers. "This is your basic course in Haleakala's Science City." She handed me the envelope. "If nothing else, it should help you get to sleep at night."

"I don't think getting to sleep is going to be a problem," I said. "Staying awake is another matter altogether."

"When you're well rested," Mala said, "I'll give you a list of things you might like to do while you're here, other than tag along with me to meetings. You certainly want to attend a luau."

"I'm going to one tonight."

"In Wailea?"

"I believe so."

"Wonderful! Another cousin is one of the dancers. Perhaps I'll see you there. It depends on the outcome of my next meeting." She looked at her watch.

"Am I holding you up?"

"Not at all. I have a little time yet, but if I get there early, I may be able to sneak in ahead of the appointment before mine. My competition for the department chair wants to meet with me." She made a face. "Dreadful man. It should be interesting."

We left the café and walked back toward the horticulture building.

"Where will you be teaching?" Mala asked.

"The college has given us a classroom in one of the buildings near the police station," I replied. "We start tomorrow. I stopped there today to introduce myself to the other instructor who'll be teaching with me."

"Oh, and who is that?"

"Detective Mike Kane. When I told him I was going to look for your class, he said he'd heard great things about you. Do you know his name?"

"Of course," Mala said with a grin. "It's a small island. Everyone knows everyone."

"How is that possible? There must be more than a hundred thousand people living here, not counting the tourists."

"I think it's closer to a hundred fifty thousand now," she said. "And maybe saying everyone knows everyone is a bit of an exaggeration. We don't know the seasonal workers, of course. Not many of the kids who come to work in hotels and restaurants stay long enough or interact with the locals enough to become familiar. And I couldn't say we know all the retirees who've decided to live out the rest of their lives on our golf courses. But for those of us whose families have been here for generations, we all know or at least know *of* each other."

"Detective Kane is a Native Hawaiian?"

"We don't use the word 'native.' His father was, or at least has Hawaiian in his background, but Mike is also a *kahuna*, a big shot. I don't know how many times he's been written up in the local paper. But I thought he was retired."

"He's retired from the police department," I said. "Now he works in hotel security, but he calls it something else."

"Loss prevention," she said, chuckling and shaking her head. "The hotels in the islands don't want you to think there's any crime here, so they renamed their security offices. It's still the place you go to report if anything's missing."

"Yes, that's the term. But I understand he also consults for the police department."

"I'm sure he does. He's famous. Probably every young police officer with a puzzling case shows up on his doorstep looking for advice."

"Well, now they'll get a chance to pick his brain in a formal setting," I said. "I'm looking forward to what I can learn from him as well."

"And he must be thrilled to have a famous writer to work with."

We had stopped outside an impressive concrete and steel building with a turquoise roof, on top of which were solar panels and small white wind turbines rotating in the breeze. A sign outside said 'IKE LE'A, which I later learned means "to see clearly."

"This is the new science building," Mala said. "My appointment is in here." She smiled softly. "I'm so happy you're here. Uncle Barrett would have loved to meet you."

"And I would have loved to meet him, too."

She sighed. "I hope I get to see you later."

"Let's plan on it."

"Well, the Wailea luau draws several hundred people. It may be hard to locate one person in that crowd."

"You look for me and I'll look for you," I said. "I'm sure we'll find each other."

But I was wrong.

Chapter Two

A'a i Ka Hula; Waiho Ka Hilahila i Ka Hale—
Dare to Dance; Leave Shyness at Home

"So, Mrs. Fletcher, how do you like Maui?"

"Leave her alone, Abbott. For heaven's sake. She just got here."

"I know that, Honi, but it doesn't take that long to form an opinion."

"From the little I've seen, Professor Luzon, it's beautiful," I said while attempting to spoon a Molokai sweet potato onto my plate. The line of diners at the luau curled across the grass, but it moved quickly. Two long buffet tables with both sides offering the same dishes split the line into four columns. I stepped forward to a large stainless chafing dish that held slices of the roast pig that had been disinterred to great fanfare moments earlier. It had been cooked in an underground oven, covered with soil, simulating the methods used by early Polynesians who populated the Hawaiian Islands.

"You must try the salad. The greens are grown right here on Maui, in Kula," Honi said.

Professor Luzon's wife had been advising me all along the buffet line, and my plate now held more food than I could possibly eat.

"Did you take some poi?" she asked.

I smiled at her latest suggestion, stepped out of the line, and said, "It all looks wonderful, but I want to leave a little room for dessert. I'll see you back at the table."

It was a beautiful, warm night with the sun sinking into the cloudless horizon. Round tables covered in linens that matched the turquoise waters dotted the grassy field, which overlooked the ocean. Earlier in the evening when I arrived, I had been seated at a table directly in front of the stage. My tablemates included the Luzons, whom I estimated to be in their mid-forties. They were accompanied by a young woman named Grace. Across from me was an older couple from Michigan, Bob and Elaine Lowell, celebrating their anniversary; and next to them was a pair of stylish ladies from Santa Barbara, Helen and Marian, whose husbands had declined to attend the luau, preferring to stay on the golf course until the last possible moment and then celebrate their game in the clubhouse bar. The two seats designated for them were left empty.

"It's nice that you brought your daughter with you," Elaine Lowell said to Honi. "At that age, our daughter never wanted to be seen with us." She chuckled.

"We don't have any children," Honi said.

"Oh, my mistake, but she looks so much like you."

"Grace is Abbott's teaching assistant. She's a graduate student in environmental science."

"I can speak for myself, Mrs. Luzon."

"Well, then, why don't you, *dear*?"

"I'm Grace Latimer. Abbott and I are working together on a sustainable food production project at Maui College as part of my master's requirements."

"Isn't that what I just said?" Honi asked.

"Honi, that's enough," her husband muttered.

I wondered whether Mrs. Luzon was irritated that Grace called the professor by his first name while maintaining a formal distance from his wife. It was clear they weren't on the best of terms.

"We're golf widows tonight," Marian said, smiling at her companion, "but we're going to have a great time, aren't we, Helen?" She took in the others at the table. "We love Maui. This is our fourth luau. It's always a great show."

"Marian is hoping one of the sexy male dancers chooses her to come up onstage," Helen said. "She's been practicing her hula."

"I have not," Marian said, fanning her red face with her hat.

"Lucky us, huh, Abbott?" Bob Lowell commented.

"I beg your pardon," Luzon replied, peering over the half-glasses he'd put on to read a brochure.

"We're surrounded by a bevy of lovely ladies. I like the male-to-female ratio at this table."

"Cut it out, Bob," his wife said, elbowing him. "You're going to make people uncomfortable."

"Why should anyone be uncomfortable? I'm just stating my appreciation for the beauty surrounding me." He grinned and winked at the golf widows. "And that includes my gorgeous wife here. I bet you'd never guess we've been married for fifty years."

"Oh, Bob!"

"And you're still smiling," Honi said with a tight smile herself, although it wasn't genuine.

"Congratulations," I said. "What a nice way to mark the occasion."

"I've always wanted to come to Hawaii," Elaine said. "It was on my bucket list." She stole a glance at her husband and lowered her voice. "Every time I brought it up, Bob would say, 'We'll come for our fiftieth anniversary.' I don't think he ever thought we'd make it, but we did. And here we are."

The musicians onstage began to play a Hawaiian tune and Elaine clapped her hands over her ears. Although our seats were considered a preferred location, they were uncomfortably close to the loudspeakers.

Bob stood and beckoned to Abbott Luzon. "The bar is open and we're taking orders, aren't we, Professor?" he shouted over the music. "So, ladies, what would you like?"

Luzon reluctantly got to his feet and pocketed his glasses. "I don't see how the two of us will be able to carry back all those drinks, Mr. Lowell."

"It's Bob, and if we have to, we can make a second trip."

"I'll help," Grace said, hopping up.

Honi rolled her eyes, but I was the only witness to her expression as the others delivered their drink orders to the men.

Bob Lowell wrapped an arm around Grace and pulled her close to him. "Atta girl," he said. "Come on, we'll get the drinks for everybody." He tried to give her a peck on the cheek but she squirmed away from him.

I rose and excused myself. "Thank you," I said, "but I think I'll take a little walk before dinner. I'm trying to find a friend. I'll pick up a drink on the way back."

Like the other ladies, I was wearing a lei of purple ginger flowers that had been draped around my neck when I arrived at the luau. I also had on a hat with a wide brim, having been cautioned that the glare could make facing the stage uncomfortable until the sun had set.

I wandered around perusing the booths of Hawaiian crafts that were set up on the perimeter of the field: wood carving, basket weaving, and the making of bark cloth, or *kapa*. A photographer had a station offering on-the-spot photos of the guests with the Pacific as a dramatic backdrop. Everywhere I walked, I kept an eye out for Mala Kapule, but as she had predicted, it was hard to locate one person in the crowd of several hundred.

I found a walkway behind the stage and ventured partway down the path, keeping track of the time so I wouldn't miss the start of the program, although the volume of the music onstage made it unlikely that I wouldn't be alerted.

The trail was a favorite of walkers, runners, and young couples with baby carriages, making for slow going. Even so, I was entranced by the pounding waves striking the rocky shore fifty feet or more below. Out to sea, boats were silhouetted against a clear sky as the sinking sun created a shimmering golden line on the horizon. Along the path, clumps of tourists paused, hands shading eyes that searched the foamy water around the rocks below.

"I see one," a little girl cried out.

I followed her gaze to catch a glimpse of the black-and-yellow head of a large sea turtle as it surfaced for a breath of air. It lifted a flipper toward the sky, its body washing against the sharp crags of hardened lava that formed the precipice and jutted into the water.

"They eat the vegetation that grows on those rocks," the child's father told her. He kept a hand on her shoulder. "Don't go any closer. See that sign? It says not to tread too near the edge."

"What does 'tread' mean?"

"It means you can't step over there where the ground is soft. If it caved in, you would fall down the cliff and into the water and drown."

"Don't frighten her," said a lady next to them, presumably the child's mother.

"I just want her to know the danger," he said as they moved on.

A woman's powerful voice announcing the beginning of the luau floated over the sound of the surf, and I retraced my steps back up the trail. She was explaining the history of the Hawaiian peoples and the significance of the celebration we were attending. I picked up a glass of punch at the bar and returned to my front-row table.

"Did you find your friend?" Elaine asked.

"No, but she'd said it would be difficult with so many people."

"Who were you looking for?" Honi asked.

"Mala Kapule. She's a botanist at the college. I'm sure that your husband knows her."

"I know her," Honi said before Abbott could respond. "But I don't see why she would be here. She must have seen dozens of luaus over the years."

"Her cousin is one of the dancers," I said, adding, "She wasn't definite about coming."

"Then I don't know why you wasted your time looking," Honi said tartly.

"Actually, I saw her," Grace said.

"You did?" I sat taller and scanned the crowd. "Where was she?"

"She was over by the tables in the back near the bar."

"Did you speak with her?"

"No. I didn't know you were looking for her. Anyway, we were busy juggling the drink orders, and she . . . well, she was having a serious conversation. I could tell she didn't want to be interrupted."

"Thanks for letting me know."

The woman onstage, whose voice had guided me back to the luau from my walk, took the microphone again and recited a prayer in Hawaiian. She was tall, her dark hair swept up in a chignon, with large white flowers pinned behind each ear. She wore a long sarong patterned with blue hibiscus blossoms. Conversation ceased as our attention was directed to the stage.

"Thank you, ladies and gentlemen. During dinner we will be serenading you with more music and hula dancing. And then after dinner, the wonderful journey of *Te Au Moana*, 'the ocean tide.' From all of us to all of you, *aloha* and welcome."

I tasted most of the dishes Honi insisted I try. I don't

know whether it was fatigue—according to my watch it was one in the morning in Cabot Cove—or simply the overabundance of food on my plate, but I had little appetite to finish.

"I'm going up for seconds," Bob Lowell announced.

"Oh, Bob!"

"Now, Elaine, I'm on vacation. How many times in a lifetime do we get to go to a luau?"

"I hope you won't be sorry later tonight," she said. "You know you have a delicate stomach."

I was surprised to hear there was anything delicate about Bob Lowell. He was a big man with a big voice, and a stomach to match. Elaine's last observation had been made to his back as he lumbered across the grass to the catering section, to return shortly with another full plate.

Later, once our dinners had been cleared—including Bob's second round—two bare-chested male dancers walked down the aisles blowing into conch-shell horns to mark the continuation of the performance. Our elegant narrator took the stage again.

"Tonight we unveil the story of Maui, the masterful and mischievous hero who became legend, and for whom our beloved island is named. Maui and his famed mother, Hina, begin this extraordinary journey."

Ukuleles, guitars, and drums joined the spoken word.

"When I was a young girl, my mother would tell me to gaze into the moon and I would see Hina making her billowing *kapa*, the precious cloth of our people. Folded into it are centuries of stories of Hawaii."

As she spoke, male dancers wearing *kapa* loincloths and shell pendants appeared, their bodies tattooed with patterns and images that I imagined were reflections of the Maui legends. They were joined by five women, each more striking than the last, wearing grass skirts and dancing the hula to traditional and very loud Hawaiian music.

"How do they move their hips like that?" Elaine asked her husband.

"I'd like to see you do that," Bob said. "Learn that dance and I'll get you one of those grass skirts."

"Oh, Bob!"

"There's a hula school in Lahaina, up the coast," Helen put in. "Marian and I took some lessons the last time we came. It's a lot harder than it looks."

"Helen practically threw her back out trying to get it right," Marian said.

"I did not."

"But I enjoyed myself," Marian added. "It's all in the hips. Your feet barely move."

The sky darkened and the insistent beat of the drums pulsed through my body. With a terrifying scream, one of the male dancers bounded onto the stage, waving a lance with flames blazing on either end. There was a flutter of wings and loud honking as birds rose into the dark sky behind the stage in response to the dancer's shriek.

"My goodness! What was that?" Elaine said, grabbing her husband's arm.

Grace leaned over. "Those are francolins," she said.

"What's a francolin?"

"They're birds that nest on the ground. He must have startled them."

"And they startled *me*," Elaine said, laughing.

Bob patted her hand.

The smell of burning oil reached our table as one of the dancers strode across the stage, lighting the tiki torches at each corner. Leaping into the air, he passed the pole between his legs and behind his back, then twirled it overhead. I marveled at how he managed not to ignite the dry grass of his costume and headdress.

The dancers appeared and disappeared in a dizzying array of colorful costume changes, the energetic acrobatics of the men alternating with the delicate movements of the women, slowly waving their graceful arms in contrast to the rapid undulation of their hips.

"Isn't she adorable?" Helen commented about a little Hawaiian girl who'd been called upon by the narrator to demonstrate her considerable skills.

"I might have been that good if I'd started at that age," Marian said.

"You're pretty good for a newcomer to the art," her friend told her.

"Have you ever danced the hula?" Marian asked Grace.

"Grace doesn't have time for such fripperies," Honi said, waving her glass in the air. "She's too busy keeping my husband working late at the laboratory."

Grace didn't respond to Honi, but I could see that it was an effort. She kept her eyes focused on Marian and shook her head. "I'm not very graceful, despite my name," she said with a small smile.

"She has other talents," Honi said.

"I'm getting another drink," Professor Luzon said, ducking away from the table.

"You might have asked if I wanted anything," his wife called after him.

"And do you?"

Honi waved her husband away with a disgusted look and stirred her drink with the straw.

The voice of the narrator rose above the music to explain the stories being told in dance.

"One day, Hina tells Maui to go catch *ulua*, the great fish, with the magical fishhook his grandfather gave him. 'But you and your brothers must not look back for any reason once the fish has taken the hook,' she says. Out at sea, the brothers feel a gigantic tug upon the canoe and paddle with all their strength into the waves. At that moment, a baling gourd floats alongside the canoe. The brothers pull it on board and it transforms into a beautiful woman. Excitedly, the brothers all look back at this wondrous sight, and the spell is broken. The fish is lost, but instead they have raised the islands of Hawaii from the sea."

"That's a neat trick," Bob said. "I only catch bass when I go fishing."

"Shh, Bob!" his wife said, poking him with her elbow.

Marian gave Bob a polite smile and returned her attention to the stage, pointing out one of the dancers to Helen. "That's the one we saw last time."

"How can you tell?" Helen asked. "He's wearing a mask."

"I remember his tattoo."

The narrator finished her tale. "Maui and the beautiful woman of the canoe fall in love. They are married and become ancestors to the Hawaiian people. This is the story of our people, guided by stars across the Pacific to make their homes on new islands and to begin new families. On a clear night you will see the constellation Scorpio. That is the magical fishhook that guided our ancient navigating ancestors to these shores. Ladies and gentlemen, *that* is the legend of Maui."

The audience broke into applause. I gathered my hat and shoulder bag in anticipation of the program's end, but Honi waved, shaking her head. "It's not over. There's at least another hour to go. They're just setting out dessert."

"I don't think I could eat another thing," I said, stifling a yawn.

"And we haven't had our chance to try the hula," Marian said. "That's the best part."

I relaxed back in my seat. The luau continued with more dancing and storytelling. Despite the volume of the music, the vibration of the drums, and the acrid scent of the tiki torches—or perhaps because of them—I felt myself nodding off. I straightened in my chair and looked around, hoping no one had noticed. I peered into my empty glass of punch. "Would you please excuse me? I'm going to get a cup of coffee. Would anyone else like one?" With no takers, I slipped from my seat and walked up the grassy aisle toward the booths that served as outdoor bars. Long tables held plates of cakes cut into small squares, and urns of coffee. I helped myself to a cup, walked farther up the field behind the bars, and turned to watch the performance, grateful to be at some distance from the loudspeakers. A cool breeze ruffled my hair and I breathed in the refreshing air.

"She's never going to give up. You know that, don't you?" an angry voice said off to my right.

I glanced over to see two men arguing in low tones. One of them was tall with an athletic build, the other older, softer, and with a shaved head.

"Did he try talking to her?" asked the taller man.

"It's too late for talking," the other replied. He was a beefy man in a colorful patterned shirt, shorts, and flip-flops, almost a Hawaiian uniform, judging by the attire of most of the men at the luau. "She'd better quit if she knows what's good for her. They're not going to put up with it anymore."

"She's not going to convince him to change his mind, even if she tries."

"If she scuttles this project, I swear he'll kill her."

They must have noticed me eavesdropping. The tall man glanced my way and drew his companion toward the path that circled the field.

I shrugged off the threatening talk and moved back toward the coffee table intent on a refill. I peered at my watch but couldn't see its face in the dark. The luau should be ending soon. It would be a forty-minute ride back to the resort before I could finally climb between the cool sheets of my bed. *Perhaps another cup of coffee isn't a good idea,* I told myself, adding, *Maybe you should have waited to get over jet lag before attending a luau.* I'd recently adopted a rule for myself: Never schedule anything important the night you arrive if you travel across time zones. Now I was thinking about extending that to two nights.

I returned to the table just as the narrator was describing the elements of a hula dance.

"We're going to send our boys and girls into the audience to select a few volunteers. Now, for those of you chosen by our dancers, please oblige them, for this is our custom. In a few moments you'll be joining us here onstage."

"Get ready, Elaine," Bob said. "They're going to want you to show off your dance moves for everyone."

"Oh, Bob!"

Elaine's husband obviously heard that plaint a lot. But it wasn't Elaine who was pulled from the table to demonstrate her hula skills. I felt a strong hand circle my wrist. "Come— you're going to be my partner," the dancer said.

"Oh, no," I said. "I'm not the right one."

"I'll do it," Marian called out.

"This is the *wahine* I have chosen," the dancer said, bowing before me. He tugged me behind him to the stage, where a small crowd of people were waiting to mount the stairs. "Don't worry," he whispered into my ear. "We'll teach you all you need to know."

We formed a long line on the stage, the lights effectively blinding us to the audience.

"Put your hands off to the side, bring your feet together, bend your knees, and smile," the narrator instructed, her voice reflecting her own wide smile. "Next, put your hands up in the air and make a big circle with your hips. As the music moves faster, make your hips move faster."

My expression must have been skeptical, but I was wide-awake now, wanting desperately not to make a fool of myself. My hula partner jumped in front of me and demonstrated the proper technique. My hands in the air, I swiveled my hips in an approximation of his moves, feeling the heat of embarrassment rise up my neck. I knew my face was scarlet.

"Hands to the side. Hands up. Turn in a circle. Aren't they wonderful, ladies and gentlemen? Let's have a big hand for all our hula dancers."

The narrator directed each couple to display their hula prowess and encouraged the spectators to vote for their favorites with their applause. I watched nervously as younger, suppler bodies than mine attempted the tricky feat, but when she pointed to me, I pasted a big grin on my face and swiveled my hips. I could imagine what the reaction would be if my friends in Cabot Cove heard about this escapade. "Jessica Fletcher dancing the hula? Never happened!"

But as my Irish grandmother used to say, *"May you dance as if no one's watching, sing as if no one's listening, and live every day as if it were your last."*

I gave my all to the hula.

Chapter Three

Ao No Hoi!—What a Terrible Thing!

Mike Kane was writing on the whiteboard when I entered the classroom the following morning an hour before our students were due to arrive. He was tall and broad in the way many Polynesian men are, with a face remarkably unlined for someone his age, which I estimated to be mid-fifties. He wore a white shirt with an embroidered placket tucked into baggy tan trousers, the cuffs of which puddled on his gray sneakers. A thick black band dangling from his neck held a pair of eyeglasses with clip-on sunglasses attached.

"Good morning," I said, putting my shoulder bag and notebook on the table next to where he'd set his briefcase. "Thanks for suggesting the luau. It was wonderful, although I must admit by the end of the evening, I was struggling to stave off jet lag."

He turned to greet me. "You couldn't have been too tired. I heard you came in first in the hula competition."

"My goodness, word gets around here quickly."

"You're on a small island," he said with a smile, although there was something in his eyes that stopped me.

"What's wrong?"

"I'm afraid I have some bad news to give you."

"Oh, dear. Has our class been canceled?"

"Nothing as simple as that. Please take a seat." He pulled out one of the chairs, held it for me, and sat opposite, taking one of my hands in both of his. His chin dipped down to his chest and he took a deep breath.

I felt the blood drain from my face, and a torrent of awful possibilities raced through my mind. What could have happened? Did he get a message from Cabot Cove? Had our sheriff been injured racing to a traffic accident or crime scene? Had there been a fire or a flood or a break-in? Would anyone even know where to reach me should some disaster occur? Had one of my friends taken ill, or worse? Seth was getting on in years. Although I cautioned him to slow down, he still insisted on keeping full-time office hours, not even counting how long he spent at the hospital visiting his patients every day. Had his heart given out? I prayed he was all right. Countless dire scenarios materialized as I waited for Mike Kane to elaborate.

"Jessica, I'm so sorry to have to tell you this."

"Yes?"

"You met Mala Kapule?"

"Yesterday," I said, slightly breathless. "I told you I was

going to stop by her class. We had coffee together afterward. I heard she was at the luau, too, although I didn't see her."

"Mala fell off a cliff on the south shore last night. The police think she was trying to climb down to where a specimen of a particular plant is growing in the rocks."

"Oh, dear. Was she terribly injured?" I asked, afraid to contemplate anything worse.

"She was badly battered by the rocks. She may have hit her head when she lost her balance. She fell in an especially difficult place for rescuers to get to. The tide is very rough on that stretch of shore. The waves come in one right after the other. There are boulders under the water that are jagged and sharp. By the time the authorities got to her, she was gone."

I let a soft moan escape my lips and felt tears start in my eyes, even though I'd known her so briefly. "So young," I whispered. "She was so young."

"Yes, but old enough to know not to go climbing in the dark of night, no matter how enticing the prize growing out of the rocks."

"Are you certain that's what she was doing?" I asked.

Mike shook his head. "That's what the police have presumed. They've labeled her death an accident."

"But you have doubts?" I let go of his hand and pulled a tissue from my pocket, dabbing at my eyes and regaining my composure. Now was not the time to get all weepy. A dozen students were about to arrive.

"Let's just say I'm reserving judgment."

"I don't know why I got so emotional on such short acquaintance," I said. "We'd barely met. I guess it's that I've been hearing about Mala for months. Her late uncle Barrett was a friend of a close friend of mine. She was so charming and sweet to me yesterday."

"You don't have to excuse your grief. Any life lost is a loss to the community," he said. He paused a moment, then continued. "In Hawaii, we believe in *'ohana.*"

"I've heard that word before. What does it mean?"

"The simple translation is 'family,' but in reality our *family* is a much wider circle than those merely related by kinship. It takes in all of those we love, all those we respect and honor. It is both our community as well as those outside it to whom we have ties. That can encompass many people." He stood and paced in front of the whiteboard.

"Was Mala part of your *'ohana*?" I asked.

He nodded. "I didn't know her, but her uncle, Dr. Kapule, was my physician. So I knew of her."

"Until I met her yesterday, that was my experience as well."

"I'm going to ride over there after class," he said.

"To the place where Mala fell?"

"Yes. Would you like to come with me?"

"Very much."

Our students began filing into the classroom.

"We'll talk more later," Mike said, turning back to the whiteboard.

I picked up my notes and reviewed them, purposely pushing my mind away from the image of Mala Kapule tumbling down the rocky precipice into the churning water below. But she kept intruding on my thoughts. I remembered the child who'd pointed out the sea turtle. Her father had warned her not to step off the path. Clearly the signs posted along the trail cautioning visitors indicated that there was a real danger of losing footing if the soft earth should collapse. Yes, Mala was passionate about botany. But would she really have been so foolhardy as to risk her life to acquire a plant? I tried to avoid the conclusion that kept forcing its way to the front of my thoughts. What if her death wasn't an accident? What if the same people who objected to her political and scientific views decided their goals were better served without her? And what if those men on whose conversation I'd eavesdropped at the luau were speaking about Mala?

There were twelve students in our class, all soon-to-be graduates of the Maui Police Department's training program. After brief introductions and expressions of our thanks to the sponsoring foundation and the police department administration—and instructions for the students to turn off their cell phones—Mike and I began teaching our course, entitled "Public Input and Criminal Investigations."

Mike's qualifications for leading the class—thirty-two years on the force and a long string of cases effectively closed—were obvious. Mine were less so. While my reputation as a mystery writer may have brought my name to the attention of the sponsors, it was more likely that my experience in helping to solve some murders over the years had prompted the invitation to become Mike's co-instructor. I never start out intending to get mixed up in a murder case, but somehow information comes my way, and before I can stop myself, I'm pursuing leads and giving advice to the police—not always well received, I might add. But clearly, someone had noticed my successes, and here I was about to tell future detectives their business.

"We're going to begin by talking about how information makes its way through a neighborhood," Mike said. "Jessica, would you like to start?"

"The nature of a community is that news travels within it in many different ways," I told the police recruits. "For an electronic generation such as yours, the obvious route is on-line, on social networking sites, in texts and e-mails, but these are far from the only ways to ferret out information when you're working a case. Leaving out the Internet for the time being," I continued, "can you give us examples of other ways you might hear news about, let's say, a series of bur-glaries?"

Hands went up and suggestions were called out.

"In the incident reports."

"On TV."

"The radio station, Native 92.5."

"In my grandmother's kitchen."

"*Maui News*, the paper."

"How about Wow-Wee Maui?" This was greeted by a wave of laughter.

I looked at Mike questioningly.

"It's a local bar."

"These are all great suggestions," Mike said. "One thing to keep in mind when you're out on the street—and you're all going to be pounding a beat on the street before you become an investigator, if you ever do—is to keep your ears open for news. Sometimes even the simplest statement you overhear can give an investigator the key to solving a case." Mike screwed up his face and pointed to a student in the third row who had been whispering to the young woman next to him while she was trying to listen and take notes.

Mike squinted one eye and called out, "'Ey, bruddah!"

The student looked up quickly.

"I saw Lenny Jingo last night giving rides in his new pickup. Whaddya tink'a dat?" Mike said in his best streetwise accent.

Those not in Mike's line of sight giggled nervously as the student Mike had called upon pointed to his chest and had a confused look on his face.

"Yeah, you! C'mon, you're supposed to be a police officer now," Mike said.

Mike's victim in the third row squirmed.

"Nothing up here, huh?" Mike said tapping his temple.

"How's something stu . . . , something like that supposed to help you with a case?" the student asked in an irritated voice.

"You tell me," Mike said. "Think about it. You're walking a beat. You're getting to know the people in the neighborhood. What does this news tell you?" He looked up at the class. "Ideas?"

"Lenny finally got his driver's license back?" someone called out.

"His *kuku wahine* died and left him her fortune."

The other students laughed.

Mike lowered his head and leaned toward the fellow he'd singled out. "Let's hear from Akamai over here."

"My name's Louis. Why'd you call me Akamai?"

"*Akamai* means 'genius.' I figured since you weren't paying attention, you already knew everything. Okay, Louis, what's your idea?"

"Well," he said, buying time, "I think—"

"That's a good start," Mike said, setting off snickers among the students.

Louis's face reddened. He cleared his throat. "Lenny Jingo never has two cents to put together," he said.

"And that means?"

"That if he's joyriding around in a new pickup, he probably borrowed it."

"Or?"

"Or stole it."

"Very good! That's why it's important to listen."

The class broke into applause. Louis stood and gave his classmates a mock bow.

"In a small town, or on a small island, anything out of the ordinary is commented on," I began. "People will talk. Sometimes they know something. Sometimes they don't. They may be guessing or even making up a story to fit the facts, but you have to pay attention. A clue may be buried in the gossip."

"You also have to be careful and judge when you listen," Mike added.

"Exactly," I said. "You cannot assume that everything you hear is true, but a rumor is a good place to start looking for the truth."

"Okay, let's get back to your favorite place, since you all usually have your heads buried in your cell phones," Mike said. "If you do go online trying to find information on our fictional burglaries, where do you go?"

"You could check out Lenny's personal page, see what photos he posted to figure out where he's been in the past few weeks," one student offered.

"Where else?"

"His friends' pages?"

"Twitter?"

"Anyplace else?" I asked.

There were shrugs all around as the suggestions dried up.

"Mrs. Fletcher, where would you look?" Mike asked.

"I would look at the news stories, blogs, and columns online," I said.

Louis groaned. "What good is that? They're only going to repeat the common knowledge."

"Perhaps," I said, "but in the Comments sections below the articles, people may make an observation or even joke about what's going on. They might not respond to the police request to call with any information, but in their need to express an opinion, they often reveal more about themselves and what they know than they intended to. You may find the names of people who know something, or who could lead you to other people who know something."

"Yeah, but what if they're anonymous or using a fake name?" someone called out from the back row.

"That's easy to trace," another student answered.

"The point Detective Kane and I are trying to make is that information can come from anywhere. If you're observant, if you file away offhand remarks in your memory bank, sometimes the pieces of the puzzle can come together."

Mala Kapule was a puzzle, I thought.

As the class continued, I wondered how I could find out more about this beautiful young botanist whose acquaintance I'd only just made, whose family and friends were strangers to me, who lived on an island I was unfamiliar with, but who, in such a short time, had already become part of my *ohana*.

Chapter Four

'Ike Aku, 'Ike Mai—Recognize and Be Recognized

Mike's car was a dusty blue SUV with a dent in the front fender on the passenger side and with the distinct aroma of fried fish inside. A plastic bag hanging from a radio knob held balled-up wax paper from a variety of fast-food places. Two empty cans of Coke occupied the cup holders in the console.

"It looks like you do a lot of eating on the run," I said, hoping it didn't sound like criticism.

"Yeah," he said as I buckled up. "Excuse the mess. My wife won't go near this car. She says it stinks. I cleaned it up for you. Not too bad now, huh?"

"As a method of transportation, it's perfect," I said, pressing a button to roll down the window.

"You don't need air-conditioning?" he asked as the car started with a groan of protest and rumbled to life.

"I'm fine without it."

"Where you from? Florida?"

"No," I said, laughing. "I'm from Maine, all the way up the East Coast, the last state before Canada."

"Never been there. Actually, the only place I been to on the mainland is California."

"So you're a Hawaiian, born and bred?"

"Relatively speaking," he said. "My father was half-Hawaiian. Like most of us on the island, I'm pretty much a mutt. Got some Portuguese, Filipino, Samoan, French, Korean—I think there's even some Irish in my blood."

"My mother was from Ireland," I said. "I knew we had something in common."

Mike gave out with a belly laugh. "Then top o' the morning to you, Cousin Jessica," he said.

"That's not a bad Irish accent you have there, Cousin Mike."

A police car passed us on the road and the driver honked.

Mike gave him a Hawaiian wave, a fist with thumb and pinkie finger extended. He was silent a moment, then said, "After class tomorrow you should come to our family picnic."

"Where is that?"

"We do a barbecue up in Iao Valley. Good food. You'll like my wife. She's a lot like you. Her name is Pualani. She calls herself Lani. Are you free?"

"I am, and I would be honored to come. Can I bring anything?"

"Just yourself," he said, grinning. "It'll save me a lot of time explaining to my wife who this woman is that I've been seen driving around with."

From Kahului, where the college was located, we took

Mokulele Highway across the island to Pi'ilani, a four-lane road that ran parallel to the southwest coast and avoided the congestion of the main street through Kihei, a neighborhood of smaller condominiums, homes, and hotels where many of the resort employees lived.

Mike parked his car in a shopping center and we made our way between two luxury hotels to reach the Wailea Coastal Walk, a mile-and-a-half trail that ran behind waterfront resorts and private condominium developments. I'd explored a small portion of it the evening before. It was midday and hot. I followed Mike's example and put on a hat, grateful that I'd thrown a pair of tennis shoes in my shoulder bag so I could change out of the dress pumps I'd worn to teach the class. The paved part of the walk radiated back the heat and the air shimmered above it as we walked past a crescent-shaped beach and down toward the field where the luau had been held.

A few runners, undaunted by the high temperature, coasted by us, but most of the pedestrians must have opted to wait for the cooler evening or early morning hours to enjoy the spectacular view. The luau field was empty, the tables and chairs gone, the stage dismantled and stored away until the next performance. We ambled around the curves of the coast, Mike taking his time and examining the vegetation along the path.

"So Miss Kapule was at the luau last night," he said, pausing to peer over a bush near a rocky outcropping.

"I can't confirm that," I replied, "but one of the women at my table said that she'd seen her talking with someone."

He moved on. "Who would that woman be?"

"Her name is Grace Latimer," I said, glancing over the

same bush that seemed to interest Mike. "What are you looking for?"

"Just admiring. Tell me about Miss Latimer."

"About twenty-five, blond, blue eyes. Pretty, but a little restrained. She doesn't smile much, but perhaps it was the company. She's a graduate student working with Professor Abbott Luzon on her master's project. The professor and his wife were at the luau as well."

"In what context did Mala's name come up?"

"I mentioned that I was looking for her. Mala had told me that one of her cousins was a dancer and that I might see her there."

"But you didn't."

"No. We never found each other. At least, I didn't find *her*. I have no idea if she was looking for me as well."

"Was there any reason why she would have avoided you?"

"None that I can think of, although she had made a point of saying we might not run across each other because of the crowd."

"How many people were there? Any idea?"

"I would guess several hundred, but the luau organizers should be able to give you a more precise number. As I understand it, everyone needed a ticket or reservation to get in."

He grunted. "You didn't make plans to meet in a particular area?"

I shook my head. "When I last saw her, she was going into an appointment in the science building and wasn't even sure if she would make it to the luau. I simply suggested that we look for each other. That was the extent of our plan, if you can call it that."

"But this Grace Latimer said she saw Mala at the luau? Did she speak with her?"

"I asked the same question. The answer is no. But that's certainly understandable; at the time, Grace didn't even know I was hoping to see Mala."

"Who was Mala talking to?"

"You'll have to ask Grace. All she said was that Mala was engaged in a serious conversation and looked as if she didn't want to be interrupted."

Mike thought about that a moment, then said, "You should tell this to the police."

I smiled. "I thought I was."

He looked down at his feet and shook his head slowly. "Sorry for the interrogation. Once a cop, always a cop," he said with a bemused expression. "Hard to break old habits."

"So I hear."

"I'll introduce you to a buddy on the force."

"Why would he even be interested if they believe Mala's death was an accident?"

"Just to cover all the bases."

"Do you think it was an accident?"

"I already told you. I'm reserving judgment."

"Just checking to see if you're still telling the same story," I said.

"You sure *you're* not a cop?"

"Maybe in another life, but not in this one."

"Yeah? You believe in that reincarnation stuff?"

"I'm reserving judgment," I said.

Mike laughed. "Touché," he said. "I don't think there's a word for that in Hawaiian."

We continued along the path overlooking the water. At one point a stone wall rose about eight feet high, obstructing our view of the land and buildings above and narrowing the walkway so that those we met coming in the opposite direction had to stand sideways to let Mike and me pass. A little beyond, a wooden bridge crossed a small ravine, at the bottom of which a trickle of water flowed down a hill and over a sandy patch of shoreline into the sea. Yellow tape marked the place where three investigators were conferring on the sand.

"How good are you at rock climbing?" Mike asked.

"Am I about to find out?"

"Let's see if we can find an easy way down."

We walked around a wooden gate meant to keep trespassers off private property, backtracked up the side of the gully until the trail to the bottom was less steep, stepped through the brush that flanked the stream, and followed the smooth gray stones toward the wider water. Mike splashed directly through the water, and after trying unsuccessfully to keep my sneakers dry, I followed suit.

The crew on the beach looked up as we approached. Mike lifted his chin, "Howzit?" he called to a man in a blue flowered shirt and white shorts.

"'Ey, Kane! I thought you pulled the pin," the man said, walking up to us. The two uniformed officers, a man and a woman, stayed by the shore.

"I got bored being retired. Besides, I heard you were praying to the goddess Uli for my return," Mike said. He turned to me. "Jessica Fletcher, meet Detective Henry Tahaki, a big-mouth cop who thinks he knows forensics."

Tahaki chuckled and reached out to shake my hand. "Aloha. Any friend of this big kahuna is welcome," he said. "Jessica, is it?"

"That's right. Nice to meet you."

"Who you got with you?" Mike asked.

"New recruits. Showing them the ropes. How often do you get a dead body to investigate on Maui?"

"Once is too often," Mike said.

Henry eyed Mike. "What brings you here? Did you know the vic?"

"Are you thinking she's a victim now?"

"Whether it's by her own hand or someone else's, she's dead," Henry said. "That makes her a vic in my book."

"Did you find evidence to sway you either way?"

"Look, brah, I got to know your position here. Last I heard you were working hotel loss prevention. I take it this isn't a social visit."

"Let's just say I'm on special assignment from the department," Mike said. "Private duty."

Our class on community involvement in criminal investigation could be considered a "special assignment," I thought, although I wasn't sure the police department would approve of Mike's using his position as an instructor to justify poking his nose into a case.

"Is Jessica here your assistant?" Henry asked.

Before Mike could answer, I piped up. "I'm his partner," I said.

Henry's eyebrows shot up. "A female private investigator? Cool. Don't see too many of those," he said.

I smiled, deciding not to correct Henry. If he filled in the blanks himself, I could honestly say that I hadn't claimed to be a private investigator. I only hoped he wouldn't ask to see my license.

"Jessica knows someone who saw Miss Kapule at last night's luau," Mike said.

"Yeah? Who was it?"

I gave Grace Latimer's name to Detective Tahaki and told him he could find her at the college. I wondered if Grace had recognized the person Mala was talking to, and thought I might ask her myself the next time I was on campus. I realized I didn't even know if Mala's companion was a man or a woman, and silently chided myself for not having thought to inquire. But of course I never expected I would need to know such information. I had no reason to think Mala was in danger, if, indeed, she had been.

"This isn't where she fell," Mike said.

Henry shook his head. "No. They found her body up the coast a bit in a place only fit for *honu*."

"That's a sea turtle," Mike said to me.

"You can't get in there without a boat," Henry continued, "and even with one, it's a bumpy ride. The rocks'll put a big gash in anything too heavy. They had to moor the rescue boat offshore and paddle in to get her."

"How long do you figure she was in the water?"

"Not sure she was. Might have just been on the rocks. But that's a question for the coroner, not me. I'm just checking out the area, see if she dropped anything, find any witnesses."

"And?"

"We checked all the neighbors. No one saw or heard anything. At least that's what they're saying. It started to cloud over around oh one hundred hours. Rained for an hour or two. She could have slipped when the ground was wet. Couldn't really tell; the rain washed away a lot."

"So you don't have a time of death?" Mike said.

Henry shrugged. "Sometime between darkness and oh six hundred, when a jogger called it in."

"You can do better than that," Mike said.

"Probably around midnight before the clouds covered the moon. If she was looking for a particular plant, she wouldn't have been able to see it easily after that."

"What makes you think she was looking for a plant?" I asked.

"I didn't see the body, but one of the rescuers said she was holding some leaves in her hand."

"Would you mind letting me see the report when you're finished?" Mike asked.

Henry shrugged. "You know where they're filed," he said.

"Don't make me go to headquarters," Mike said. "E-mail me a copy. You can do that."

Henry nodded but didn't look too happy.

"*Mahalo*," Mike said to him.

"Yes. Thank you, and nice to meet you," I said to the detective. I waved to the other officers, who were watching us.

"Not much new there," Mike said under his breath as we left the beach.

"I'd like to see where she fell," I said, trying to keep up with Mike's pace.

"We're on our way there now."

"Why did Detective Tahaki call you 'brah'?" I asked.

"It's our word for 'bro,' like mainland slang for 'brother.'

A lot of what you think is Hawaiian is just our version of the way an English word is pronounced. Like 'fadda' for 'father' or 'eriding' for 'everything.' "

"I'm going to have to listen carefully," I said.

"Stick with me. I'll teach you. Before you leave, people will think you're a real *kama'aina*."

"That sounds Hawaiian. Does it mean someone who lives here?"

"Yeah. A local. See? You're picking it up already. All you really have to know is *aloha*, *mahalo*, and that it's bad luck to whistle after dark."

"I'll keep it in mind," I said. *"Mahalo."*

"A'ole pilikia. That means 'no worries,' but most people simply say 'you're welcome.' "

We traipsed up the stream, climbed the side of the ravine, and walked through the gate and back onto the trail. The wet footprints we left on the path evaporated almost immediately in the hot, dry air, and soon my sneakers were dry as well. A short way ahead, around a curve, more yellow tape alerted us to the site from which the police believed Mala had fallen. The grass there was matted; more than one pair of shoes had beaten it down. The trampled edge was across from a grassy area that bordered a condominium development. A wood-sided porch jutted from the second floor of the building, and a little boy in a straw cowboy hat leaned over the railing watching us. Thick black hair jutted out from beneath the hat. The lenses in the round, rimless glasses he wore caught the light and gave the impression that no eyes were behind them.

Bushes bordering the walkway on what Mike called the

makai side of the path—that's the sea side—blocked access to a rocky ledge, and a sign warned pedestrians to stay clear of where the soft earth had been disturbed. Apart from the sandy soil and a few crushed cigarette butts, there wasn't much else to see. Mike ducked under the tape and carefully maneuvered himself onto the ledge so he could peer down into the cove.

"How could a jogger have seen her?" I asked. "You can't see to the bottom of the cliff from here."

"Maybe he took a break sitting on this ledge," Mike said. "That's the only way. Unless someone from one of the early-morning outrigger canoe trips alerted him to call the cops."

I stayed on the path but walked a short distance back the way we'd come to see whether the angled approach allowed me to spot where the sandy soil might have collapsed. I paused in the shade of a palm tree, part of the condominium's landscaping, grateful for a little respite from the sun.

"Do you see any vegetation growing out of the rock?" I called to Mike.

"No, but that doesn't mean it wasn't there before she picked it."

"Maybe she wasn't trying to pick anything at all," I said. "Maybe she just grabbed onto a bush to stop from falling."

"Yeah, that's possible."

"Like this one," I said, moving to where a tall, full bush with dark red flowers sat close to the path's edge. Mike joined me.

"See?" I said, pointing to a broken branch. "This is what Mala might have grabbed when she started to fall."

"Which begs the question of why she would have started

to fall in the first place. She was young and healthy. It doesn't ring true to me that she'd simply lose her balance."

"Whatcha lookin' for?" a young voice interrupted.

I shaded my eyes with my hand and looked up to the wooden railing where I'd seen the child, but he was gone.

"I'm over here." He stood on the sill of an open glass door that led to a small patio under the deck where a little table and two chairs were set up.

I waved. "Hi. Does your mother know where you are?" I asked. "I'm not sure she'd want you to come outside without her." I was thinking that I wouldn't want to live in such a dangerous location if I had a small child.

"I'm allowed," he said, stepping down onto the grass and walking toward me. "I can go as far as the tree." He pointed to the palm.

"Tell you what," I said. "You stay where you are and I'll come to you."

I crossed the grass and guided the boy back to the patio. Cool air from the condominium flowed through the open door.

"Is your mother home?" I asked.

He shook his head.

"There must be someone at home with you."

"Tutu is, but she said not to bother her. She has a my, a my-something."

"A migraine?"

"Uh-huh."

"Those are pretty painful," I said, "but still, I think she'd like to know that you're outside."

"What's your name?" he asked, which made me smile. He certainly was a direct little fellow.

48

"I'm Jessica Fletcher."

"My name's Kona."

"Like the coffee?"

"Like the place on the Big Island. But my daddy calls me Koko. You can call me Koko, too."

"Nice to meet you, Koko."

"Found a new friend, huh?" Mike said, easing his big body into one of the patio chairs. "Could use a break from the sun. You have any water with you, Jessica?"

"I have a couple of bottles in my bag," I said, "but the water's going to be warm."

"As long as it's wet," he said. "Take a seat. We can spare five minutes."

"But we don't know who lives here." I groped around in my bag for the small water bottles I'd tossed in it that morning.

Mike shrugged.

"You know me," Koko said. I now could see large brown eyes through the thick lenses of his glasses.

"Yes, we do," I said, taking the other chair and handing Mike a bottle, "but I would feel better if you went inside and told Tutu that we're out here on your patio."

Koko looked down at his feet. "She gets angry when I wake her up."

Mike chuckled. "Guess we better let your grandma sleep, huh?"

Koko grinned at him. "What's the yellow ribbon for?" He waved at the crime scene tape.

"A lady fell and hurt herself," Mike said. "We want to make sure no one else goes there and gets hurt—like you. Promise me that you won't walk over there."

Koko shook his head. "I won't. I'm not allowed to go on the trail, only as far as the tree."

"Good boy. You listen to your *tutu*." Mike took a sip of his water and swiped a hand across his damp brow. "Henry indicated they questioned everyone in the neighborhood, and no one heard anything last night," he said to me.

"I heard something last night," Koko said.

Mike leaned forward in his chair and gave Koko a little smile. "What did you hear, Koko?"

"I heard the rain."

"Oh, it woke you up, did it?"

"No. I was already up. The birds woke me up."

"Birds?" Mike said.

Koko nodded. "The loud ones. I hear them every morning, and last night when—"

"There you are, Koko. I've been looking all over for you." A woman in a yellow apron stood in the open door. "You're letting out all the cold air. Get in here this minute." She glared at Mike and me. "And who are you?"

Mike stood and gave her a mild smile. "Investigators, ma'am."

Her angry expression changed to regret. "We heard about it. Just awful. I've been saying for years that they need to build a fence along that path."

"What's awful, Tutu?" Koko asked.

"Nothing you need to know about. Get inside, little one. It's time for your snack." To us, she said, "You can sit as long as you like."

"We'd like to ask you a few questions if you don't mind," Mike said.

"I already told the police I went to bed at ten and slept through to this morning. Didn't see anything. Didn't hear anything. Sorry."

Koko started to say something, but his grandmother ushered him inside and closed the glass door.

Mike sat again. "What do you think?" he said.

"I think Mala might have fallen down the cliff before the rain came," I said.

"Why do you say that?"

"The birds Koko heard. At the luau last night, a noise disturbed birds that nest on the ground behind the stage and they flew into the air making loud noises. Grace Latimer said they were francolins. Maybe francolins were nesting here, too. Mala's presence might have roused them. Perhaps she screamed. If she did, it might have startled the birds into calling. They're certainly loud enough to wake a little boy. It could point to the time she fell—or was pushed."

Mike grimaced. "I'll hold off on the second half of that statement," he said, "for the moment. Meanwhile, let's go look and see if we find any evidence of the birds."

But whether or not we found a nest, I was convinced that the birds already knew what I only suspected: that Mala's death was no accident, that she didn't go rock climbing at midnight, that someone wanted to shut her up—permanently. That realization overrode the heat of the day and sent a chill through me.

Chapter Five

Kōkua—Help or Assistance

Mike was in a hurry to get home. He bought take-out sandwiches for us at a fish restaurant in a shopping center and, before dropping me off at the small resort where I was staying, reminded me that I was invited to his family picnic after class the next day.

I took my paper-bag lunch out to the lanai, a shaded patio off my room with a view of the bay, and sat at a round metal table to unpack my meal. The sandwich—grilled fish with lettuce, onion, and tomato—was delicious, but so spicy that I was grateful Mike had gotten me an iced tea as well. The warm breeze, combined with our morning exertions and a filling meal, made me sleepy. I changed seats, relaxing back into a padded wicker chaise, and soon dozed off, visions of Mala and the rocky cliff and a flock of loud birds fighting for space in my dreams.

She was teetering on the edge of the rock, peering down

into the water. I tried to call to her to be careful. She looked up and waved to me. Just then a flock of francolins rose into the air, startling her. Mala's arms wheeled, her body tipped sideways, and she tumbled out of my sight down the precipice. The birds shrieked, their calls piercing in the night.

I awoke with a start, the dream fading but leaving a persistent sense of unease. The sun was high, the afternoon heat oppressive. I could still hear the birds calling. No, that was the telephone in my room. I pulled myself out of the chaise, shaking my head to clear the remnants of my daytime nightmare, and walked to the bedside table.

"Yes?" I said, snatching up the receiver. "Hello?"

"I'm sorry to disturb you, Mrs. Fletcher, but someone left a message for you at the front desk this morning. My apologies if no one informed you earlier. Would you like us to have it delivered to your room?"

"Thank you for offering, but I'd prefer to pick it up," I said, thinking I could use a little walk. "Is the café open?"

"Yes, ma'am. It's past lunchtime, but you can get a snack. Dinner service begins at five."

"I'll be there in a while."

"We'll have your message at the front desk. My name is Jack. If for any reason I'm not here, Eileen will have it at her station."

I thanked him and hung up the phone. I briefly debated changing into a bathing suit. A swim would surely clear the cobwebs, but I decided a cup of tea would do the same without the bother of undressing and then dressing again for dinner. I checked the contents of my shoulder bag for a book in case I wanted to read, and reminded myself to stop at the newsstand to replace the water bottles Mike and I had consumed.

The resort where the foundation was putting me up was situated on Maui's north shore and maintained a rack of bicycles for the convenience of its guests. Since the college was a short ride away, a bike was going to be my preferred choice of transportation, as long as it wasn't raining. If the weather didn't cooperate, there was a bus stop a block away, or the bellhop could call me a cab. The main lobby, an open-air space, faced the street, but the café in the back overlooked Kahului Harbor. I stopped at the front desk for my message and was handed a white envelope with the college's return address and my name printed on the front.

"Would you like to sit outside?" the hostess asked when I approached her podium in the café. A pin in her lapel read: LIVE THE ALOHA SPIRIT.

"That would be lovely."

She led me to a table for four, shaded by a large umbrella, and pulled out a seat for me. "May I get you something to drink? We have POG, piña colada, iced tea, or you can choose a drink from the menu on the table."

"What is POG?" I asked, settling my bag on the seat next to mine.

"It's a Hawaiian specialty, a fruit punch made with passion fruit, orange, and guava juices."

"That sounds wonderful. I'll have that."

The hostess left to put in my order, and I opened the envelope, pausing only to decide if the handwriting on the front was male or female. Female, I decided.

Dear Mrs. Fletcher,

It is urgent that I speak with you about Mala Kapule.

I'm working in the laboratory all day today, and I'd appreciate it if you wouldn't tell anyone that I contacted you.

—Grace Latimer

Grace had included a room number in the new science building under her name.

I looked at my watch just as a waiter in a pink aloha shirt delivered an icy glass of punch sitting on a white doily-covered plate. The juice and his shirt were the same color and I briefly wondered if the uniform had been chosen to match the drink.

"My apologies if I've kept you waiting, madam," he said.

"You haven't kept me waiting at all," I said. "I just remembered an important appointment. I'm afraid I have to go."

"Would you like me to put the POG in a go-cup for you?"

"That would be perfect," I said. "Thank you so much. And please bring me the bill as well."

I left the fruit punch in my room, not wanting to juggle drinking and steering at the same time, and hurried to where the bikes were parked. I was still wearing the tennis shoes I'd changed into for my late-morning hike with Detective Kane. After checking out a bike at the front desk, I headed off to find Grace Latimer.

The campus was quiet when I pedaled in, most of the classes having finished for the weekend. I hoped Grace was still there. She seemed like a diligent type and her note had indicated that she would be working all day, but the clear sky and balmy winds might have tempted her away from her tasks to enjoy the outdoors.

One pair of the science building's glass doors was locked, but the other was open, and I entered the cool, empty hallway. I checked the room numbers, counting down until I found the lab where Grace was working. She was alternately leaning over a microscope and making notes on a pad in a room with a battery of microscopes arrayed on aqua tables with gray tops. Her blond hair hung lankly, and she chewed on the thumbnail of one hand while she used the other hand to fiddle with a focus wheel.

I knocked softly on the side of the open door so as not to startle her, and entered the room. "Grace?" I called softly.

She turned and looked at me, a confused expression on her face. "Oh! Mrs. Fletcher. I almost didn't recognize you."

"I'm sorry to interrupt your work, but your note used the word 'urgent' and I came as soon as I could."

Grace jumped up from her seat and met me at the door. "Please come in," she said. "Sit anywhere." She leaned over the threshold, glancing left and right, then shut the door.

"You've heard about Mala, I assume," she said, taking a seat next to mine.

"Yes. Mike Kane told me this morning. We're teaching a class together."

"The retired detective?"

"Yes."

"Boy, I'd love to hear what *he* has to say about this."

"He isn't saying much at all," I said. "What do *you* know?"

"Me? I wasn't there when she died. I left the same time as you and Professor Luzon and his wife."

"But your note said you wanted to speak with me about Mala." I dug in my bag and pulled out the envelope she had left for me at the resort.

"Oh, that. I guess that when I heard that they found her body, I went into shock, had to speak to someone. Still creeps me out to think about it." She shivered. "Did the police tell you anything?"

I wondered if she had news to tell me or was more interested in what *I* knew. I figured that if she knew that the police believed Mala's death to be an accident, she might withhold information rather than draw attention to herself. I decided to answer her question with one of my own. "How did you learn of Mala's death?"

"Abbott told me."

"Professor Luzon?"

"Yes. The college administration got in touch with him right after the police notified them."

"Why would they contact Professor Luzon?"

"He's the head of the department now. Hadn't you heard?"

"When did that happen?"

"They made the announcement yesterday afternoon."

"What time was this?"

"It was right in the middle of our class on horticulture and landscape maintenance. I was so excited. A lot of fuss was made. It's going to be in the paper, I'm sure. Mala wanted the job; everyone knew that. She might have had a chance if she wasn't so outspoken. There's a lot of politics in academia. People don't expect it, but it's there."

"There aren't many fields in which politics doesn't play some part," I said.

"Abbott knows how to play the game; I'll give him that. He made the case for our work in sustainable agriculture being especially critical to the Hawaiian economy. Money always talks when you're trying to promote your position."

"You don't mean . . ."

"No. No. I don't mean he bribed anyone or anything like that. It's just he kept the big picture in mind."

"What big picture is that?" I asked.

"The college administration is acutely aware of Hawaii's difficulties. The legislature is always financially pressured."

"It would seem to me that every state legislature struggles with finances. Is Hawaii's any different?"

"It is and it isn't. As an island state, it's very difficult for us to maintain the same standard of living as the mainland. You can see why. Almost everything has to be shipped in."

"That must make it expensive to live here."

"Well, that is some gross understatement," she said with annoyance.

I felt my eyebrows rise but decided I wouldn't take offense.

Grace seemed not to realize she had been rude. She glanced down at her thumbnail and continued talking. "The more we can grow, nurture, and manufacture, the less our reliance on imported goods. Of course, the hippies who just want to live off the grid and skip paying taxes give our efforts a bad name. What we want to do—Abbott and I—is develop *systems* for sustainability and export our knowledge to the rest of the States. It could be big. Very big."

"So you're saying Professor Luzon's economic proposals landed him the chairmanship?"

"Well, no one is confiding in me, but that's my take on it."

"Tell me, what does this have to do with Mala Kapule's death?"

Grace picked at her ragged fingernail and shrugged. "She may have gotten wind of the announcement— or maybe Abbott told her himself. It must have been a terrible blow to her ego."

"You're not seriously suggesting that Mala threw herself off a cliff because she wasn't given the chairmanship of the department, are you?"

"I don't know that she actually jumped, but it's possible the news was so upsetting that she didn't look where she was going."

"Tell me again when you saw Mala last night?"

"Just what I told you, when we were getting the drinks."

"You said she was in a serious discussion with someone. Do you know who that person was?"

Grace nodded. "I think so. He looked to me like her boyfriend, or at least the guy who *was* her boyfriend. I heard they broke up recently."

Now I felt I was getting somewhere. "What is this boyfriend's name?"

"Carson Nihipali."

"And what does *he* do?"

Grace's thoughts seemed to have drifted off onto some

other topic, so I asked again. "Does Carson Nihipali work here at the college?"

Grace burst out with a short laugh. It was the first time I'd seen an expression on her face that wasn't glum. "Sorry. Carson's as far from academic as you can get," she said, still amused at my question. "He's a 'surfer dude,'" she said, putting on an accent. "And to support his obsession, he works as a deckhand on one of the sunset cruise ships."

He didn't sound like the type of person I'd have expected Mala to find attractive, but I knew enough not to prejudge a man by his occupation or preoccupation, and especially by the description given by someone who clearly felt herself superior.

"Can you tell me where I might find Carson Nihipali? Do you know where he lives?"

"No idea at all," Grace said, the look of displeasure back on her face. "But here, I'll write down the name of the ship he works on. It's out of Lahaina, on the other side of the island. Have you been there?"

"Not yet," I said, "but I'm sure I can find it." *Or a cab driver can find it,* I thought, taking the paper on which Grace had written "Maui Ocean Star."

She stood. "I'm afraid I have to get back to work," she said. "Sorry if you think I wasted your time."

"You haven't wasted my time at all," I said. "I appreciate your getting in touch with me."

But as I pedaled back to my room at the resort, I wondered why Grace had written me that note. Did she think I knew Mala better than I actually did? Was she expecting to deliver the bad news herself? Some people delight in being the first one to pass along information without regard to whether it will—or perhaps even *because* it will—upset the listener. Grace knew something she wasn't telling me. I was convinced of that. But would whatever she knew shed light on Mala's death? That I didn't know, but I was determined to find out.

Chapter Six

ʻO Wai Kou Inoa?—What Is Your Name?

Jack was no longer at the front desk when I returned to my hotel, but Eileen was.

"I'm interested in taking tonight's sunset dinner cruise on the *Maui Ocean Star*," I told her.

"Do you have a reservation, Mrs. Fletcher?"

"No, but I'm hoping they can accommodate one person at the last minute."

"Would you like me to call and try to reserve a space for you?"

"I would appreciate that very much. I'll also need a taxi to get to Lahaina."

"That won't be a problem."

While Eileen called the cruise company, I went back to my room to change and to check my e-mail. I opened my laptop and paused. I needed to notify Seth Hazlitt of Mala's death. Over the years Barrett Kapule had written so glowingly of his niece that I was certain Seth felt that he knew her, too. But that news would be better delivered by telephone than in an e-mail, and it was already close to midnight in Maine, too late to call.

Instead, taking the advice I'd given my students that morning, I looked to see whether the local newspaper already had a story about Mala's death and what, if any, reader comments might have been left. I logged onto the *Maui News* site. There was a headline in the local news section, "Woman's Body Found off Wailea Coastal Walk." When I clicked on it, a short article came up:

A 32-year-old woman, a possible drowning victim, was found unresponsive at the base of a cliff off the makai side of the Wailea Coastal Walk this morning. Kihei firefighters responded to the call at 7:25 a.m. Air One was called in to confirm the location. Rescuers borrowed a private kayak to reach the woman. She was transported to shore, where medics pronounced her dead. The woman's name was not released.

There was a link to share the story on social media but no place to put in comments. *Got that one wrong, Jessica,* I told myself. The newspaper's blogs and columns online did have links for comments, but no one had written about Mala so far, not surprising given how recently she had died and that she hadn't been named in the article.

The phone rang as I slipped a sweater over my shoulders in anticipation of cooler nighttime temperatures. It was Eileen from the front desk.

"I'm sorry, Mrs. Fletcher. I was unable to make a reservation for you. The sunset cruise is fully booked. However, the lady who answered the phone said that occasionally there were no-shows and that if you wanted to stop by, there might be an extra seat at the last minute. No guarantee, though."

"Oh, dear," I said, wondering if I was going on a fool's errand in choosing to put in an appearance without a reservation. On the other hand, if my powers of persuasion were sharp, I might be able to talk myself onto the boat. At worst, I could have dinner in Lahaina, wait for the cruise to return, and hopefully get to speak with Mala's former beau Carson Nihipali. Of course, this was assuming that he was working this night. If he wasn't . . . well, I didn't have other plans anyway.

"I think I'll take that chance," I told Eileen.

"In that case, the cab is here and is available whenever you are."

I thanked her, checked my shoulder bag for necessities in the event I was marooned in Lahaina for the evening, and walked to the hotel lobby.

The cab waiting for me was an older-vintage white sedan with a detachable lighted sign on the roof that read AAA TAXI and a slightly askew sign on the door bearing the same name and a phone number. The bellman held the door for me and I slid onto the cracked red leather bench seat in the back. A pine-tree-shaped air freshener dangled from the rearview mirror and filled the cab with a medicinal aroma. The driver's taxi license, which hung from his headrest, was laminated in plastic so scratched it was difficult to read. But the picture showing the gap-toothed smile of the driver matched the face of the man sitting behind the wheel.

"Good evening, Mrs. Fletcher," the driver said, tugging on the peak of his ball cap. "I'm Elijah. I'll be your chauffeur tonight. Would you like a bottle of water?" He lifted a cardboard soda carrier holding two bottles of water. Tucked into other spaces were bags of macadamia nuts and three granola bars.

"No, thank you," I said, "but it's kind of you to offer."

"Not kind," he said, shrugging. "The water is two dollars a bottle, the nuts are five, and the granola bars are three apiece."

"Since I'm going to dinner, I think I'll skip a snack right now," I said.

"Sure thing. I'm driving you to Lahaina Harbor, the Banyon Tree Park, right?"

"I'm taking a sunset dinner cruise," I said. "Does it leave from the park?"

"From the harbor right behind it. Which one you on?"

"The *Maui Ocean Star.*"

"Very nice. You will enjoy it. Going to be a clear night. Bright moon."

After our initial conversation, Elijah concentrated on his driving, while I relaxed in my seat, buckled in, and watched the scenery pass by as we made our way to the west coast. Once we were out of town, the storefronts and strip malls were replaced by fields of sugarcane and other vegetation that bordered the highway. On my right, the flatland rose to become the sharp outlines and brown peaks of the West Maui Mountains. Across the valley was the broad flank of the volcano Haleakala. On top, I knew, was the high-altitude observatory about which Mala had been so concerned. I sighed. It would be terrible if her passion to preserve such an ecologically and culturally important site had somehow brought about her death. But I knew that the politics of academia that Grace had referred to paled in comparison with the partisan battles that took place when valuable land and millions of dollars were in the balance. When the stakes grew that high, anyone seen as trying to impede "progress," no matter how legitimate their cause or how valid their arguments, might get crushed in the process—or in Mala's case, get pushed out of the way.

At Ma'alaea, the road curved around to the north, revealing a spectacular expanse of water that had been only a distant view earlier. Marching up the mountain to my right was a line of wind turbines, their huge sails slowly twisting in the winds that swooped in from the sea and cut up the valley to Maui's north coast.

Since he'd been silent for so long, I was surprised when Elijah asked me a question.

I leaned forward. "I beg your pardon?"

"See our wind farm there?"

"Yes, I was just noticing it."

"They're trying to figure out a way to cut back on the oil that has to be brought in. Gas is very expensive here, you know."

"And will the wind energy be able to replace it?"

Elijah shrugged. "The wind maybe covers ten percent of the island's needs. Me, I have solar panels on my house, but they don't help fill the gas tank."

"I guess not."

"You here on vacation, Mrs. Fletcher?"

"Actually, I'm here to teach a class," I said, "but I'm hoping to fit in some recreation time."

"A class? Where are you teaching?"

"Our classroom is on the Maui College campus, but the course is part of training for police recruits."

"No kidding? Maui College, huh? Any chance you know my cousin? She teaches there—or she did."

"Who is your cousin?" I asked as my eyes again took in the plastic-covered license affixed to his headrest. I reached out and tilted it to read his name through the scratches. ELI-JAH KAPULE. "Are you related to *Mala* Kapule?" I asked.

"Oh, yes. Mala was a teacher at the college. She taught about plants and stuff like that. Very sad news about her today. They said she fell off a cliff this morning trying to pick a flower."

"You're Mala's cousin?"

"You know her? I mean, you knew her?"

"Not well, but yes, I knew her. We had coffee together yesterday. I'm so sorry for your loss. She was a lovely young woman. Now that I think about it, she mentioned that she had a cousin who drove a cab."

"Several cousins, actually. Me and my two brothers. We are Triple-A Taxi. It's not our initials or anything. We thought up the name so we'd come first in the phone list. Clever, huh? Works, too. We got a good business."

"Was Barrett Kapule your father?"

"You knew Uncle Barrett, too?"

"I didn't know him personally," I said, "but he was a long-time friend of a close friend of mine."

"Uncle Barrett, he was an old man when he died. It was

sad, but he had a good long life. But Mala, she was too young to be taken. We have a phrase in Hawaiian. '*Oia la he koa no ke ano ahiahi; 'oia nei no ke ano kakahiaka.* It means, 'He is a warrior of the evening hours; but this person here is of the morning hours.' She had much more to do, more things to accomplish. It is a terrible loss, not just for our '*ohana* but for all Maui, even all Hawaii." Elijah fell silent again. Was he wiping away a tear?

I wanted to ask him more about Mala, about her friends he might have known and perhaps others who didn't hold her in such high regard. But I held back. I didn't want to intrude on his grief. Instead, I asked, "Do you know when her funeral will be?"

He shook his head. "Probably next week sometime. The plans haven't been finalized yet."

"Did Mala live with family?"

"Not for some time now. She was independent, you know. But I know Auntie Edie will want to have a celebration of her life. The celebration takes a little time to prepare. They need to make a lot of leis for the family and people who come. And there's always a big table of food. It's not like a *haole* funeral, all somber. In a Hawaiian funeral, we have music, hula, singing, maybe a video of her. We have so many cultures, so many religions, we mix them up. We take what we like from each one."

"Do you think it would it be all right for me to attend?"

"If you knew Mala, you should come. She would want you to. She loved the old ways, the traditions. Only thing is . . ." He paused. "Can I tell you something?"

"Yes. Of course."

"Please don't wear black. In Hawaii we don't wear black to funerals. White is okay. Aloha clothing is better."

While we were speaking, Elijah had driven through the beginnings of the city of Lahaina. We moved slightly inland away from the chain of beaches and I began to see strip malls and storefronts again. Elijah turned left and then right onto Front Street, which was crowded with automobiles and tourists. We inched forward until a huge banyan tree came into sight; a group of children played tag around its many low branches and hid behind the ropes of aerial roots reaching to the ground.

He pulled to the curb and pointed. "There's too much traffic to get you right in front, but if you go around the park, there will be a row of kiosks along the harbor. The one you want has a little red awning."

I thanked him and held out my credit card.

He shook his head. "No money," he said. "Not from you. It's a gift from Mala."

I tried to object, but he was adamant. "I'm living the aloha spirit today," he said, tapping a button on his lapel that echoed that sentiment. "You enjoy your cruise, and call me if you need a ride back to the hotel." He handed me his card. "If I don't see you again tonight, I hope I see you at my cousin's celebration."

"I'll make certain to be there."

"Good. Have a nice cruise, Mrs. Fletcher, and take care. You are in our *'ohana* now."

Chapter Seven

Okole Maluna!—Bottoms Up!

The *Maui Ocean Star* kiosk was unattended, but the crew of the catamaran was escorting passengers aboard. Two young women—one blond, one brunette, both with deep tans—held clipboards and checked off the names of paying guests as they arrived.

I walked down the wooden gangway and drew near the brunette. Her badge read, BITSY.

"Name, please," she said with a bright smile.

"I'm Jessica Fletcher, but you won't find my name on your list," I said.

Bitsy cocked her head and looked at me with a disappointed expression. "I'm afraid we're fully booked, Ms. Fletcher."

"Yes, I know. The desk clerk at my hotel in Kahului told me, but she also suggested that if I stopped by in person, you might be able to accommodate one more."

"That's a long way to come," Bitsy said, sighing. "You're sure you're by yourself? No one else is going to show up at the last minute?"

"All alone," I said. "And I promise I won't eat much."

She laughed. "If you can wait while I finish with those who have reservations, I'll go check with the captain. I'm pretty sure I can convince him to fit you in."

"I'll count on your charm," I said.

I walked back up the gangway and perched on a bench near the kiosk, watching the preparations being made to ready the ship for the evening's sail. As Bitsy and her blond colleague continued to check in passengers, my attention was drawn to their male counterparts as they geared up to cast off. There were three of them in my line of sight, all in dark green polo shirts and khaki slacks, the same uniform worn by the young women. They bustled about the large two-hulled boat, untying ropes, carrying supplies inside, and ushering guests along the slippery decks. I had no way of knowing whether one of them was Mala's former boyfriend Carson Nihipali but hoped that he was there that night. Grace Latimer had called Carson a "surfer dude." Was that the same as "beach bum"? She hadn't said it in a kindly way, although maybe I was reading something into her comment. I try not to do that, but sometimes I fail.

I wondered at the sort of life these men led on Maui. It was clearly a healthy way to live, being physically active and out on the water in the fresh air. Of course, the Hawaiian sun could do damage, but I assumed that they protected themselves from its most harmful effects. The sun and my fair skin have never been on especially friendly terms.

A taxi pulled up and a couple got out, arguing. "We're going to miss the boat; I just know it." I'd heard that woman's voice before. I strained to get a better look at them. The familiar voice was one half of the older couple from Michigan, Bob and Elaine Lowell, who'd been at my table at the luau. I stood to greet them as they headed toward the catamaran.

"Hello there," I said.

It took a moment before they recognized me.

"Jessica, right?" Bob said, snapping his fingers. "Now, this is a pleasant surprise, indeed, isn't it, Elaine?"

"It's good seeing you again," I said. "Are you going out on the sunset cruise?"

"If we're not too late," Elaine replied. "Bob is such a dawdler. Are you on the cruise, too, Jessica?"

"I'm hoping to be. I just showed up but don't have a reservation. They're trying to accommodate me."

"Heck, there's got to be at least one extra space," Bob said. "Don't you worry. I'll make sure that you're on the cruise. It'd be great to have *two* lovely ladies on my arm."

"Oh, Bob!"

"Please," I said, "you two get on board and don't worry about me. I'm sure they'll take good care of me. Go ahead, now. I'll catch up with you later."

Bitsy had disappeared onto the catamaran. When she returned, she checked in the Lowells and waved for me to join her.

"The captain said okay," she announced. "I told him your name and he asked whether you were the famous Jessica Fletcher who writes mystery novels. If you are, he'd like you to be his guest."

"That's very generous of him," I said, embarrassed. "I do write mysteries, but as for being famous, I don't know about that . . ."

A short, wiry man yelled from the deck, "Hey, Bitsy, let's move it. It's supposed to be a sunset cruise, not a sunrise trip."

"Better get on board," Bitsy told me, laughing. "Never pays to get the captain mad."

I crossed the gangway onto the catamaran and noticed a row of shoes lined up on the deck. One of the young deckhands met me and said, "Rules, ma'am. Shoes and socks off. Safer for you and less wear and tear on the decks."

Barefooted, I gingerly made my way along one of the side decks to the front of the vessel, where the other guests had gathered. A young couple took turns photographing each other with a cell phone. Two middle-aged gentlemen leaned on the railing observing activity on other docks that serviced the cove. A couple with a daughter whom I pegged at about twelve years old tried to cajole their child not to pout and to enjoy the evening. The Lowells stood talking to the man who'd called out to Bitsy and whom I assumed was the captain, although he wasn't dressed like one, no jaunty white hat with a peak or blue blazer with gold bars on the shoulders or sleeves. Instead, he was in the same green and khaki as his crew. He broke away from the Michigan couple and came to me.

"Mrs. Fletcher?" he said, shaking my hand.

"Please call me Jessica."

"I'm Charlie Reed, owner and captain of the *Maui Ocean Star*. Welcome aboard."

"It's nice to meet you. Thank you so much for agreeing to take me on at the last minute."

"You're very welcome. It's a pleasure to have you as my guest, Jessica. I read lots of murder mysteries, and yours are some of my favorites. Recognized you right away from your picture on the covers."

"I'm flattered," I said. "This is a magnificent boat, if that's the proper description."

"Thank you. There's nothing else like it on Maui. I have to admit, it's my baby. I had a hand in designing every inch and personally sailed her back here to Maui from the California shipyard where she was built."

"I'll look forward to exploring your baby," I said.

He laughed. "You do that," he said pleasantly. "She has quite a lot to show you. I'm honored to have you on board. I'm sure my crew will see to your every need."

"Hey, Charlie," one of the hands called out.

"Please excuse me now," he said to me. "We're about to set sail."

Most people moved downstairs to the large covered cabin, in which eight tables were set up with napkins and bowls of nibbles. As the Lowells passed, they urged me to come along. Bob said, "Don't miss out on the free food, Jessica."

I laughed and said, "Save some for me. I'll be there shortly."

I remained on the catamaran's bow and observed the deckhands smoothly carrying out their tasks as Captain Reed used the engines to back away from the pier, turn, and head for open water where he could unfurl the sails. I tried to decide which of the crew was Mala Kapule's former beau

Carson Nihipali and used my imaginary powers to envision each of them with her. I finally settled on the tallest of the three. He was a handsome fellow, tanned and trim and with broad shoulders and a shock of unruly dirty-blond hair that rested on his ears and neck. A bit older than the others, he had light blue eyes with fine lines radiating out from the corners, a result perhaps from squinting into the sun—or maybe from smiling. He was busy curling a length of rope and getting things shipshape, as they say.

I debated how to approach him. He'd finished his chore, tucking the last loop of the line in place, and walked toward the stern. I wasn't sure what to say. Did he know of Mala's death? If so, would he resent my bringing it up to him? Since they were an ex-couple, it was possible that he hadn't been informed of her passing. If he had, he obviously hadn't gone into a grieving shell; he was here working.

"Good evening," I said as he reached me.

"Hi," he said, flashing me a boyish grin. "Enjoying yourself?"

"Very much. It's a beautiful night for a sail."

As he started to walk away, I said, "Excuse me, but are you Carson Nihipali?"

He turned and gave me a strange look. "Yeah," he said, drawing the word out.

"I apologize if I've mispronounced your name," I said, "but I'm still trying to get the hang of the Hawaiian language."

He cocked his head. "You said it just fine. Do I know you?" he asked, a smile still playing on his lips.

"No. We've never met, but I was a friend of Mala Kapule."

"Mala?" He shook his head, his smile gone. "You knew her?"

"Not well, but we did strike up a friendship. I was saddened by her sudden death. I understand that you and she were close."

His face mirrored the debate he was going through.

"I only mention it," I said, "because someone told me about your relationship with Mala and that you worked here on the *Ocean Star*. You know about the . . . about the accident?"

"I heard," he said shaking his head. "I couldn't believe it."

"It's hard to accept. Had you seen her recently?"

"No."

"Really?"

"Why would you ask?"

"Because someone thought they saw you with her last night."

"Yeah, well, they were wrong. Look, I'm sorry about what happened, but I have to get back to work."

His comment struck me as oddly cold.

"Hey, Carson, Charlie needs another bag of ice for the bar," Bitsy called to him.

"Could we find some time to talk?" I asked. "I'd really appreciate it."

"I can't. Sorry. You can see I'm busy."

"It doesn't have to be now. Perhaps after we get back to the dock? I'd be happy to buy you a drink."

"I don't know." He hesitated, then changed his mind. "No, I don't think so. I have to go."

I watched him disappear down into the cabin and tried to sort out my initial reaction to him.

I'd obviously taken him by surprise, and his hesitancy to talk about Mala was understandable considering the circumstances. Still, there was something off-putting about him that stayed with me as the cruise progressed. Not that those thoughts were all consuming. It was a magnificent night on the water. Bitsy's coworker brought me a mai tai, an island specialty, which I sipped while watching the sun sink below the horizon, turning the sky and Pacific Ocean into a rainbow of colors that can be enjoyed only in tropical paradises like Maui.

I decided to join the others in the cabin and found that most of the people were crowded around the bar enjoying what seemed like a never-ending supply of drinks served up by members of the crew, including Bitsy and Carson. The array of appetizers on the bar and tables was impressive— cheese and crackers, vegetable crudités, prawns with cocktail sauce, California rolls, pork sliders with mango sauce, mushrooms stuffed with crabmeat, and teriyaki chicken skewers— enough to constitute a meal in itself, but we were told that a full dinner would follow.

The Lowells insisted that I join them at their table. Bob was in an expansive mood, becoming more so with each successive drink. He took to telling jokes, some bordering on the risqué, which brought forth an "Oh, Bob!" from Elaine. I enjoyed their company but had trouble focusing on the conversation. My attention kept shifting to Carson, who passed through the cabin numerous times. When he took over behind the bar, he engaged the passengers in light-hearted banter, with which he seemed comfortable, but each time I saw him, his eyes avoided mine.

The boat anchored in waters close to a rock cliff, the crevices of which hosted nesting petrels. Belowdecks, a lavish buffet was laid out on the counter together with a selection of wines. We queued up to fill our plates and glasses. I wasn't hungry anymore, so I went easy on my selections, grateful to find a tub of ice with water bottles at the end of the line. Not wishing to be rude, I rejoined the Lowells at their table.

The passengers scattered once dinner was served, most of them going topside to eat and enjoy the evening breeze. When dessert was served, Bob came back from the bar with a second helping of chocolate chip cookies and vanilla ice cream and almost sent the plate flying into Elaine and me when he tripped and stubbed his big toe. Apologizing for the colorful language that spilled from his mouth, he hopped to his seat and examined his foot.

I noticed that Carson was alone at the bar and took advantage of the opportunity.

"Delicious dinner," I said.

"Oh, thanks," he said as he busied himself placing used glasses into a dishwasher rack.

"I really would appreciate having some time to speak with you," I said. "The offer still holds to buy you a drink when we're back in port."

"It's kind of you," he said, "but I don't think so. Thanks anyway."

I knew that I had limited time before others came to the bar.

"It was such a surprise the way Mala died," I said, keeping my tone pleasant and nonconfrontational.

He adopted a thoughtful expression. "I couldn't believe it," he said, "although Mala was—well, she was a real free spirit." He shook his head, summoning up his smile again. "Climbing down a rock ledge to grab a plant. That's Mala."

"Is that what you've heard about how she died?"

"Yeah, sure. Isn't that what happened?"

"There's some question about it."

"Really?" His voice reflected his skepticism. "What question?"

"Well, Mala was a somewhat controversial figure, wasn't she?"

"You mean about plants?"

"Actually I was thinking more about the telescope up on Haleakala. She told me that it's a contentious issue on the island."

"That's for sure," he said. "Charlie—the guy who owns this ship—he's always talking about it." He lifted the full rack of dirty glasses and added it to a stack of crates.

"Does he agree with Mala that putting the telescope on the volcano is a bad idea?"

"Just the opposite," he said, laughing. He concentrated on filling another rack with dishes and flatware, perhaps hoping I would take the hint and leave. When I didn't, he said, "I heard them say that you write mystery novels."

"That's right."

"Are you going to write a book about the telescope and the volcano?"

"Goodness, no. I'm here on Maui to teach a class to police recruits. I just happened to be at the luau the night Mala died. She was there, too."

"Was she? Since we broke up we didn't talk much."

"I thought you might have been there, too. It seemed as though everyone on Maui was."

"Nope! I was working. No time for luaus." He turned his back to me as he added the rack to the pile.

"I looked for her, but we never connected," I said. "I should be honest with you. I'm asking about her because I wonder whether Mala really died as the result of an accident."

He spun around and started to respond, but we were joined by others at the bar, and I knew it was time to end the conversation.

"Look," he said in a low voice, and leaned toward me. "I don't know anything about how she died. Maybe you can make it up in a book. All I know is that we had a great relationship while it lasted and I'm sorry that she's dead. Now, excuse me. We're on our way back, and I have responsibilities up on deck."

I went back to the Lowells' table, where Bob had gathered a few other passengers and was entertaining them with stories. His wife, Elaine, looked at me and winked. "He is a handsome devil, isn't he?" she said.

"Who?"

"That young crew member you were talking to at the bar. I think he has eyes for you."

Her husband heard the comment and said, "He's too

young for women your age." He directed it at his wife, but I knew that he'd included me in his comment.

"As though all those young cuties in bikinis walking around the beach don't catch your eye, Bob."

"Different for a man," he said. "Nothing wrong with an older guy taking up with a younger gal."

Elaine rolled her eyes and said to me, "I noticed him at the luau. All the women were looking at those big shoulders and blue eyes."

"He was at the luau?"

"Oh, I'm pretty sure. Couldn't help but notice him. You didn't?"

I shook my head.

"Well, I could see that you were tired last night. A bit of jet lag, I guess. I was, too. Of course, Bob was bright-eyed and bushy-tailed, like he always is. Wanted to party into the wee hours. I don't know where he gets his energy. Me? I was asleep two minutes after the luau."

She continued talking about him, but her words went by me as I wondered why Carson Nihipali had insisted that he hadn't seen Mala lately and was adamant that he hadn't been at the luau.

Determined to enjoy the sail back to the dock at Lahaina, I tried to put aside what I'd learned from Elaine Lowell. It was possible that she'd been mistaken about him. Perhaps it was another handsome blond surfer who had caught her eye. Not that it meant anything in and of itself. Mala's death was thought to have occurred later that night. But what nagged at me was his denial. Professor Luzon's assistant,

Grace, had also identified Carson as the man she thought she'd seen talking with Mala. Was she wrong, too? If it had been Carson, why wouldn't he admit it? Why had he said he'd been working?

I was the last passenger to gather my shoes before disembarking and getting into vans that would take us back to our hotels, a nice bonus offered to guests by Charlie Reed. I'd hoped to travel in the van driven by Carson Nihipali, but it wasn't to be. I did stop to chat with the skipper of the *Ocean Star* before leaving.

"You have such a wonderful crew," I said, "so pleasant and accommodating."

"They'd better be that and more," Charlie said, holding my elbow as he escorted me down the gangway. "I only hire men and women who enjoy being with people."

"That hiring philosophy certainly pays off," I said. "I was especially impressed with a young man named Carson."

Charlie laughed. "Everybody loves Carson," he said, "especially the ladies. He's older than he looks, you know. He must be pushing thirty. My other deckhands are just out of college. I figured Carson would add a little maturity to the staff, but he's just as flaky as the rest of them. If the surf is up, I can't always count on a full crew. Now, let me make sure you don't miss your ride."

I was about to ask the skipper if Carson had worked the previous evening's cruise when he changed the subject. "It was a pleasure having you aboard, Jessica. Would you sign a book for me if I got it to you at your hotel?"

"I'd be delighted," I said, and told him where I was staying.

He repeated it to the driver as he helped me into the van.

The Lowells were in the same vehicle that would take me back to my hotel. Bob Lowell sat between his wife and me and draped his arms over our shoulders. Although it made me uncomfortable, I decided not to say anything.

"Everybody have a good time?" he asked.

"It was lovely," I said.

"That is some boat," he said. "Could probably sail it around the world. Reminds me of a joke. This sailor comes into a bar and . . ."

Fortunately, the hotel where the Lowells were staying was the first drop-off. It was situated on a vast expanse of land that sloped down to the ocean and was where the luau the previous night had been held.

"How's this for an idea?" Bob said as he and Elaine climbed over me to get to the door that the driver slid open. "We have dinner together tomorrow night, my treat, and then we find some show to take in, maybe a hula-dancing show. You can show off your stuff again. That was some demonstration. They can't only have hula-dancing at luaus, right?" He asked our driver, who nodded. "See? They do have other hula shows. Are you up for it, Jessica?"

"I'm afraid I have another engagement," I said, feeling that my little white lie was justified.

"How about the next night?" he called out as the driver started to slide the door closed.

"Sorry," I said, "but I can't think that far ahead. Too many mai tais."

Another white lie.

"Well," Lowell said cheerfully, "you know where we're staying. Give us a jingle."

I nodded and waved good night as the van pulled away, and was glad when we reached my hotel. As I walked to my room I found myself mumbling, "Oh, Bob! Oh, Bob," and had to smile. They were nice people, but as my dear friend Seth Hazlitt might say, "I'd hate to be seated next to him on a long flight."

Seth! He didn't know about Mala yet. That was a call I'd have to make tomorrow.

Chapter Eight

He Ali'i Ka 'Āina. He Kauwā Ke Kanaka—
Ancient Hawaiian Saying Meaning:
The Land Is a Chief, Man Its Servant

My intention upon returning to the hotel was to climb into bed and get a good night's sleep. But it wasn't to be. Mike Kane and I had to teach another class in the morning even though it was Sunday. The police department hadn't wanted to take our students away from the more hands-on training that was conducted during the week.

I'd prepared a lesson plan I would use during the class and spent time going over my notes, jotting down additional ideas on a lined pad of paper. The problem was that my attention kept shifting from the material at hand to Mala Kapule.

While the consensus seemed to be—at least at that juncture—that she'd been victim of an unfortunate accident, Mike Kane had questioned the finding. The instincts of a man of his caliber and experience—a highly respected detective who was still revered by members of the Maui Police Department after having retired—were not to be ignored. Nor, to my mind, were my own reservations, despite my brief acquaintance with Mala. Over the years, I'd learned to give more credence to my intuition; call it a hunch. Of course I believe in facts and evidence, and there was nothing to prove that Mala had died at someone else's hand—at least not yet. I've always enjoyed a statement that former New York senator Daniel Patrick Moynihan once addressed to a colleague who was spewing erroneous information: "You're entitled to your own opinions, sir," the eloquent senator had said, "but not to your own facts." Facts are always to be respected; however, one's inner feelings were to be heeded, too.

I wrote down the word "Motivation" on a fresh page and underlined it twice.

One of the subjects I intended to introduce at the Sunday class was the question of motive in a murder investigation. Not that Maui had many murders to solve. In fact, there were few, if any, in recent history. Nevertheless, a police department has to prepare for all eventualities, and with that logic, I could reasonably raise the topic. Then, too, motive applied to every crime; my counsel on why a town's rumor mill merited attention was still valid. I had examples from my own life that had too often transported me from the writer of murder mysteries to an active participant in the solving of real murders. I wouldn't mention to the class that one of my good friends back home in Cabot Cove often chides me about becoming entangled in real crime. Of course, Seth Hazlitt knows that it was never my intention to become involved. It just seems to happen. He would say it again, I was sure, if I let him know my suspicions about Mala's fall. Better to simply tell him the official police version—as of now—rather than upset him with unsubstantiated innuendo, no matter how earnestly I believed it. I made a mental note to call him in the morning. I couldn't put it off any longer.

I jotted down a number one next to "Motivation" and wrote "Relationships" on the next line.

Relationships between a victim and a murderer often aren't obvious. What might have seemed to be a healthy and positive association—even a loving one—could be cast in a very different light by a careless comment from someone who knew both parties. In Cabot Cove, a small town growing larger with each passing year, casual conversations at Sassi's Bakery, Mara's Luncheonette on the dock, or the bar at Peppino's Restaurant could be a rich vein of useful observations for someone engaged in solving a murder, if that someone was tuned in to what was being said. Did the victim owe money to another person? Was he or she involved in a business deal gone bad? Was the wife or husband in what appeared to be a picture-perfect marriage entangled in a secret love affair that was discovered by the spouse? A suspect who claims never even to have met the victim can be shown to be a liar by a friend who in an off-the-cuff remark over a drink reveals that she'd seen them together.

Of course, I wasn't in Cabot Cove, where I might overhear a comment that would shed light on Mala's death. I knew only what I'd been told and what she'd said.

I hadn't looked at the packet of materials she'd given me over coffee on the day we'd first met. She'd certainly been passionate about the cause she espoused concerning the construction project atop Haleakala.

I put my pad down and began perusing the clippings and position papers contained in the envelope.

The telescope was a $300 million venture, with most of the funds coming from the United States government. Hawaii's two senators had done a good job of lobbying for the money. A number of lawsuits had been filed by Mala's group and another that opposed the telescope, and these had caused repeated construction delays. The contractor, Cale Witherspoon, the lowest bidder, whose company was based in Los Angeles, claimed that the holdups were costing taxpayers $750,000 a month. He also stated that unless construction was resumed soon, $146 million in federal stimulus funds would be withdrawn.

Money! There was a lot at stake financially, especially for Mr. Witherspoon's construction firm. He was quoted as saying, "I have dozens of people sitting on their hands doing nothing—and being paid, I might add—while this pathetic group of do-gooders stands in the way of scientific progress. They ought to be ashamed of themselves. What's more important: advancing scientific knowledge and creating well-educated men and women, or protecting pretty flowers and cuddly little animals? As for violating Hawaiian myths and sacred grounds, Maui isn't your great-grandfather's Hawaii. This is the twenty-first century." A photo of him accompanied the article. He was a big, rawboned man wearing a white ten-gallon cowboy hat and fringed deerskin jacket, someone whose physical presence warned that he was not a man to be trifled with, a my-way-or-the-highway kind of guy.

His statement had been unnecessarily harsh, and I wondered whether he'd crossed the line and had insulted men and women of Maui who might be on the fence about the project.

There were statements from representatives of the University of Hawai'i, who also criticized citizens like Mala for standing in the way of science and education. One such spokeswoman cited a special grant of $20 million attached to the telescope project from the federal government to train Hawaiians in what was termed STEM: science, technology, engineering, and mathematics. In fact, that was the focus of the new science building on the college campus, the one where Mala had an appointment, and where I had found Grace Latimer working in the lab.

From what I read, the telescope would be the largest solar telescope in the world, fourteen stories high and five stories deep, requiring a forty-foot excavation. Its purpose was to enable astrophysicists to study solar wind and solar flares and how they influence the earth's climate, an impressive undertaking to be sure.

The final item I pulled from the envelope was a long interview with Mala in the *Maui News*. A wave of sadness swept over me as I saw her photo, her large, beautiful brown eyes reflecting the sort of grit she demonstrated in leading the protest against the solar telescope. During the interview she said:

Haleakala is a precious site for all Hawaiians. It is known as the House of the Sun, or *Ala hea ka la*, the path to call the sun. For many Hawaiians Haleakala is the physical manifestation of the goddess Pele, and there was a time when only priests were allowed to set foot in the crater. The land belongs to the Hawaiian people and hosts a trove of biodiversity they have protected for centuries. No one, not even our government, has a right to build on it without their permission. Maui has already accommodated the scientific community with the high-altitude observatory currently installed on the summit. Now this sacred temple will be further trampled by men and women for whom the site is meaningless, except for their own selfish interests. There comes a time when we must say "Enough!" The telescope must be stopped at all costs for the sake of the Hawaiian people.

A spokesman for the University of Hawai'i was quoted at the end of the piece: "I find it ironic that Ms. Kapule, herself a scientist and academician, would take such a vehement stand against the pursuit of knowledge."

By midnight the day had caught up with me, and I undressed and got ready for bed. But I continued to think of Mala and her demise and found myself hoping that she had indeed died in an accident brought about by her interest in the flora of Maui. But that was purely a selfish desire on my part. If she had slipped and fallen, I could mourn her death, celebrate her life, and get on with my own.

But if she'd died at someone's hands, it meant spending what time I had on Maui going through the painful process of trying to understand why she'd been killed and who'd killed her.

If Mala had been murdered, the pain for her family and friends was compounded by another perspective: It was a betrayal of the aloha spirit, that yearning to dwell in harmony and love that Hawaiians strive to live by.

Chapter Nine

'O Ka Manawa Kēia No Ke Ko'ala 'Ana!—
It's Barbecue Time!

The scenery surrounding the road leading into the famed Iao Valley was lush and green, steep tree-covered mountains reaching skyward, shading the ground from the sun's intense rays. I leaned back in Mike's SUV and let the cool breezes coming in the open window soothe me. It had been a tense morning, starting with my call to Cabot Cove.

I had searched for the right words—gentle ones to soften the blow—to deliver the news of Mala's death to Seth, but I had failed. Instead, thanks to a faulty telephone connection, I'd ended up shouting that Mala had fallen to her death.

"What do you mean, she fell on her hip?" came Seth's annoyed voice.

"No, Seth. Mala fell off a cliff. I'm so sorry to have to tell you this. She was such a lovely young woman. She died from her injuries."

"What did she lie about?"

When I finally got across the message that there had been a dreadful accident and that our mutual acquaintance had perished from her fall, there was silence on the line. "I'll call you later," he said. Even with the static interference, I could hear the grief and sadness in his voice.

After we hung up, I opened my laptop and quickly wrote Seth an apologetic note. It was morning in Hawaii but afternoon at home. Seth would probably be cooking an early dinner for himself. He might be poring over the sections of the Sunday paper he'd saved to give a closer read, or opening a book he'd been planning to start, or perhaps reviewing charts for patients he would be seeing in the coming week. These were his quiet hours, a relaxing interlude after a busy week and before another one began, a time I knew that he treasured. And I had broken into his peaceful Sunday with a grim announcement.

Our Sunday class hadn't gone smoothly either. Perhaps resentful that the police department was co-opting their weekend, our class of police recruits was in a foul mood. I also sensed that many of them were suffering from the effects of a Saturday night spent in obviously more entertaining pursuits.

Mike and I struggled to keep their attention, reminding them to quiet down, doing a virtual song and dance to pique their interest until the former detective threw up his hands, parked himself in a chair in front of the whiteboard, and sat seething until the chatter died and an uncomfortable silence took its place.

"I would have been happy to sleep late this morning," he finally said. "I'm sure Mrs. Fletcher would have, too. We didn't need to haul ourselves over here to try to pound some valuable information into your hard heads. If you don't want to be here, leave. Don't waste my time, her time"—he pointed at me—"and yours gossiping about who passed out from too many jiggle shots.

"You're supposed to be *cops*. Some people may say that word with derision, but I say I was a cop—I *am* a cop—with pride. A cop knows how to work a scene so it reveals its secrets. A cop knows who to watch and who can be ignored. Cops know, no matter how tough the situation, they can rely on fellow cops to watch their back, to support them, to face danger together, to protect the public." He paused, and his voice, which had been rising, fell back to almost a whisper. "But I don't want you at my back if you don't have enough respect for the job that you whine about having to work on the weekend. Let me tell you something—those criminals out there, they don't know about taking the weekend off. It's maybe their favorite time to steal, to get drunk and punch someone, to wreck a car, to pull out a knife. So get used to it."

Mike slapped his knees and stood, an ironic smile on his face. "I could tell you some really disgusting stories of stuff that goes down on the weekends, but I think I'll let you find that out for yourselves. And now, if you think you're grown-up enough to sit quietly for—" He made a show of looking at his watch. "For the fifteen minutes we have left in our class, I'll turn it over to Mrs. Fletcher."

All eyes turned to me. *Thanks a lot, Mike. That's some act you want me to follow.* But I managed to get through the quarter hour remaining, going over the material to be covered and putting lists I'd prepared up on the board, grateful to hear the tapping of keys as the recruits took notes.

"Tough class today, huh?" Mike said as we drove through a thickly forested section of the steep road.

"I have to admit," I said, "when I was a substitute English teacher in my former life, there were some days it didn't pay to get out of bed. Today, it looked like it was going to be one of those days, but you managed to get them back on track. Of course, that was a pretty dirty trick turning them over to me after you had whipped them into submission."

He chuckled. "I thought you handled it pretty well. You know, in a sense it was a really good lesson for them. You showed them how to hold tight to a goal under difficult circumstances. It's a lesson they're gonna have to learn pretty fast on the job. A cop's best quality is don't-give upness."

"You're adding words to the dictionary?"

"It should be one. 'Stubborn' doesn't quite cover it. Can't tell them to 'bird-dog' it. These kids don't know what a bird dog is. In this business, you only get places if you don't give up. Yeah, 'don't-give-upness.' I like it. So do I call up Webster and tell him to put it in his next edition?"

"If you can call up Noah Webster, who's been dead for a hundred and seventy years, you're a better man than I am, Gunga Din."

Mike Kane howled and pounded the steering wheel.

"Hey," he said as he passed a slow-moving truck, "did you notice that I cleaned up this buggy for you?"

"As a matter of fact, I did," I said. "I'm flattered, although all the fast-food wrappers added character to it."

"That's what I always tell my wife, Lani, but she doesn't see it that way. I'll tell her what you said."

"Please don't," I said. "I want her to like me."

"Oh, no fear on that score. I've told her all about you. She's dying to meet you."

As we drove into the valley, I kept swiveling my head to take in the verdant landscape that rose majestically on either side of the road. It was like entering a primordial jungle, and I wondered whether dinosaurs once roamed here. We pulled into a parking lot shaded by trees, where Mike found a space at the end of a long line of vehicles. Families carried large coolers and boxes of food. One man carted a portable grill, his two youngsters following with bags of charcoal.

"Here we are," Mike announced. "Iao Valley." He pronounced the name "EE-ow."

"From the way it's spelled, I would've pronounced it 'Eye-AY-oh,'" I said.

"You'll get the hang of the Hawaiian language," he said. "There's Lani and our group over there."

I looked in the direction he pointed and saw two dozen men, women, and children gathered around a large kettle barbecue on the banks of a wide, fast-moving stream. Dozens of other large groups also congregated around barbecue grills.

"You have a large family," I commented as we walked in that direction.

"Not all blood relations," he said, "neighbors, too. Everybody becomes family at the Sunday cookout."

Mike's wife saw us and closed the gap. She gave her husband a quick kiss on the cheek and extended her arms to me. "So this is the beautiful woman who's been keeping my husband occupied," she said with mirth in her voice. She wore a flowing, vividly colored yellow-and-red dress. Her inky black hair was worn short, her round face was free of lines, and her smile was high wattage.

"I'm afraid that I've been trying to spend as much time with your husband as possible to learn from him. His instincts are impressive."

"Instincts about crime," she said. "He's not always so instinctive when it comes to more mundane things like picking up after himself around the house." She winked at her husband and linked arms with him. "Come, join us, have a chi chi."

I asked what a chi chi was as she led me to a table where two oversized thermos containers stood amid dozens of plastic cups.

"A classic Hawaiian drink," Mike answered. "Vodka, pineapple juice, coconut cream, and a little sugar. You'll love it."

After handing me my drink, he turned in a circle, arms outstretched, and proclaimed, "Is this not the most beautiful place on earth?"

"It is lovely," I said.

"Four thousand acres of untouched beauty," he said. "Look over there. The Iao Needle."

He pointed to a green-mantled rock that jutted straight up into the air.

"More than a thousand feet tall, taller than the Eiffel Tower. Hawaiians consider it a symbol of Kanaloa, the god of the underworld."

I laughed. "There seems to be a Hawaiian god for everything."

He laughed, too. "Part of our charm. With so many gods looking over us, we're always safe. Come, meet the others."

The next hours flew by quickly. It was a spirited group. The children were full of energy but well behaved, listening to their parents when they were getting out of hand. I never learned of the relationships between many of the people, but that didn't matter. The warmth that prevailed was immensely satisfying, and I thoroughly enjoyed myself. The men in the group cooked enough meat on the grill to feed every Hawaiian god within miles, and a combination of the chi chi and food made me sleepy.

"I'm going to take a stroll," I told Mike.

"Don't go too far," he said. "There's a storm brewing at the headwaters of the stream. It can flood before you know it. We'll be packing up soon."

"I'll keep you in my sight," I assured him and set out along the streambed. A number of older children frolicked in the water, and some teenagers jumped from rocks into a spot where it widened and appeared deep enough for them to not be hurt.

I passed other "families" enjoying the pristine day and

being together. Many waved to me and said, "Aloha," and I returned the greeting, which now came naturally to me. The friendliness reminded me of Cabot Cove, where waves from both friends and strangers were frequent as one walked through town.

I looked back to see if Mike was summoning me, but he was busy tossing a Frisbee with another man. I went a little farther but stopped when I saw a familiar face, Charlie Reed, the owner and skipper of the *Maui Ocean Star*, on which I'd enjoyed my dinner cruise the previous evening.

"Well, hello again," he said. "Didn't expect to see you here."

"I'm here thanks to my teaching partner, Mike Kane," I said. "He was good enough to invite me to join his family."

"Oh, yeah, right. Kane, Detective Kane," he said. "He's supposed to be some sort of a legend on Maui."

It didn't sound as if he was impressed with Mike's celebrated reputation.

"He's quite a man."

Reed's nod was noncommittal. "Say," he said, "I have your book in my car. I was going to send it over to your hotel. How about signing it right now?"

He fetched the book and I inscribed it to him, citing his magnificent catamaran and the cruise I'd taken on it.

"Thanks, Jessica. Are you, uh—?"

I cocked my head.

"Are you involved in some way with what happened to Mala Kapule?"

"I'm not sure what you mean by 'involved.' "

"Rumors are floating around—I mean, some people are

saying—uh, that she might not have been the victim of an accident. The cops questioned me, too. That was annoying. Of course, I was out on the water, so I wouldn't know anything about how she died."

"Really? As I understand it, the police are labeling her death an accident."

"That's a relief. Mala was a pain to a lot of people, but to think that someone might have killed her is—well, it's ridiculous. Don't you agree?"

"As a matter of fact—"

A brilliant bolt of lightning slashing through the sky on the horizon was followed by a succession of thunderclaps. We both looked up.

"That's some storm coming our way," he said, tucking my book inside his jacket under his arm.

"So Detective Kane warned me."

"You were saying," he said.

"Oh, yes. It's true that the police think Mala was the victim of a tragic accident, but I understand enough doubt exists to keep the case open." I watched his face carefully.

"Doubt? Who has doubts?"

"I wouldn't really know. I'm a newcomer here."

He laughed. "Doubts! It's absurd."

"Is it? You said a moment ago that Mala was a pain to many people. I think that's how you put it."

"Sure. Everybody knows that. She and her group of bleeding hearts have kept the telescope project from going forward. They've been standing in the way of progress at every step. That telescope is good for Maui and for Hawaii in general—bring in lots of money, create jobs, do good things for the island, especially the native population—but nobody could get through to her. She was a pain in my a— Never mind. Every time progress was made, she and her lawyer friends would file another suit in court and everything came to a standstill again."

"She was passionate in her beliefs," I said.

"Obstinate, you mean, inflexible, like everyone else who agreed with her. We tried to talk sense into them, but it was useless, and—"

More lightning and thunder interrupted him, and a sudden strong gust of wind sent my hair flying.

"Mr. Reed," I said, "when you say that 'we' tried to talk sense into them, who do you mean?"

"The committee," he replied. "Everyone with a stake in the telescope belongs to it: our elected officials, the university, businesspeople, everyone. We've been fighting Kapule's group from the beginning. Maybe now that she's dead, things will ease up and it can go forward."

The callousness of his attitude startled me.

Charlie must have sensed that his comments might be offensive and covered it with a laugh. "Now, don't take me wrong," he said, "I'm really sorry that she died. Beautiful girl. Aside from our differences about the telescope, I liked her, liked her a lot."

"I'm sure she would have been happy to hear that."

I heard my name called and looked back to see Mike Kane headed in our direction, waving his arm.

"I think Detective Kane and his family are getting ready

to leave. You'll have to excuse me. It was nice to see you again," I said, not sure that it was.

"Same here, Jessica. Thanks for signing the book." He thumped his fist on my novel underneath his jacket.

I intercepted Mike and we walked back to where people were hastily packing up supplies.

"Sorry to interrupt you," he said, "but once the rain comes this stream will be overflowing within minutes. Can be dangerous. I saw that you were talking to Charlie Reed."

"Yes. He had me sign one of my books. I met him last night on his catamaran."

"The sunset cruise."

"Yes, it was a lovely experience."

"He talk about the telescope and Mala Kapule?"

"Just now, yes. He was no fan of her efforts to stop its completion."

Mike gave a snort. "That's putting it mildly. He's one of the biggest financial supporters of a so-called committee that's been fighting her group every step of the way."

"Sounds as though there are some very powerful people on that committee. I'm sure they have a lot more money than Mala and her supporters do."

"True, but from what I've heard, she was some tenacious lady."

I helped Mike's family and friends pack picnic supplies in the cars and had delivered my final load when the rains came, a torrent, sheets of water being tossed about by the increasing wind.

"Just in time," Mike said as we ducked into his SUV. His wife was in the car that had brought her to the cookout, and she waved at us as we joined a procession of vehicles leaving the valley.

"I'm sorry that you have to drive me back to the hotel," I said as he leaned forward to better see through the windshield.

"Not a problem," he said. "You have plans for later?"

I hesitated before I admitted, "Nothing specific. I was thinking I might stop by Mala's home."

"Why?"

"Oh, I don't know, just to pay my respects, maybe gain a sense of how she lived, feel close to her."

"That's as good an excuse as any," he said.

"What do you mean?"

"You're convinced that she didn't fall off that cliff by accident, aren't you?"

I gave him an ironic smile. "You're reading my mind."

"Maybe you're reading *my* mind. Know where she lived?"

"No."

"I can find out easily enough."

"Oh, Mike, I've taken you from your family too much already."

"Lani will understand. I'll call her."

I was pleased that he offered to go with me, and didn't protest any further. He called on his cell phone and left a message on his home answering machine: "Driving Mrs. Fletcher to see where Mala Kapule lived. Don't hold dinner for me in case we run late. Love you, baby."

Obviously the Kanes had a solid, trusting marital relationship, much the same as my husband Frank and I enjoyed when he was alive. I love being around couples who exhibit that sort of easy acceptance of each other and their individual needs and aspirations. It was a bittersweet moment. I sighed at the remembrance, sat back, and enjoyed the sound of rain pelting the roof of the SUV. I was content; I was not the only one who suspected intrigue behind Mala's untimely death.

Chapter Ten

E Komo Mai—Welcome, Come In

Mike checked the telephone directory and got Mala's address, which he told me was close to the airport and the college and not far from where I was staying in Kahului.

I had assumed that he would have asked the police for the information, and said so.

"Yeah, I could have called in for it, but sometimes if you do it yourself, it's faster," he said. "Also, this way we don't raise any eyebrows. Not that anyone would have objected, but they don't have to know my business all the time."

Twenty minutes later we pulled into the driveway of an unassuming two-story house with a fancy red sports car in the carport.

Mike whistled. "That's some set of wheels."

The rain had stopped, and a young man and woman

who'd been sitting on the small porch in front stood at our arrival and came down the three steps to greet us.

"*Aloha*. I'm Mike Kane. This is Jessica Fletcher."

"*Aloha*," the woman said. The man shook Mike's hand.

"This was where Mala Kapule lived?" Mike asked.

"Yes," replied the woman. "You're friends?"

"Not exactly," Mike said.

"I knew her," I said, "but not well. We met at the college where she taught."

"You're aware that—?"

"That she died?" I said. "Yes. Are you related to her?"

"Cousins," said the man. "I'm Joshua. This is Lily."

The sound of voices from inside the house reached us. Lily said, "Other cousins."

"I'm so sorry for your loss," I said.

"I've heard your name," Joshua said to Mike. "Is this an official visit?"

"I'm former Maui PD, retired, so this is more like an unofficial visit. Mrs. Fletcher wanted to see where Mala lived and—"

I completed Mike's statement. "I wanted to extend my condolences to the family, and I have a letter from a friend back home for Mala's aunt, Mrs. Barrett Kapule, but I don't know where she lives. Perhaps one of you could give me directions to her home."

"You can give it to Auntie Edie right now. She's inside," Lily said.

"Oh, thank you." I reached into a pocket in my shoulder bag and withdrew the letter from Seth that I had promised to deliver. His words of condolence were about his friend

Barrett, but now the Kapule family had a second bereavement to contend with.

"Would you mind telling us what you've been told about Mala's death?" I asked.

The two looked at each other before Lily turned back to me. "There doesn't seem to be any question about that. Cousin Mala tripped and fell off a cliff while going after some type of plant. That's what the police told Auntie Edie."

"You're right," Mike said. "That's the way it's on the books."

"I hear a big 'but' in that," Joshua said.

Mike shrugged. "It's only been a short time since she died," he said, "and it's always been my experience that a case shouldn't be closed until every angle has been looked at, every possible cause of death ruled out."

Another glance passed between the couple before Lily asked, "Are you suggesting that Mala might have killed herself?"

Mike shook his head. "I didn't say that, did I?"

"Then do you think someone else killed her?"

"I'm not suggesting anything," he said.

There was an awkward moment of silence finally broken by Lily. "Did you wish to come inside?"

"I wouldn't want to intrude if this is a bad time," I said, not adding that I was hoping that we'd be asked. "If it is, we can come another day."

"It wouldn't be an intrusion," she said, "but let me tell them that you're here."

They both went inside, leaving us in front of the house with the sky threatening again. While we waited to be admitted, I took note of the garden in the small yard. It was artfully arranged with a mix of flowers and plants with interesting foliage. I stopped to admire a small tree with red brushlike flowers. "This is beautiful," I said to Mike.

"It's an *ohiʻa* tree," he said, "native to Hawaii. Most of our plants and flowers were brought here from someplace else over the centuries, but this tree is Hawaiian-born. There's a legend about the *ohiʻa* tree. Would you like to hear it?"

"Of course," I said smiling.

"The goddess Pele turned a young man named Ohiʻa into a tree when he declined to become her lover. You see, he already loved another woman named Lehua. Lehua begged the gods to reunite her with Ohiʻa. But instead of returning Ohiʻa to human form, they made Lehua into the beautiful blossoms that bloom on the tree. That's why we say never to pick the flowers. If you do, it will rain—the tears of the separated lovers."

"That's charming."

"I thought you'd like that one." Mike pointed out another plant with delicate white flowers with pink centers and edged in the same hue.

"The plumeria," he said. "We use those in our leis."

"I'm impressed with your knowledge of plants," I said.

"Being a cop doesn't mean not being interested in other, less nasty things."

Lily came out on the porch and beckoned to us. We climbed the steps and went through the door into the living room, where three other of Mala's relatives, an elderly woman and two young girls, were seated at a table piled high with flowers.

"They're making leis for Mala's celebration," Lily said.

One of the girls was leafing through what looked like a photograph album. "I like these," she said.

"This is Auntie Edie," Lily said of the elderly woman, who had left the table to greet us. "You wanted to deliver a message to her."

"I'm sorry to meet you at such a sad time," I said, introducing myself and Mike.

Barrett's widow was a small woman with a heavily lined face and dark circles under her eyes. Her voice was deep and raspy, a smoker's voice. After we had expressed our sympathies, I offered her the envelope. "This is a letter from a dear friend of mine, Seth Hazlitt. He asked me to deliver it to you personally."

"Ooh, Seth," she said, taking the letter and tapping it against her palm. "Barrett spoke so fondly of him. They corresponded on the computer, you know. At the end, Barrett's eyes were not so good. He liked that he could make the type very large on the screen. It let him write lots of letters. You and your friend are welcome here, Mrs. Fletcher. Come, sit down. Can I get you something to drink? Pineapple iced tea perhaps?"

"Sounds refreshing," I said, speaking for both of us.

Mike took a seat on the couch next to Joshua. While Mrs. Kapule went to the kitchen, I ambled over to the table to see the pictures the girls were looking at in the album. It was a series of photographs of Mala at various ages.

"She was very beautiful," I commented.

"Yes," replied the older girl. "See, here she is at her graduation. I made that lei for her. She taught me how."

"It's lovely. You're very talented."

"And this is her with an old boyfriend."

I bent over to peer at the picture.

"Yes, she was beautiful," Mala's aunt said, coming into the room with two glasses. "She was beautiful and headstrong. I understand you were her friend, Mrs. Fletcher."

I took one of the glasses. "Did Mala tell you about me, Mrs. Kapule?"

"No. Elijah mentioned you," she said, handing the other glass to Mike. "And call me Auntie Edie. Everyone does."

"I will if you'll call me Jessica."

"How did you know my niece, Jessica?"

I explained my brief relationship with Mala and my subsequent introduction to her nephew the cab driver.

"Elijah is a good boy," Auntie Edie said.

"He was very kind to me."

"And Mala was . . . well, you couldn't hold that girl down," she said, taking her seat again at the table. "Barrett was very proud of her. I'm glad he's not here to see what happened." She shook her head sadly. "She didn't always recognize when people were taking advantage of her. I sometimes thought . . ." She trailed off, picking up a blossom and stringing it with other flowers.

"What did you sometimes think?" I prompted.

"Look, Auntie Edie. Look at this picture. We could use this one," the younger girl said.

The old woman leaned over the album and peered at the photograph that the child had pointed out. She ran a finger under one eye, wiping away the moisture. Reluctantly, I wandered back to where Mike was talking with Joshua and Lily.

"I assume the police have been here," Mike said.

"Only briefly" was the reply. "They wanted to make sure that there would be someone here so that no one took advantage of Mala's absence, you know, break in and steal things."

"You're staying here?" I asked.

"Some of us cousins are taking turns," he said.

"I rode with one of your cousins the other night, a taxi driver named Elijah."

"That's my brother. Me and Elijah and my other brother, Matthew. That's our business. Transportation."

"Do you think it would be possible for Mrs. Fletcher and me to see Ms. Kapule's working space?" Mike asked.

"I don't see why not," he replied. "It's upstairs. You say you're a retired police officer?"

"Right. A detective."

"And you think that Mala's death might not have been accidental."

"As I said, I'm just covering all the bases."

"Follow me."

We left our pineapple iced teas in the kitchen and followed Joshua up narrow stairs to a landing on the second floor. An open door to the left revealed Mala's bedroom. I stepped inside while Mike talked with her cousin. There wasn't much room for more than a bed, nightstand, and small dresser. A curtain covered the opening to a closet. It was pulled to one side. Most of the closet's contents were what I'd expect Mala to wear to teach her classes. Mixed in were what her cousin Elijah had called "aloha clothing," colorfully patterned shirts and dresses with the characteristic large flowers and leaves. In a clear plastic garment bag there were a diaphanous blue silk dress and a lightweight cashmere scarf draped over a hanger. Both items still bore their price tags. I was startled to see how expensive they were, more than I would have expected her to be able to afford to spend on a college professor's salary. The floor of the closet held a few pairs of flats and flip-flops and two shoeboxes with designer names on them. I knelt and lifted the cover off one. Inside was a pair of platform high heels of a type I'd seen only in pictures taken on a red carpet.

The fancy car in her driveway and costly clothes in her closet were a surprise. They made me realize how little I actually knew about Mala Kapule. How could I have presumed to understand someone I'd met only once? True, Seth had been sharing her uncle Barrett's e-mail messages for some time, but Dr. Kapule had painted an idealized picture of his niece and her accomplishments. After all, why should he share anything about her that wasn't approving?

I had taken Mala at face value, a dedicated scientist and academician, one with the zeal to do what she thought was right. Her seeming tilting at windmills by supporting a position on the Haleakala telescope that defended the rights of the indigenous peoples of Hawaii only raised her image in my eyes. I've always admired idealists, even if their causes were ultimately unsuccessful.

I pondered Mala's closet. Perhaps she was borrowing the clothes for a special event. Or maybe she had saved for a long time to be able to treat herself to such luxuries. Of course, it was possible she had received one or more of these things as gifts. It wouldn't be unusual for a woman as beautiful as she had been to attract a wealthy admirer. The discovery added to my picture of Mala, but rather than bringing her into focus, it made the image fuzzier.

I crossed the hall to a much larger room that she had used as an office. Mike and Joshua had preceded me into what was a laboratory of sorts. Although the space was relatively large, it could barely contain her huge collection of books, which filled the floor-to-ceiling bookcases. Additional volumes were stacked neatly on the tile floor. One of the drawers of a four-drawer tan file cabinet was open. A picture window dominated one wall. In front of it was a workbench on which two microscopes, vials of liquids, and an assortment of plants under Plexiglas covers were arrayed. An open laptop computer and a printer sat in front of the chair. I nudged the mouse, and the computer's screensaver came to life, a moving collage of brightly colored flowers that swirled about the screen, merging into one, then separating.

"Is this where she did her research?" I asked.

Joshua nodded. "She spent half her life in this room. She really loved what she did, but she was usually a little neater than this." He retrieved a balled-up piece of paper on the floor and dropped it in the wastebasket.

I spotted a sheet that was still in the printer tray. It was a meeting notice for the group Mala spearheaded in opposition to the telescope. It was to be held at a restaurant in Wailuku.

"Mind if I take this?" I asked.

"Sure," he said. "Go ahead. Look around. I'll be downstairs if you need me."

He left Mike and me alone in the room. In his absence, I sifted through other papers on Mala's desk, finding several bills and an unopened envelope from an engineering company in Oregon. I bent over the wastebasket to pluck what Joshua had tossed out. I open the crumpled paper, smoothing it out on the desk. "Look at this, Mike."

"What did you find?"

I stepped back so he could read the message Mala had crushed.

I know what you're up to. You're asking for trouble. Keep it up and you'll end up buried at Haleakala.

"Somebody didn't like her much," he muttered.

"One of many people who resented her opposition to the telescope," I commented. "She mentioned to me that she'd received nasty e-mails. Do you want to give this to Detective Tahaki?"

"Yeah, Henry should see this." Mike stuffed the paper in his pocket. "I don't know that he'll do anything about it, but I'll show it to him anyway. Let me know if you find anything else."

There was a soft noise at the door, and Auntie Edie stepped softly into the room, looking around, her eyes moving from the shelves to the glass terrariums to the microscope.

"You must have been very fond of Mala," I said to her.

She didn't verbally respond, but her eyes took on a glassiness as she trained them upward. Mike and I watched as her lips moved silently, as though speaking to an unseen person in the room.

"She knows," she finally said, taking a deep breath and nodding emphatically.

"Pardon?" I said.

"She knows," she repeated.

"Who knows?" Mike asked.

"Uli."

"The goddess?" Mike said.

"Uli knows everything. She knows what happened to Mala."

I started to say something, but Mike raised an index finger to stop me.

"Those who did bad things to Mala also pray to Uli. She knows who they are. They will be punished."

She looked from Mike to me without saying any more and walked from the room.

"What was that all about?" I whispered to Mike.

"Uli is our heavenly mother," he said in hushed tones. "She was married to our creator, Eli Eli. Hawaiians believe that Uli beholds all justice and righteousness. Nothing escapes her all-seeing eye. When she gave instructions from above, the *kāhuna* always nabbed their man. The police have benefited many times, thanks to Uli."

"Has she ever helped you as a detective?" I asked.

"Sure. I've had suspects spill their guts because they're convinced that Uli tells them to. I'm not a religious man, Jessica, but I don't discount anything." He surveyed the room. "We done here?"

"Yes. For now."

We said good-bye and thanked Auntie Edie and Mala's cousins before leaving the house and getting into Mike's SUV.

"What's next on your agenda?" he asked.

"I'd like to revisit the place where Mala fell," I said, thinking aloud, "but I need to go there at night."

"Okay."

"Oh, I didn't mean to suggest that you drive me."

"You don't want me to tag along?"

"But I've taken you away from your wife and family long enough."

"Lani's used to me being away. No problem. I'll give her a call and tell her we're going to have dinner. She can join us, if she wants. That sound good to you?"

"It sounds wonderful."

But Lani declined our invitation, preferring to stay home to watch *Masterpiece* on PBS. "Have a good time," I heard her tell Mike before he snapped his cell phone shut.

"Please remind me to buy your understanding wife a special present before I leave Maui."

"She'd be flattered," he said.

"What would she like?"

"I'm the wrong person to ask. I may have solved a lot of crimes over the course of my career, but I never seem to pick the right gift for Lani."

"Then you won't be of any help in the gift department."

"Afraid not. But I do have one suggestion."

"Which is?"

"Ask the goddess Uli. She knows everything."

"I just might do that."

Mike navigated the SUV through traffic and started whistling a tune.

"Didn't you tell me it was bad luck to whistle?"

"Only after dark. It's not dark yet."

Chapter Eleven

Pūpūkahi I Holomua—Unite to Move Forward

Had Mike not offered to take me to dinner, I would have opted for something simple at the hotel, maybe room service. Knowing where to eat when traveling is always problematic unless someone you trust gives you a recommendation. Without that, you tend to end up in a place that's convenient (and maybe not with the best food) or a touristy restaurant whose dishes are budget busters.

But with a Maui legend leading the way, we ended up in a tiny café off the beaten track, where Mike was greeted like one of the numerous Hawaiian gods. The woman who owned the spot was also the chef and prepared for us what Mike said was her specialty, opah, a rich, creamy baked moonfish that Mike said was the Hawaiian good-luck fish, often given as a gift. It was delicious.

The rain had resumed and came down in torrents during

dinner, but by the time we'd finished the entrée it had stopped again. We lingered over strong coffee and a dessert that the owner called *kalamai haupia*, pudding that was more the consistency of Jell-O. She told us that it was a secret recipe using masa harina, corn flour of the type used to make tortillas. I would never have ordered it on my own, but the result was sublime.

"I never want to eat again," I said as we bid farewell to the owner and went to Mike's SUV. The sun had just set, painting the sky with vivid streaks of red and orange and yellow. I stood by the open passenger door and took in the spectacular beauty of the horizon.

"Do you ever get tired of the sunsets?" I asked.

"I wouldn't say I'm tired of them, but I don't much notice them anymore—unless, of course, I'm with a visitor who does."

Mike was in a chatty mood as we drove toward Wailea and the coastal walk, which ran behind the south shore's condominiums and resorts, including the one at which Bob and Elaine Lowell were staying. With any luck we wouldn't run into them.

The sky was blanketed with stars by the time we left the car and headed for the place from which Mala had fallen. Fallen? Had she fallen, or had someone pushed her to her death? While I regarded our destination as the scene of the crime, I had a sinking feeling that Mala's death might never be considered anything but a tragic accident. In the murder mystery novels I'd written, the crime is always solved in the final pages and the murderer brought to justice. But I knew only too well that in real life things didn't always work that way. Many murders go unsolved every day, and years go by with the family and friends of the victims never enjoying that sense of closure we hear so much about. Sometimes, through dogged work by a detective obsessed with a particular murder, a cold case becomes hot again and the perpetrator is made to pay for his or her crime. But that doesn't happen frequently—not frequently enough to suit me.

The heavy rain had soaked the ground, making it mushy as we walked across the vast grassy field toward the path, the beam of Mike's flashlight swinging back and forth in front of us. Mike's previous talkativeness had abated. He was silent as we navigated the narrow walkway, and I didn't say anything to break the mood. There was a pleasant chill in the air; a refreshing breeze came off the water.

We reached the spot where the police said Mala had fallen. The grass was still trampled; the rain had slicked down the blades. A vision of her going over the edge came to me, and I shuddered involuntarily.

"You all right?" Mike asked.

"I'm fine. I was just envisioning Mala falling to her death on the rocks below."

"Not a pretty picture."

I took a few tentative steps toward the edge. Mike grabbed my arm. "Hey, we don't need a second body down there," he cautioned.

I looked down at my shoes, then at the grassy edge. "Something bothers me," I said, almost to myself.

"What?"

"This is where Mala supposedly fell," I said.

"Right," Mike concurred.

"But—"

"But what?"

"Look at the ground. If she had slipped, the grass would have been mashed down at the very edge. But it isn't. It's trampled down here a few feet from the edge, undoubtedly by at least two pairs of shoes, but isn't flattened where she would have lost her footing."

"You mentioned that there were various pairs of shoes before, Jessica, but that doesn't prove anything. Some of the prints were probably made by cops with big feet."

"You may be right, Mike, but I remember what you said the first time we came here, that you couldn't fathom why someone as young and physically fit as Mala would lose her balance."

"Maybe she was high on some drug."

I shook my head. "Somehow I don't believe it. Mala struck me as someone who didn't like to lose control. But I guess it's a question we should ask."

"The other alternative is that someone pushed her," he said flatly.

"I'm more convinced than ever that that's what happened. Maybe not a deliberate shove, but her fall had to have involved others. The way I see it, after she was pushed, she grabbed this bush and went over the edge grasping the leaves. That's why it was assumed that she'd died while trying to climb down to pick a plant. It's probably the same plant that's up here."

When he didn't say anything, I turned and faced him.

"Am I right?" I asked.

"You are very right," he said. "The scenario you're painting matches perfectly with what I've been thinking since the morning we first came here."

"You've had that opinion all along?" I said.

He nodded, and the moonlight caught the mischievous grin on his face. "You're probably assuming that I'm just saying it to make it sound as though I don't want to be outdone by you."

"I wasn't assuming that at all," I said.

"But if you were, you're wrong. To be honest, I wanted to see whether a famous writer of murder mysteries would pick up on something like that. Well, you have, and I'd be more comfortable if you would take a few steps back."

I did as he suggested. "Behind that pleasant facade, Detective Kane is a devious man."

He bowed slightly. "Deviousness is an important asset for any detective, Jessica."

"Like don't-give-upness?"

"Precisely. Don't-give-upness and deviousness. Both sides of the coin. I take your comment as a supreme compliment."

"You devil," I said, and started to laugh.

"We make a good team," he said.

"I'm flattered to be a part of it."

"There's something my teammate should know," he said.

"Which is?"

"When I checked my cell phone after dinner, I saw that Detective Tahaki e-mailed me the coroner's report."

"On Mala?"

"Yup. Good man, Henry. I knew I could count on him."

"What did the report say, Mike?"

"It seems that the autopsy on Ms. Kapule wasn't very instructive. There was no alcohol in her bloodstream. She had numerous abrasions on her head and body, some of which held traces of the sort of lava rock where she fell. Her lungs were clear, suggesting she was already dead before the body washed into the water. The foliage in her hand was of a type consistent with bushes throughout the island, including up here. Toxicology report to come."

"Were there any wounds that might have been inflicted before she went over the edge?"

"By her murderer, you mean?"

"Yes."

"Nothing definitive."

"But if she was pushed, wouldn't there be marks on her body?"

"I don't see how, unless she struggled."

"Of course, if someone bumped into her and she lost her footing on the wet grass and fell, is that murder?"

Mike smiled. "Good questions, Mrs. Fletcher. Like I said, we make a good team. Come on, I'll drive you back to your hotel."

The thought of getting back to my room, where I could take a hot shower, get dressed for bed, and curl up with a good book until sleep arrived, was a welcome contemplation. It had been an eventful day: my difficult call to Seth; the challenging class that morning; the barbecue in Iao Valley; visiting Mala's home and meeting her family; the pleasant dinner; followed by the disturbing visit to where Mala had met her death. It was a lot to contemplate and I was exhausted.

Mike walked in the direction from which we'd come and

disappeared around a bend, but I remained transfixed near the grassy edge of the path. It was almost as though Mala were standing next to me, peering down at the rugged lava rocks and swirling waters below. I was deep into this reverie when I suddenly sensed someone behind me. Before I could turn, a pair of hands gripped my shoulders. I screamed as the hands pulled me back, almost causing me to lose my footing. There was a loud flapping of wings as startled birds rose in the air, making such a noise that I couldn't hear myself think.

The grip was released, and I spun around to be face-to-face with a tall man with a square, chiseled face on which a thick mustache curved down around the edges of his mouth.

"Who are you?" I said, struggling to catch my breath.

"I should ask you the same thing," he said.

"Why did you come up behind me and frighten me like that?"

"To keep you from going over the edge."

The man wore a white terry-cloth bathrobe over pajamas and slippers.

"Well," I said, "you might have meant well, but you could have at least said something to warn me instead of just grabbing me."

"What are you doing here at night?" he asked, his arms folded over his chest.

"I was— I'm here with—"

Mike suddenly appeared. "Are you all right, Jessica?"

"Yes, I'm fine," I said. "This gentleman surprised me, that's all. And apparently my reaction woke up the birds."

"Those francolins make a racket; best alarm clock there is." Mike lifted his chin at the man. "What did you want?"

"I asked what she was doing here," the man said.

"Taking a walk," Mike said. "It's public property. You live here?"

"That's right." He pointed to the house where we'd met Koko and his grandmother.

"You're Koko's father?" I said.

"How do you know my son?" He tilted his head, appraising me.

"Look," Mike said, "Mrs. Fletcher and I are here because of what happened to her friend, Mala Kapule, the lady who went over the cliff. You know about that?"

"Of course I know about it. I was afraid that this lady was about to suffer the same fate."

I looked past him and saw Koko in his pajamas and straw cowboy hat standing on the patio. Moonlight reflected off his glasses.

"We haven't been formally introduced," I said, extending my hand. "Jessica Fletcher."

He hesitated before accepting my greeting and giving me a tentative shake but had no compunction about reaching for Mike's outstretched hand.

"Kane. Mike."

"You the ones who spoke to my son a day or two ago?"

"That's right," I said. "He's a charming little boy."

This brought forth the first smile from the father. "Warren Mohink," he said.

"Pleased to meet you," Mike said. "You and your wife must be proud of your son."

"He doesn't have a mother," Mohink said. "She died a few years ago. My mother lives with us and takes care of Koko while I'm at work."

"You work near here?" Mike asked.

"The Thompson sugar mill. I'm a production manager."

"As long as we're standing here," Mike said, "let me ask whether you saw or heard anything the night Ms. Kapule died. Mrs. Fletcher and I already asked your son when we met him."

"The kid don't know anything," Mohink said quickly—too quickly, as far as I was concerned. "He was sound asleep all night. Hope he didn't tell you different. Kona's got a big imagination, makes stuff up." He waved his hand behind him. "This week he's a cowboy. Next week could be Batman. Happens all the time since his mother died. We told the other officers and that lady who came that we didn't see or hear anything."

"What lady was that?" I asked.

Mohink shrugged. "Said she was friend of the woman who died. Wanted to know if we'd seen it happen. I told her the same thing I'm telling you."

"What did she look like?" Mike asked.

Mohink yawned. "She looked like a woman, that's all, nothing special about her. Kind of blond, maybe. I wasn't really paying attention. Kona was driving me crazy crying and trying to hide under his bed. I left the lady with my mother and went inside."

"Would you recognize her if you saw her again?" I asked.

"I don't know. Look, it's late. I gotta work tomorrow."

"Of course," I said. "Sorry if I overreacted when you came up behind me."

125

"Just didn't want to see you go over the way she did. I'll say good night now."

"Good night," Mike and I said in unison.

We watched him cross the expanse of lawn leading to his house.

"But, Daddy, I wasn't—"

"Not now, Koko." He ushered his son inside and closed the sliding doors behind them.

We headed back to where Mike had parked his car at the hotel. Halfway there I stopped and wrapped my arms about myself.

"You all right?" Mike asked.

"I just have this hunch that the boy knows more than he told us the day we met, and the adults in his life are trying to keep him from talking about it."

"You think he saw something?"

"I don't know," I said as we resumed walking. "Even if he does know something, getting him alone won't be easy. His father is as protective of the boy as the grandmother was. And of course a child doesn't always understand what he sees."

We didn't say much else on the drive back to my hotel.

"I can't thank you enough for indulging me," I said as he pulled into the parking lot.

"No worries, Jessica. What do you have on tap tomorrow?"

"I'm going to attend the meeting of the group that Mala was involved with, the one protesting the construction of the telescope, but that's not until seven at night. No plans before that."

"I have to put in some time at the hotel where I work, but I'll be free in the afternoon."

"I've imposed upon you enough, Mike."

"Nonsense. You obviously want to spend the day digging deeper into Mala's life and whatever might shed light on her death. I'm at your disposal. After all, we're now a team."

"Okay," I said. "Tell you what. This team member wants to go back to talk to Koko. Nothing may come of it, but I want to try. I can do that in the morning. If the weather is good—and I can't imagine that it won't be—I'll bicycle over there."

"That's a pretty long ride."

"Not as long as the ride down Haleakala after the sunrise."

"True. You planning to do that?"

"Not tomorrow, but maybe one day. I may also go back to the campus to speak with her colleagues. The head of the department was in competition with her for the position. Of course, he had won the position before she died. Then, I—"

"Whoa! Pretty ambitious day you have planned, Jessica."

"What's the alternative, sit by the pool and get sunburned?"

"That's an appealing alternative to me, but I get your point. How about I pick you up tomorrow sometime after lunch. I'll call you with a specific time."

"Sounds like a plan to me."

"Good. Get yourself some rest. Looks to me like you're in training."

I entered my room, flipped on the lights, closed the drapes, and got into my pajamas and the robe provided by the hotel. I opened a novel I'd started and read a few pages, but I couldn't concentrate. I kept seeing Koko's face in the window, looking passively down at me, and wondered what secrets his mind harbored.

"That boy knows something," I said aloud to myself, "and I want to know what it is. I *have* to know what it is."

Chapter Twelve

E Kala Mai Ia'u!—Excuse Me!

I awoke the next morning to the ping of raindrops against the sliding glass doors. So much for riding my bike. I padded across the room and parted the drapes. Although it was raining, the sun shone brightly. Within minutes the rain stopped and a lovely rainbow arched across the horizon, a positive sign for the new day.

On my way to the hotel restaurant I stopped in the gift shop and bought a colorful blouse to augment my Hawaiian wardrobe, tucking it in my shoulder bag. I was seated at a table overlooking the bay. I had a busy day planned and ordered a big breakfast—pancakes, bacon, orange juice, and coffee—to fortify myself for the ride ahead. The dinner with Mike the previous night had done what big dinners always do to me—left me feeling famished the next day. The pancakes were delicious, but I still rank the blueberry version at

Mara's Luncheonette in Cabot Cove to be superior, maybe out of simple loyalty to my hometown establishments.

My hunger sated, I reserved a bicycle at the front desk and strolled toward my room, intent on changing into my new purchase, when I felt an odd prickle, as if there was someone watching me. I looked around but didn't see any faces turned in my direction. The hotel lobby was crowded. Local artists had set up displays of their works, and I joined the crowd perusing the tables of jewelry, *kapa* cloth scarves, and other artistic creations. I was particularly charmed by a series of color photographs of underwater creatures taken by a pleasant fellow named Scott Mead. One work really caught my eye. It was of a giant sea turtle, a magnificent specimen, just like the one the little girl had pointed out prior to the start of the luau. Was that only three days ago?

The photograph was made even more lifelike because it was printed on aluminum, which altered the look of the piece as the light source changed. The artist took great pains to explain this unusual method of printing, a technique he'd learned while working with aluminum in the aerospace industry. He moved an overhead spot, showing me how the appearance of the water and the animal changed depending upon the angle of the light striking the metal. Intrigued, I handed him my credit card and arranged to have the framed photograph sent to my home in Cabot Cove, where I had the perfect spot for it in my office. I felt good after making my purchase. For the first time since arriving on Maui, I'd partaken in something pleasant and unique to the island that didn't involve the controversy over Mala's death.

As I headed back to my room in preparation for my bike

ride to Wailea and my hoped-for interview with Koko, I passed a heavyset man, his face buried in a newspaper, standing next to an events board. "Excuse me," I said, stepping closer. "I just want to read this." Without a word, he turned and walked away.

There were three items listed: The Rotary club's luncheon would be held in the restaurant at noon; a Maui produce company was sponsoring its annual conference over the next few days; and a press conference was scheduled at nine thirty that morning in one of the public rooms, hosted by the Witherspoon Construction Company. That morning's rainbow had indeed been a good omen. I had intended to seek out Cale Witherspoon, who'd delivered what I considered unnecessarily insensitive comments in the newspaper article that Mala had included in my packet of materials. Instead of having to go to him, he was coming to me. That rainbow was prescient.

I changed into my new aloha shirt and killed time before the start of the conference by checking the Internet to see if Mala's family had posted a date for her celebration of life. I didn't find that, but I did see an article in which she had been identified by name as the victim of a tragic fall. Several comments below the article, bylined by Joe Luckey, were from bereaved students, mourning the loss of their beloved professor. One comment labeled "Anonymous" wrote: "The committee will be real happy that she's no longer around for them to trip over. Speaking of trips . . ." Another reader chastised Anonymous: "Nice comment, you no-name chicken. Her death is not funny. She was a true champion of Hawaii and what the Aloha Spirit really means." Anonymous responded: "Aznuts! Science is more important than legend. She was babelicious, I'll give you dat." The remaining comments were reciprocal insults, and I was disappointed not to see anything that Mike and I could follow up on.

I closed the computer and took out the papers Mala had given me, refreshing my knowledge of the controversy. Confident that I had a passing familiarity with the subject, I found the room where the conference was being held and took a seat in the back row. A TV crew and a local radio station had arrived earlier and positioned their microphones at a podium along with the hotel's mike. A smattering of men and women, who I assumed were reporters, had taken seats in the front, while a hotel staff member busied himself making last-minute adjustments to the podium and chairs behind it. A table with breakfast pastries, sliced fruit, pitchers of orange and pineapple juice, and a coffee urn had been set up against a wall.

I'd been there only a few minutes when Cale Witherspoon arrived, flanked by two younger men, both wearing suits and ties and sunglasses, which struck me as pretentious considering they were indoors. If Witherspoon had been the president of the United States, I would have pegged his colleagues as Secret Service. They had that fierce protective look about them. One was tall and carried himself like an athlete. The other was shorter; his suit looked too small on what appeared to be a weightlifter's body. The taller one looked familiar, although I couldn't peg where I'd seen him before. A middle-aged woman clutching a clipboard trailed behind them and took the aisle seat in the front row, putting her bag on the seat to her left, effectively signaling that she didn't want anyone to sit beside her.

Witherspoon, dressed in the same outfit he'd worn in the photograph that accompanied the article about him—large white cowboy hat, fringed tan deerskin jacket—took his place in the front of the room and looked around. He might have been handsome in his youth, but his features were now coarse from age and perhaps overindulgence.

Apart from the reporters and broadcast crews, only a few other people were present when the shorter man who'd accompanied Witherspoon stepped to the podium. "Thank you for being here," he said in a surprisingly high voice. "What we have to say today is important for every citizen of Maui. Without further ado, Mr. Cale Witherspoon has an announcement to make."

Witherspoon, who was even larger than he appeared in his photograph, took the podium, smiled, and said, "I hope y'all treat yourselves to the goodies over there on that table. Somebody told me that if you want to get the press to cover something, you've got to feed 'em." His laugh at his comment was a lonely one in the otherwise silent room.

"All right," he said after some throat clearing, "I've asked y'all here today because, as the head of the company charged with building the solar telescope up on Haleakala, it's my pleasure to announce that it looks like the Court of Appeals is about to grant the most recent motion our lawyers have filed to lift the existing restrictions on the construction and allow this great project to go forward. This is good news not only for Witherspoon Construction; it's good news for the people of Maui. Let's hear it for Maui!"

If Witherspoon had been expecting a cheer, he was disappointed. He continued, "As y'all know, there have been objections. A small group of misguided people have stood in the way of progress. They didn't understand the importance . . ." His voice had taken on an angry tone. He glanced down at the woman with the clipboard in the aisle seat; she shook her head very slightly. Witherspoon coughed into his fist. "Now, I have the greatest respect for the Hawaiian native people and certainly support anyone's right to voice their opinions. This is America, after all. But I believe this project will benefit everyone in the state—in the country for that matter—and especially the native people of Hawaii. I'm hoping they'll come to see that in time. Anyone is welcome to talk with me about this. My door is always open. I listen to all views." He checked his associate in the front row again, and this time she was nodding.

"I'd like to take this moment to extend my sympathies to the family and friends of Miss Mala Kapule, who died in a tragic accident this past weekend. She was a worthy opponent, and a fine representative of the Hawaiian natives. I didn't agree with her views, it's true." He chuckled at his own admission. "Y'all know that. But I hold no grudge, and feel real bad about what happened to her. All of us at Witherspoon Construction join me in sending our condolences. Terrible thing. Terrible thing when a young person dies. If y'all have any questions, I'll be happy to answer them."

It seemed to me that he was making an effort to be charming in his comments about Mala's death. At least he didn't say anything insensitive or mean-spirited, but I couldn't help feeling that he was elated that a major obstacle was now out of the way. It was as if Mala had been a piece of statuary standing between Witherspoon and Haleakala and had been bulldozed into dust, paving the way for Witherspoon to proceed. I tried hard to give him the benefit of the doubt—I don't like to judge people's motives harshly—but my dislike of the man was instantaneous.

The few reporters at the front of the room vied for his attention and asked their questions about what the court ruling meant and what timetable was now in place for proceeding with construction. Witherspoon answered them smoothly, although he had to ask one of the men who'd arrived with him about some technical issues.

A young woman, who was not part of the press contingent, raised her hand. "What about Haleakala?" she asked. "It's a sacred site. What are you doing to protect it? I read that this project isn't good for the land and the ecology."

Witherspoon laughed as he said, "You really shouldn't believe everything you read, ma'am." He looked at the reporters in the front row and added as an aside, "Not meaning what you good folks write, of course," before going back to the woman's question. "There's already a development on top of Haleakala. And there's been no grievous damage to the crater. People can still visit this dramatic and important site. There's hundreds of tourists coming up every week, maybe even every day. I'd worry more about litter and pollution from all those cars than about a bunch of scientists going about their business. Looks like the judges agree with me, which is why we are close to saying we're ready to roll. The sacred ground up around the volcano will be just as sacred after the telescope is built and operating. Having it there to contribute to our understanding of the solar system and its effect on our weather means human progress. That's good for Maui. That's good for all of Hawaii."

He fielded a few more questions before thanking everyone for coming and reminding them to enjoy the food spread. Flanked by his colleagues, Witherspoon was first at the table, where he picked up a piece of pastry and was chomping on it when I joined him.

"Mr. Witherspoon?" I said.

He covered his mouth with his hand to keep crumbs from falling as he finished the Danish. "Yes, ma'am."

"My name is Jessica Fletcher."

"Well, hello there, Miss Fletcher. Glad you were able to be here this morning."

"I was a friend of Mala Kapule."

"Were you now?" His face took on a somber expression. "Real sorry about what happened to your friend."

"Thank you. You mentioned that her death was a tragic accident."

He nodded at me, his head going up and down continuously like a bobblehead doll's.

"You stated this as a fact. How can you be so sure—"

"That's not my judgment, you know. It's in the police report, public record. So I'm only repeating what the police have said, and I trust their expertise."

"You don't find it strange that the person who was most active in opposing your project turns up dead just as a court is about to make a ruling in the case?"

"I hope you're not thinking that I had anything to do with her demise. The police have said it was an accident. Therefore, it was an accident."

"That's a preliminary finding," I retorted.

"And you expect it to change? I've heard the rumors,

Miss Fletcher. There's always some paranoid folks who'll see things that aren't there, like those conspiracy buffs who think every assassination was some sort of plot."

"Well, I'm not a conspiracy buff, Mr. Witherspoon, but the theory that Mala's fall might not have been an accident is held by some very substantial people."

"Including you?"

"As a matter of fact, yes."

"And why are you tellin' *me* this?"

"As a key figure in the debate over the future of Haleakala—"

"There's no debate over the future of Haleakala, Miss Fletcher, only the delaying tactics of those who want to throw a wrench in the works. What does it concern you?"

"I don't like to see young people die."

"Who does?"

"You should know, Mr. Witherspoon, that while I'm here on Maui, I'm determined to get to the bottom of Mala's death."

"Then maybe it's time for you to go home, Miss Fletcher. This is not your business."

"I'm not planning to go home, Mr. Witherspoon. You can insist this death was an accident, but I believe it to be suspicious, and I'm not the only one." I debated using Mike Kane's name, but given Mike's position as a former police officer, I didn't want to get him in trouble with the department. Our "investigation" wasn't official. Also, it wasn't my place to speak for him.

"Look, you're not with the police. What's your position here?"

"I'm a writer."

"A newspaper? What newspaper?"

"I'm not with a newspaper. I write books."

"And you're writing a book about this?" He was incredulous.

"That's not my intention. I'm simply a private citizen who wants to know what happened to a friend."

The taller of Witherspoon's colleagues who'd overheard our conversation said to the contractor, "We have to go, Cale. The meeting."

"Right, right," Witherspoon said. To me, he said, "I've enjoyed our little chat, Miss Fletcher, and I wish you all the best in looking into your friend's death."

"You could help."

"Oh, really? In what way could I help? And make it quick. I have a meeting to get to."

I cast around for a reason to extend our discussion. It was unlikely Witherspoon would have put himself in jeopardy by killing anyone personally. But by the looks of the men who worked for him, it wouldn't surprise me if Mala's death had been a contract killing. I needed more time to assess the man to gauge how far he would go to protect his interests. "I'd appreciate meeting with you to help me understand the background and recent developments in the Haleakala project."

"All you have to know is that it's going forward."

"What happened to the open door you boasted about? Anyone can come and talk to you, you just said."

"I don't have time for this," he said, making a show of looking at his watch.

I was about to admit defeat when I looked at his taller assistant—I suppose you could call him that—and had a moment of recognition. If I wasn't mistaken, he was one of the men I overheard at the luau. My mind flashed back to the conversation that night.

"Did he try talking to her?" he asked.

"It's too late for talking," the other replied. He was a beefy man in a colorful patterned shirt, shorts, and flip-flops. "She'd better quit if she knows what's good for her. They're not going to put up with it anymore."

"She's not going to convince him to change his mind, even if she tries."

"If she scuttles this project, I swear he'll kill her."

I pulled myself back into the present moment.

"Excuse me," I said to the young man. "Weren't you at the luau the night Ms. Kapule fell to her death?"

He looked to his boss before turning and walking away.

Witherspoon gave me a baleful look. "You mind some advice, Mrs. Fletcher?"

"Go ahead."

"I suggest that you enjoy your stay here on Maui like any other tourist. Stick to writing a magazine article or something. Maybe I'll buy a copy when it comes out. Don't worry that pretty head of yours about things that don't concern you. You'll be flying outta here back to where you come from. Have yourself a good trip and let the Hawaiian people enjoy the sorta success that the Haleakala telescope will give 'em. Excuse me. I've got another appointment."

What arrogance, I thought as I watched him and his acolytes leave the room.

I was poised to depart, too, when a man who'd been sitting with the other reporters approached. "Jessica Fletcher?" he said.

"Yes."

"My name is Joe Luckey, the *Maui News.*" He pronounced his name "LOO-key" and handed me his card.

"Yes?"

"I'm writing an article on Mala Kapule and the Haleakala telescope project."

"Oh?"

"Some of the people I've interviewed mentioned that you were here on the island and have been—well, I suppose you could say that you've been delving into the circumstances surrounding her death."

"Mind if I ask who told you that?"

"Not at all. I heard it from one of Ms. Kapule's family members."

I thought back to when Mike Kane and I visited Mala's house and wondered whether one of her cousins had been the source of that information.

"Could we talk for a few minutes?" he asked.

"I really have nothing to say to the public about Mala Kapule's unfortunate death," I said, "other than it's tragic to lose any young person and especially someone with such intelligence and promise."

"But I'm told that you and Detective Mike Kane are trying to prove that she might have been murdered."

"We're hardly in a position to do such a thing. Any investigation remains in the hands of the authorities."

"Nevertheless, I hear you're asking questions," he replied.

"People are talking about it. Maui's not a big island, Mrs. Fletcher."

"I'm beginning to find that out," I said. "I know you're working on your article and I respect that, but I have nothing to contribute. It was nice meeting you, Mr. Lucky."

He gave a boyish grin. "Mr. Lucky. That was a TV show, wasn't it? My name is LOO-key."

I smiled and shook his hand. "My mistake," I said.

With a disappointed expression, he turned away.

I was about to take my leave when it occurred to me that there might be something to be learned from this young reporter. After all, it's what I'd been teaching police recruits— take in any and all information from anyone, including those who are doing nothing more than circulating unsubstantiated rumors.

"Mr. Luckey," I called out, pronouncing his name correctly this time, "I apologize if I was somewhat curt. I'm having a change of heart. I would be happy to speak with you. Perhaps we can help each other."

"That's great, Mrs. Fletcher. Can I buy you a cup of coffee?"

"There's coffee over there," I said, pointing to the table with breakfast items. "Might as well take advantage of it."

With a cup of coffee and a glass of pineapple juice—Joe Luckey also fortified himself with two pieces of raspberry Danish—we settled in a corner of the room. He turned to a fresh page in his slender reporter's notebook, removed the cap from his pen, and asked, "What have you uncovered about the way Ms. Kapule died?"

I had to make a fast decision about how much to share

with him. The answer was as little as possible, although I also knew that in fairness I had to offer something in return for learning what, if anything, he had come across.

"I have to warn you, I don't have anything concrete. There's a question of where she actually fell. It's not clear from the markings on the ground precisely where she ended up going over the edge. And while my knowledge of her personality is only from short acquaintance, I find it hard to believe she was collecting plant samples in the middle of the night."

He made a note in his pad.

"But that's conjecture, Mr. Luckey. Please don't report it as fact."

"Oh, I would never do that, Mrs. Fletcher. And please call me Joe."

"And I'm Jessica. Now, what have you heard about Ms. Kapule's death in your travels around Maui?"

"Just the usual scuttlebutt. Mostly, I hear that you and Mike Kane are working together."

"You know Detective Kane?"

"Sure I do. The big *kahuna*. Hollywood used to use that term to refer to surfers. But here on the islands, it's always meant an important person. Mike's a *kahuna*. Any time there's a tough case, the police call on him for the answer. Another reporter on the paper wrote a profile of him a few months ago. Great guy!"

"He certainly is. We're teaching a course together for the new class of police recruits. What did you think of Mr. Witherspoon's comments this morning?"

He laughed. "He's a big blowhard, Jessica, a real *moke*, but I suppose he's got a right to want to push the telescope on Haleakala forward. There's lots of money involved. And as the lowest bidder, he probably doesn't have the reserve some of the other bidders had."

"*Moke?*"

"Hawaiian for a big, tough guy."

"Sounds appropriate. Money is a powerful motivator," I said.

He started to write but stopped and looked up at me. "Are you suggesting that he might have had something to do with Ms. Kapule's death?"

I held up my hand and said, "Let's not start reading things into our conversation."

"I wouldn't blame you if you felt that way. Witherspoon sure had a motive for wanting to see Mala Kapule dead."

"You need more than a motive to charge someone with murder. He certainly wanted her to stop interfering in the construction of the telescope. Beyond that, I don't think we can say. There may have been others with different motives. Let's not go jumping to conclusions."

"Sorry." He cocked his head at me. "You write books about murder."

"That's right."

"You ever do books about true crime?"

"No. I only write fiction. Why do you ask?"

"Well, I thought that if Ms. Kapule's death was murder, I might try to write a book about it."

"I think that would be a good idea," I said, "provided it *was* murder. We don't know that."

"Right, right. I just mean that if—you know, just thinking out loud."

"I understand. Have you spent time with the group opposed to the telescope?"

"I went to one meeting and reported on it as part of a longer piece."

"I'm going to a meeting tonight," I said. "I'm sure it will be different without Mala there."

"She was a tough leader."

"You knew her?"

"Met her a few times. She was no-nonsense, about protecting Haleakala, I mean. Stopped anyone cold if they even tried to express a different point of view. Have you been up there?"

"To Haleakala? No, but I would like to see what it's like."

"It's pretty impressive. Bus companies run trips up there for the sunrise. Lots of people go up by bus and come back down on a bike. You ever ride a bike?"

I laughed. "If you're asking, am I too old to ride a bike, the answer is no, I'm not too old. A bicycle is my principal means of transportation back home in Maine, and I've been doing some cycling since coming to Maui."

"Then you definitely should take the sunrise trip, Jessica."

"I'll think about it, Joe."

He made a face. "That's what my mother says when she wants to stop me from arguing with her. Okay. Don't go, but you'll be the one to miss out. Don't say I didn't tell you."

I laughed. "All right, all right. You've convinced me. I'll make the arrangements at the front desk. Now, let's get back to the subject at hand. Anything else you can tell me about what your research for your article has uncovered?"

"Afraid not." He looked down at his notes. "I guess we

really didn't give each other much information, but I appreciate your time."

"It was my pleasure."

Before we left the room, he wrapped two pieces of pastry in a napkin and slipped them into his backpack. "A snack for later," he said sheepishly.

"Better than letting it go to waste," I said.

"Witherspoon was right about that. The press loves to get fed. We just don't like to admit it."

We parted in the lobby, agreeing to stay in touch if we learned anything. I doubted I would share anything more Mike and I might discover with a reporter. Joe's goal was to get a story into print, and mine was to fit together the pieces of the puzzle of Mala's death. They were two strictly independent and, to a certain extent, selfish goals. I wanted to know if the Mala I'd met was the same exemplar her uncle had raved about, and if someone had killed her, what was the reason? Was it politics, jealousy, greed, revenge for some perceived slight? The numbers of motives were legion. But if her death was not an accident, there had to be an answer to the question *why*.

I looked at my watch and decided it was too late to bicycle to the south shore in the hope of being able to speak with Koko. Mike Kane was due to pick me up at one. Maybe he would agree to drive there.

My room phone was ringing when I walked in.

"Hello?"

"Hi, Jessica. It's Bob Lowell here."

It took a moment for me to recognize the name.

"Yes, hello, Bob. How are you? How is Elaine?"

"Me and my sweetie are just fine," he said in a booming voice. "Here's why I'm calling, Jessica. Elaine and I are going to take that sunrise bike trip tomorrow up to the volcano, Hali-something-or-other. Thought you might like to join us."

"How nice of you to think of me," I said. "In fact, I was just talking with someone else about that trip, but I haven't decided yet whether or not I'll have the time to fit it in."

He laughed heartily. "Now, don't be scared. I'll be there to protect you and Elaine. But you've gotta take this trip. Everyone says it's a must-see. You know the old saying, 'When in Rome, do like those Romans do.' It's supposed to be the best deal on the island. I like a bargain as much as the next man." Another laugh. "You could write it up in your next murder mystery, have somebody fall into that volcano or something. The missus and I already made our reservations. Not sure I'm keen on having to get up at three in the morning, but I'm an early riser anyway. This'll just be a few hours earlier. I'll probably end up carrying Elaine halfway down. She's not much of a bike rider."

I heard, "Oh, Bob," in the background.

"I'll keep it in mind, Bob," I said, "but I'm not ready to commit to going. Thanks for reminding me. My best to your wife."

Biking down Haleakala with Bob and Elaine Lowell was not high on my list of things I wanted to do. But Bob was right. It was certainly a popular excursion. Ironically, Mala herself had suggested it to me. Since the volcano, and Mala's work to preserve its sacred status for the people of Maui, could be at the root of how and why she died, it did make sense to see what she felt so keenly about. I debated the pros and cons of scheduling something that required me to forgo a good night's sleep but finally talked myself into it.

I went to the front desk in the lobby, where the cultural exhibits were still drawing crowds, and noticed the heavyset man still holding up a newspaper. *He must be a very slow reader,* I thought, *or else a man waiting very patiently while his wife shops.* I asked Eileen to cancel the bike I'd rented for the day and queried her about the Haleakala excursion.

"I'm considering taking the sunrise bike trip up the volcano," I told her. "What do you think?"

"Oh, you'll just love it," she said. "When would you like to go?"

"What do you suggest?"

"It's supposed to be a good weather day tomorrow. The forecast for later in the week is iffy. You really want to be up there when it's clear or you'll get fogged in and see nothing."

"Then tomorrow it will be." I realized I'd forgotten to ask Bob Lowell which tour company he'd booked with. It wasn't worth calling him back, however. I figured if they were going tomorrow, we'd meet up at the top anyway.

Eileen booked my reservation, gave me some verbal instructions, handed me some written material, and wished me a pleasant ride. I took a chair in the lobby and was perusing the handouts when Mike Kane strolled in. His Hawaiian shirt this time was white with silver palm trees on it.

"Is it one o'clock already?" I said.

"It is, unless you're still operating on Maine time. What do you have there?"

I showed him the brochures and printed instructions about the trip to Haleakala.

"When are you thinking of going?"

"Tomorrow."

"Sure you want to?"

"I'm not sure, but I've already made the reservation."

"I'd never talk you out of it, but I will say that riding a bike down those roads can be dangerous. A few years ago they banned tour companies from offering bike rides from the summit. Too many fatalities. You don't come down off the volcano on bike paths, you know. You share the narrow road with all the cars and trucks, navigating the twenty-nine switchbacks. It's a scary ride."

"I'm pretty handy with a bike," I said. "I use one all the time back home. I have to. I don't drive."

Kane's eyes widened. "You don't drive?"

"No, and I never wanted to. I admit it's sometimes inconvenient, but I've always managed. I do have a pilot's license, however."

His eyes became a little wider. "What else is there to know about this woman named Jessica Fletcher?"

"Just that I had a conversation with Mr. Cale Witherspoon today and find I don't like the man, not one bit. Feel like taking a ride to see if we can have another talk with a little boy named Kona, also known as Koko?"

"I'm available all afternoon," he said, taking my hand and pulling me up from the chair. "But if you develop a sudden hankering to fly a plane, count me out. Flying scares me to death."

Chapter Thirteen

***He Aha Ka Meahou?*—What's New?**

As we drove, I recapped for Mike the brief comments Witherspoon had made at his press conference and my subsequent conversation with the builder.

"Sounds as though you're not a member of the Witherspoon fan club."

"You're safe in saying that, Mike. I found him condescending and arrogant. I probably can think of some more adjectives, but I'm trying to be polite. Oh, I also spoke with a young reporter named LOO-key. He spells it like 'LUCK-ee.'"

"I know the guy," he said. "He called my cell phone while I was on my way to the hotel. Told me he'd just spoken to you."

"He certainly didn't let any time go by."

"He's a nice young man. I've met him a couple of times. He's hot on the Haleakala story. Could do worse than to have a reporter on our side."

"He wants to write a true crime book about Mala's death, provided, of course, that murder was involved."

"If we prove that someone did kill her, I hope he acknowledges us in his book. That would impress my wife."

"Just learning the truth will be sufficient acknowledgment for me."

We took our now-familiar route south, parking in the shopping center outside the hotel and walking across the field where the luau had taken place to access the narrow path leading to the house in which Koko lived with his widowed father and grandmother.

"What do you hope to accomplish?" Mike asked.

"I'm not sure, but I have a strong hunch that the boy might have seen something the night Mala died and is afraid to tell anyone."

"So your idea is to keep showing up until you wear them down?"

"Something like that."

As we approached what I now thought of as the scene of the crime, Mike said, "Why don't we try the front door this time. Maybe it will change our luck."

"If we don't see anyone in back, we can—"

The house came into view, and it was obvious that something had happened. A patrol car with its lights flashing could be seen on the road in front, and two uniformed officers were on the patio with Koko's father.

"I hope no one has been injured," I said as we left the path and stood on the edge of the lawn. One of the officers recognized Mike, waved, and came to us. "'Ey, Kane," he said.

"Hey, braddah," Mike replied. "You've got a problem here?"

"Not anymore. The man who lives here has a little boy, Kona—adventuresome tyke. We know him well. Mohink's mother usually takes care of the kid while Dad's at work at the sugar refinery, but she's sick; so he brings the kid to work with him. Seems while he's not watching the boy sneaks off and disappears into the sugar fields. Nothing new; he's done it before, loves the field for some reason. Anyway, Dad calls us and we send a team to search for the kid, find him hiding there. The father's real upset, as you can imagine. I told him we're gonna have to start charging him a finder's fee the next time. Can't have the little fella making a habit of this. Anyway, we follow Mohink and his son back to make sure they get settled in. Didn't want to see anyone get hurt. Pop is one angry dude."

"Can't blame him," Mike said.

"Father and son are both in the house now?" I asked.

"Yes, ma'am. 'Ey, Kane, what are you doing here?"

"Taking a walk with Mrs. Fletcher."

He introduced us.

"I hear you're working private on the Kapule case," said the officer. "Hope it pays well."

Mike laughed away the comment without saying anything. But as the officer turned to leave, Mike asked, "Heard anything new on it?"

The officer stopped and shook his head. "Detective Tahaki says it was an accident, only I do hear that the ME asks why would she climb down to pick a plant already growing on the top?"

"These scientists, you never know what they see," Mike said.

"I guess." The officer, whom I pegged to be in his late twenties, started to leave, then came back to us. "There was one other thing." He looked at me and then Mike.

"You can talk in front of her."

"Just thought I'd pass along a little scuttlebutt, you know."

"What's that, brah?"

"Some of the guys I hang out with, you know, have a few drinks with after work, they say that she was some hot *wahine*."

"Is that so?" Mike said.

"Not that I'd know firsthand, but some of the guys—"

I kept my mouth shut and tried not to look interested in what he was saying.

"I know, I know," Mike said, "some of the guys heard that from somebody else."

"That's right, Mike. Just thought I'd pass it along."

"*Mahalo.* Appreciate it."

When the officer had left to rejoin his partner at the house, Mike said, "Hate to hear rumors like that about a woman."

"I agree it isn't fair," I said. "A beautiful woman is often a victim of unkind remarks. Coming from a woman, I might chalk it up to jealousy. I'm not sure of what motives men would have."

"Bragging, most likely. Making themselves look like big *kahunas*, in the know about something they have no experience with."

"Even so, remember what we taught the recruits, to pay attention to even scurrilous rumors. You never know when there's an important bit of truth in them."

The officers departed the patio, leaving the father alone.

I sensed that he was debating whether to join us. I waved. He did nothing.

"Probably not a good time to talk to him," Mike said. But as we started to leave, Mohink stepped off the patio and took deliberate strides in our direction. He reached us, and I was aware of the intense anger etched on his square face. The officer had said that he was angry at his son, which I could understand. But his expression of rage went far beyond that.

"Get off my property. Now!" His lips were curled and his fists tightly balled at his sides, as though he was ready to physically strike at us.

"Now, hold on," Mike said. "Mrs. Fletcher and I were—"

"I don't give a rat's ear what you were doing," Mohink ground out. "Do it someplace else. Leave me and my kid alone. I'm sick and tired of people spying on me."

"Mr. Mohink," I said, "we're not spying on you. Detective Kane and I simply wanted to speak with Koko about the night a woman fell to her death."

His rage instantly subsided. "That's right," he said to Mike, "you're a detective."

"Retired," Mike said pleasantly, "but still active, especially when a murder might have been committed."

"Look, sorry I came on so strong. It's just that this has been a stressful day. My son came to work with me and—"

"We heard all about it from the officer," I said.

"Well, kids can drive you crazy, huh?" He forced a smile, although his jaw was still tightly clenched. "I gotta get back to work. He keeps pulling this stuff, he's gonna make me lose my job."

We watched him trudge across his lawn and disappear inside the house.

"That's a man who has trouble controlling his temper," I said. "He was ready to brawl until he remembered that you were law enforcement. The other night when he came up behind and scared me, he said he was protecting me from falling. It didn't seem that way."

"I'd like to know more about him," Mike said as we re-traced our steps to the car.

"Why do you think he believes he's being spied on?"

"Could be just paranoid. Thinks everyone must be as interested in him and his activities as he is himself."

"I wonder if it's something else."

Mike took out his cell phone when we'd gotten in his SUV and dialed a number.

"Ani, my love," he said to whoever had answered. "Mike Kane here . . . Doing just fine, thank you . . . and you? . . . Good to hear that . . . Ani, I need a favor . . . What? . . . No, I'm not looking for one of those police T-shirts . . . They're ugly . . . Ani, run a background for me on a guy named Warren Mohink . . . What? . . . No, nothing specific, just whether he's had run-ins with the law . . . Right . . . Happy to hold."

He put his cell on speakerphone and we waited until she came back on the line.

"Warren E. Mohink," she said, "male, forty-one, works at Thompson Sugar Refinery, widower, one child."

"Sounds like him," Mike said. "Has he ever been a bad boy?"

"A few times, Mike. Before his wife died there were two

domestic violence calls from his house made by the wife. She was bruised but ended up not pressing charges. Two other incidents, both in bars, fights, the usual. Both times charges were dropped. Anything else I can do for you?"

"How did his wife die?"

"Let me see what it says. Okay, she drowned. Her hubby, Mr. Mohink, and she were snorkeling. He was questioned, but the ME ruled it an accidental drowning. Anything else I can do for you?"

"Give me a kiss the next time I'm in headquarters."

"Hey, I don't want any trouble from Lani."

"She told me to say that. Any *meahou* about the Kapule case?"

"Are you involved with that?"

"Just dabbling," Mike said with a laugh.

"And I'm a professional hula dancer," she said.

"You've got the hips for it," he said.

"I'll let that pass," she said. "Call anytime."

"I'd say Mr. Mohink could use an anger management class," I said.

"Looks that way."

"Do you mind swinging by the college on our way back?"

"For?"

"I want to see if we can catch up with Professor Luzon. I don't know if you're aware that he was named department head the afternoon Mala died."

"You said that she wanted that job."

"She wanted it, but she didn't harbor any illusions about getting it. She knew that her controversial stance about the telescope and Haleakala would stand in her way."

"Do you think she might have confronted the professor about it?"

"I don't know, but it would be interesting to find out."

Mike pulled out of the parking spot and slowly drove from the lot. As he reached the fringe of the property, I asked him to stop.

"What's the matter?"

"See that woman on that bench?"

"Looks like she's crying."

"I know her. I sat with her and her husband at the luau. Give me a minute."

I got out of the car and approached Elaine Lowell, who had indeed been crying. As she saw me draw near, she attempted to dry her eyes and sit up straighter.

"Elaine," I said, taking a seat next to her on the bench. "Remember me? It's Jessica. I'm sorry to see you so upset. What's wrong?"

"Nothing," she said, and began to cry again.

I placed my hand on her shoulder and allowed her to gain control. "Is there anything I can help you with? Has something happened to you? To your husband?"

"It's—it's Bob," she managed.

"Is he ill? Did he have an accident?"

She shook her head and used another tissue. "They just don't understand him," she said. "He wouldn't mean anything by it."

"By what, Elaine?"

"The chambermaid. She said that he tried to grab her. That isn't Bob. He loves people, that's all, likes to give everybody hugs and kisses."

"Oh, my," I said, thinking back to the luau when Bob hugged Grace Latimer and tried to kiss her on the cheek, and his tendency to wrap his arms around women, including me. "Is he in trouble because of it?" I asked. "With hotel security or the police?"

"The security man talked to him about it. The chambermaid complained to him, and he had to do something, I suppose. He warned Bob not to touch her again. She said she wouldn't press charges, thank goodness, but she's been assigned to another wing. She's not mean or anything. I thought she was sweet. She just doesn't understand my husband."

"Sometimes people take displays of affection the wrong way," I said, hoping to calm her. "It sounds as though everything's been settled." I injected cheer in my voice to boost her spirits. "Where is Bob now?"

"He was mad after speaking with the security man and said he was taking a walk." She looked away from me and spoke as though addressing someone else. "Oh, Bob, I've *told* you that women don't like to be hugged by strangers."

I glanced back to where Mike remained in his SUV. "I have to be going, Elaine. Someone is waiting for me over there. I'm sure that everything will work out just fine."

She sniffled and blew her nose. "Thank you, Jessica," she said. "You're a good person."

My thought as I slipped into the passenger seat was that I probably wouldn't be seeing the Lowells the following morning on the trip up to Haleakala and the bike ride down. Nice as they were, the idea didn't displease me. And even though I experienced a twinge of guilt, I also felt relief knowing I wouldn't have to spend a day with Bob Lowell.

"What was that all about?" Mike asked as he headed for the college.

I gave him a brief explanation.

"It happens," he said. "Every once in a while, a tourist at the hotel where I work has a little too much to drink and gets frisky with a female staff member or somebody else's wife. That demon rum can turn the most placid individual into a raving lecher."

"Mr. Lowell is a nice man, at least what little I know of him. And I don't think that drinking is the cause of his behavior. He's just—well, he's just too gregarious for his own good, especially with women." I smiled. "Oh, Bob!"

"What?"

"Nothing. Just talking to myself."

Chapter Fourteen

Mai Wahapa ʻA Mai ʻOe Iaʻu—Don't Argue with Me

Although it was growing late in the day, the Maui College campus was busy as we drove in, and it took some time to find a parking space near the new science building with ʻIKE LEʻA on its sign.

"Tell me about this Professor Luzon," Mike said after turning off the engine.

"I met him and his wife at the luau. I didn't know it at the time, but apparently that afternoon he'd been named head of the horticulture department, a post that Mala coveted. When we parted, Mala and I, she said she had a meeting with her competition. That may have been Professor Luzon. I'd like to know whether he'd spoken with her between the time his appointment was announced and her death."

"Was there bad blood between them?" Mike asked.

"Not that I'm aware of. It was Professor Luzon's teaching

assistant, Grace Latimer, who told me she saw Mala at the luau."

"The name you gave to Detective Tahaki."

"That's right. Grace is a graduate student in the school. She all but suggested that Mala may have committed suicide because of losing the chairmanship, something that makes no sense to me at all. Grace is also the one who told me she saw Mala's former boyfriend that night. He's a deckhand on the *Maui Ocean Star*, the sunset cruise I took. His name is Carson Nihipali. Did I pronounce it correctly?"

"You're getting the hang of it," said Mike. "Tell me more about this ex-boyfriend."

"Handsome, sure of himself. Ms. Latimer called him a 'surfer dude.'"

"Plenty of them in Hawaii. Did you discuss Mala with him?"

"I tried to, but he wasn't eager to have that conversation."

Mike looked out the window and rubbed his chin.

"You're thinking?" I said.

"Yeah. I'm thinking about what that young cop at the kid's house said, that Ms. Kapule was a 'hot *wahine*.' I wonder how many boyfriends she had and how many of them may have had a reason to hold a grudge."

"That kind of gossip shouldn't be too difficult to uncover," I said.

As we approached the building's entrance, Mike said, "Maybe you'd rather speak with the professor alone."

"Oh, no. I think having a retired detective with me adds some gravitas."

"Gravitas? Me?" he said, chuckling. "That's a first."

I checked the names on a board in the lobby and saw that Professor Luzon, now a department chairman, had an office on the second floor. We pushed against a tide of students coming down the stairs and made our way down a long hallway with open doors on either side as classes emptied for the evening. Ahead of us, a small group was clustered in front of a closed door. I wondered why they hesitated to knock or enter until angry voices from inside reached us. A man and a woman could be overheard arguing.

"You don't know what you're talking about," the man said. "You never do."

"Don't lie to me, Abbott. I wasn't born yesterday," the woman yelled. "She bats her big blue eyes at you and you heel like some pathetic puppy. And don't think I don't know about the others."

"Damn it, Honi, keep your voice down. This is where I work."

We'd found Professor Luzon's office, and he and his wife were having a very public argument, unaware of the audience it was drawing just beyond the door.

"Ladies and gentlemen," Mike said in a low voice. "Don't you think we should give these people a little privacy?"

I caught exasperated looks flashing between several of the students who'd been eavesdropping, but clearly they were not about to challenge a man the size of Mike Kane, and they began dispersing just as Honi's next volley came through the door: "No, Abbott, this isn't where you *work*; this is where you seduce all those wide-eyed innocents who go gaga over the esteemed professor. You're incorrigible."

I wasn't sure what to do—knock and interrupt their fracas or stand in the hall until one of them stormed out. I didn't have time to make a decision because the door flew open. Honi Luzon stood staring at us. "Get a good earful?" she said.

"We and a good number of the students," Mike said.

"I'm sorry, Mrs. Lu—"

Honi didn't stay for my apology. "His majesty, the chairman, will see you now. Excuse me," she said, and pushed past us, striding down the hall, unmindful of the faces that turned to see who she was and the whispers she inspired as she passed.

Mike and I peered through the open door. Luzon was standing at the window with his back to us.

"Professor Luzon?" I said.

"My office hours are over."

"We're not students," Mike said.

Luzon turned. His face was crimson, and he visibly shook.

"What do you want?" he snapped.

"If this is a bad time, we can—"

"Mrs. Fletcher, right? From the luau?"

"Yes, and this is Mike Kane, retired detective."

Luzon struggled to bring himself under control. He went behind his desk and said, "Come in." Whether he was aware that we'd overheard the argument with his wife wasn't evident; he probably preferred not to know.

"What can I do for you?" he asked, but I was certain that he didn't care.

"Just a few minutes of your time," I said. "I suppose I should start by congratulating you on your promotion."

"That cannot possibly be the purpose of your visit."

Deciding that directness was the best approach, I responded, "You are correct. Former detective Kane and I are working together to try to paint a more complete picture of the death of your colleague Mala Kapule."

My statement got his attention. His eyes widened as he groped for his next words. "Please sit down," he finally said. "I only have a few minutes, however."

"And that's all the time we'll take," I said, ignoring the chairs he pointed to. "Professor Luzon, we were wondering whether you'd had the opportunity to speak with Ms. Kapule the day that she died."

He adopted an exaggerated expression of deep thought. "No, I . . . I don't believe I did." He pulled a pair of glasses from his breast pocket and carefully put them on. "Why do you ask?"

"I spoke with your assistant, Ms. Latimer, and she wondered whether Mala was so upset that she'd lost out on becoming chairman of the horticulture department that she might have—well, might have taken her own life."

He guffawed. All the anger seemed to drain out of him. "That's ridiculous," he said, smiling. "Grace said that? Not a very scientific conclusion."

"Yes. I agree that it's far-fetched, but I did think it was worth mentioning. You didn't see Mala the night we sat together at the luau?"

"No."

"Ms. Latimer said that she did, and since you went together to fetch the drinks, I thought perhaps you might have been with her when that occurred."

"No," he said, "I never saw Professor Kapule that night."

"That afternoon perhaps? Mala and I had coffee, after which she left me for an appointment in this building. She said she was going to meet with her competition. Wouldn't that have been you?"

"Her competition for what? I have said that I didn't see her, and that answers your question. I get the impression that I'm being grilled." He directed that last statement at Mike, who'd said nothing so far.

"That's hardly the case. Mrs. Fletcher and I are just trying to clear up some lingering questions about Ms. Kapule's death. I'm sure you'd like to have those questions answered, too, considering that you were colleagues here at the college."

"Well, of course. We were all shaken and saddened at Mala's demise. She was a fine scientist and a talented teacher, much beloved by her students."

Luzon sounded as if he was rehearsing a eulogy he'd written for Mala's funeral.

"But from everything I've heard, her death was an accident, if a bizarre one." He shook his head ruefully. "Just like Mala, scrambling down a dangerous cliff in search of some bit of vegetation." He again shook his head. "Probably *Cryptostegia grandiflora*. She was on a campaign against that one. So unnecessary. So tragic."

"Professor Luzon," I said, "you and Mala worked in the same department for years. You must have known her pretty well. Is there anyone you can think of who might have held a grudge against her, someone who was angry enough to have pushed her off that cliff?"

Luzon cleared his throat. "The university informed me that the police have labeled her death an accident. I generally accept the conclusions of the authorities. The appropriate authorities. But if I had to guess, I'd say it was someone who was adversely impacted by her stand against the telescope on Haleakala. But that's assuming she was pushed. That's not what I have understood." He looked over his glasses at me and added, "Anything else?"

"I don't think so," I said. "We appreciate your time."

"Not at all," he said affably. "Thanks for stopping by."

As we were on our way out the door, I turned and said, "Please give my best to your wife."

Luzon's face turned red. "I'll do that," he said.

We got in the car. Before Mike started the engine he said, "I gather the woman he was arguing with was his wife."

"Yes, Honi Luzon. It's safe to say from what we heard that they were arguing about another woman."

"More like other *women*," Mike said.

"Are you thinking what I'm thinking?"

"Probably. I'm thinking that if Mala Kapule was one of those other women, that would give both Mr. and Mrs. Luzon a motive."

"I hope not. If that's the case, he certainly wasn't broken up about her loss."

"Those kinds of guys wouldn't be. It's all about the chase, not about the woman herself."

"That's a pretty negative view of your fellow man, Mike."

"Yeah, well, there's good guys, and there's other guys. Luzon doesn't come off like a good guy. You going to the meeting of Mala's group tonight?"

I nodded.

"And you're still planning to go up to Haleakala a few hours later and bicycle down?"

"It's on my agenda."

"I'd be happy to drive you there the day after tomorrow."

"I appreciate that, but I'm assured that the best view will be available tomorrow. Afterward the weather will be less predictable."

"I'll give you that. You do need a clear day to appreciate it."

"I know I'm cramming a lot in, but this is my thinking: As long as I'm here on Maui I might as well do what the tourists do. Frankly, I'm looking forward to it."

"You're not going to get much sleep tonight. You know those buses leave in the wee hours."

"I know."

"Just do me one favor."

"What's that?"

"Be careful. It can be dangerous, especially when you're tired."

His warning accompanied me into my room, where I pulled out a notebook in which I'd been jotting down my thoughts and started adding more.

Chapter Fifteen

Ono!—Delicious! Sometimes Combined as *Ono-licious*

I had a few hours before the meeting of Mala's opposition group and was grateful to spend quiet time in my hotel room. After leaving our brief and somewhat awkward confrontation with Luzon, I was concerned that we were spinning our wheels and getting nowhere. That Mike's other plans would preclude our being together that evening and the next day was a double edged sword. Having the legendary Maui detective at my side made the point that the questions I was asking weren't frivolous. I've interacted with a number of detectives over the years, and as fine as many of them were, none impressed me more than Mike. He was a gentleman in every sense of the word, a man with a pixyish smile and twinkle in his eyes to accompany a keen mind, as well as a devoted family man with an appreciation of the human dilemma.

On the other hand, allowing Mike to get back to his family life and regular business concerns assuaged my guilt at taking him away from his wife and his job. I hoped his involvement with me didn't jeopardize either relationship. I remembered I had promised myself—and him—that I would find a nice gift for Lani as thanks for sharing her husband's time, even though he assured me she was accustomed to his odd hours and just as happy to follow her own interests by herself. I also had to admit that the prospect of not having him at my side was liberating in a way. I've had many discussions with Seth Hazlitt and other friends in Cabot Cove about how today's frenetic lifestyle, fueled by all the technology that surrounds us, takes away from precious time to think. I needed think time. We all need think time to avoid making some of the mistakes we humans are prone to.

I reflected on that first morning when Mala and I enjoyed coffee together. She was a beautiful woman who undoubtedly had a number of beaus, including the deckhand on the *Maui Ocean Star* Carson Nihipali. He'd gone out of his way not to talk about Mala and the particulars of her death. Of course, I'd caught him when he was working, not the best time for confidences. But I sensed a coldness in him that bothered me. Had he been one of many boyfriends, as the young police officer had hinted? If so, was he aware of his competitors for her attention? Mike Kane's question was apt: Could one of them have harbored enough resentment to have taken the drastic step of getting rid of her altogether?

But let's say that Mala had fallen to her death during an argument with a boyfriend. It could well have been an accident, an argument that got out of hand, even a situation in which she felt threatened, backed away, lost her footing, and tumbled down to the rocks and surf below without being pushed. If that was the case, whoever accompanied her on the trail was guilty of nothing except callous disregard and failing to alert someone. If you were questioned by the police and lied about what you knew, that was a crime, but it wasn't murder.

Reviewing the possibilities, I realized that I was limiting myself to looking for a romantic reason for her death. A more realistic possibility was Mala's staunch opposition to the telescope on Haleakala. There was big money involved, not only for someone like Cale Witherspoon and his construction company, but also for the university and the island of Maui. There were powerful forces lobbying to see that the telescope was built, and from what I'd gathered, many of the island's movers and shakers, including Charlie Reed, were putting their money where their mouths were, funding a series of legal skirmishes designed to overcome Mala and her smaller group's efforts to kill the project.

Some of my thinking, and the notes I was making, focused on Professor Luzon. Mike and I had overheard his wife, Honi, accusing him of infidelity. The tension at the luau between Honi and her husband's graduate assistant, Grace Latimer, was palpable. Had Luzon been having an affair with Grace? If so, what bearing would that have on Mala Kapule's death? Unless Grace was jealous of Luzon's attentions to Mala, assuming they existed, and wanted to rid herself of a rival. Grace had asked to see me after Mala died. Was she just probing to see what I knew? I doubted that there was a connection between Luzon and Mala, apart from her desire to become chair of the department. The day I met her and she was heading off to a meeting with her opponent for the chairmanship, presumably Luzon, she referred to him as a "dreadful man." But if they weren't romantically involved, could academic rivalry have been so heated as to lead to a physical confrontation? There was a lot to ponder. I needed a walk to get my blood flowing. I left my room through the French doors and ventured along the shoreline of Kahului Bay, breathing in the fresh air and enjoying the late afternoon sun. A narrow beach rimmed the water, curling around the harbor. To my right in the distance was a ferry slip, and beyond it, a long pier at which a large cruise ship was berthed jutted into the water. Others were also enjoying the quiet beginning to the evening—a family with children, an older couple slowly walking hand in hand, young joggers, and a few solitary men and women gazing out over the peaceful beauty of the water. The slanted rays of the sun spun a kaleidoscopic effect on the water, reminding me of the way I felt seeing the sea turtle photograph I'd purchased. I reveled in the experience. This was the way one was supposed to feel when visiting Hawaii, and I was very much in the moment.

But all good things must come to an end, and soon I found myself back in my room changing clothes before taking a taxi to the restaurant where Mala's protest group was meeting.

To my delight, Elijah Kapule was my cab driver.

"Good to see you, Mrs. Fletcher," he said as he opened the rear door for me.

"Nice to see you, too," I said. "Have plans for Mala's funeral been set?"

"Yes, ma'am, day after tomorrow." He handed me a sheet of paper on which the details were printed. "You'll be there?"

"I'll make a point of it," I said as I slid onto the backseat.

"Remember. No wearing black."

"I'll remember."

The restaurant was only ten minutes away, but since I'd left the hotel a little later than planned, I worried about disrupting the meeting in progress.

"You still have my card?" Elijah asked as he scurried around to open my door.

"Yes, of course."

"Call me for your ride back to the hotel."

"I'll do that, Elijah. Thank you."

The restaurant was in a strip mall, flanked by a clothing shop that boasted "authentic Hawaiian shirts" and a tobacco store whose sign assured shoppers that its prices were the lowest on Maui. I walked into the dining room but didn't see any large group.

A pretty Asian woman approached and asked if I wanted a table.

"I understand there's a group that meets here regularly concerning Haleakala and the proposed telescope. Professor Kapule from the college was a member."

"Oh, Ms. Kapule. So sad what happened to her."

"Yes, it certainly was."

She led me to a small private room at the rear of the restaurant, where a dozen people were seated at a long table. A middle-aged man got up and came to me. "Can I help you?" he asked.

"My name is Jessica Fletcher. I was a friend of Mala Kapule."

"Oh, yes, I heard about you."

"You did? From Mala?"

"No, from others. Are you here for the meeting?"

"If you don't mind a stranger sitting in."

"It's fine. We have no secrets. Come, sit. We're just ordering drinks."

I sat in the chair the man pulled out for me and smiled at the others at the table. A waitress took my order for pineapple iced tea.

"We have a guest today," the man announced. "This is Jessica Fletcher."

There were murmurs of greeting.

He turned to me. "I'm sorry I didn't introduce myself. James Feary. I'm the attorney for this group. How did you know Mala?"

"I don't want to mislead you. I only met her once, the day she died, but her uncle Barrett was a close friend of another friend of mine back in Maine."

He smiled. "Doc Barrett," he said fondly. "That's what we all called him, a wonderful physician and a fine person."

"How did you happen to hear my name?"

He started to explain when someone at the end of the table tapped her water glass with a spoon and said, "Maybe we should get some business out of the way before dinner. As we all agree, this is a sad occasion without Mala. She gave voice to our concerns, and now that she's no longer with us, we have some tough decisions to make."

I wasn't sure that I should be there. I didn't belong to this group, which had obviously been meeting for a long time and had an agenda about which I knew little aside from what I'd been told by Mala and from comments I'd picked up on since arriving on Maui. But no one seemed to mind my presence, and a spirited discussion ensued about the direction the group should take without her. While their words were filled with conviction, I sensed a deflated attitude that didn't match the energy of what was being said.

While the conversation proceeded, I took in the others at the table. One handsome young man eventually caught my attention. He was seated behind a large gentleman who'd blocked him from my view. It was the student who'd spoken with Mala at the conclusion of her class and with whom she'd seemed annoyed. What was his name? Dale. That was it. As I recalled their brief moment together, I remembered that she'd curtly dismissed him, and I'd wondered why. Was he an annoying student who demanded more of his professor's time than she was willing to commit? That was the conclusion I'd come to, and I had forgotten about him until this evening.

After we'd consumed drinks, the waitress took dinner orders. Since I hadn't eaten yet, I took the opportunity to try this new-to-me restaurant and echoed what the man next to me ordered, assuming he knew the menu better than I. It was a wise move. I was served *lau lau*, a combination of salt butterfish, pork, and chicken, wrapped up in a ti leaf. It was delicious.

The serving of the food didn't get in the way of the debate, which had started off calmly but eventually morphed into something more heated. Some at the table were determined to carry on the group's advocacy, while others took the position that since Mala was no longer around to spearhead the movement, the group should be disbanded. As one woman said, "Let's face it. We're on the losing end. Let them build their ridiculous telescope. I've had it."

A few echoed that sentiment, while others vowed to fight on in Mala's name. That was a lovely thought, but I questioned whether Mala's memory would be sufficient to carry on with any hope of success against the more powerful money interests. As I listened attentively to both sides arguing their points of view, I felt distinctly out of place. While I found the debate interesting, as my niece Tracy Macgill might have said, I had no horse in this race. I didn't know whether the educational values and scientific gains to be achieved by the telescope outweighed the concerns and considerations of the volcano's place in the history and religion of the Hawaiian peoples, not to mention its impact on the ecology of Haleakala. My purpose had been only to see whether anyone at the table would have light to shine on Mala's death, and as the evening wore on, I increasingly doubted whether that would be the result.

After the dinner bills were paid and the meeting broke up, those who'd attended gathered in small knots to continue the conversation that had dominated the table. I spotted Dale and was making my way toward him when the man who'd greeted me at the door, James Feary, waved to me. "Sorry you had to come into the group at this late stage," Feary said. "When Mala was spearheading it—back when her commitment was strong—we thought we had a good chance of killing the Haleakala project. Now? I'm not so sure. We seem to be—" He stopped, searching for the right words.

"Am I understanding you correctly? You just indicated that Mala's commitment might have waned. I was unaware of that. Had it?"

"It wasn't always obvious, but I knew her a long time."

"When I met Mala just after arriving here on Maui, she was filled with enthusiasm for the cause you and the others are championing," I said. "That was only a few days ago."

"Oh, yes, she could be a real spitfire."

"'Could be'? Wasn't it genuine?"

His shrug was noncommittal.

"Why had she lost faith?" I pressed.

"You know how it is when money enters the picture."

"Do you mean the money that the opposition was throwing at the project to defeat her and this group?"

"That, and Mala finally having achieved some personal financial independence."

"I'm not sure I understand," I said.

"I'm not telling tales out of school," he said. "I've been working to settle her estate."

"You were Mala's attorney, too?"

"Attorney and accountant. I was pleased when she started receiving consultant's fees. Teaching doesn't make anyone rich. I think she decided that it was time to move on with her life. While protesting the telescope on Haleakala was certainly a worthwhile endeavor—is still a worthwhile endeavor—it didn't pay all the bills or set up a secure retirement."

I immediately thought of the luxury clothes in Mala's closet that I had found so puzzling. Perhaps this was the explanation.

"How nice that she was able to earn extra money by consulting. Was she consulting with a company here on Maui?"

"No. It was a company on the mainland, in the Northwest somewhere, I believe."

"Oregon?" I said, remembering the unopened envelopes on Mala's desk in her house.

"That's right. Douglas Fir Engineering, Inc."

"Douglas Fir? Like the tree? That makes sense. She was a botanist."

"I don't know what they do, but they were generous. She opened a separate account at the Central Pacific Bank exclusively for the wire transfers she received from the company. She did very well with them. Her account grew quickly. We were able to invest some of her money for the future. Now, of course, there is no future for her."

"I assume that Mala had a valid will."

"Of course. I saw to that. She kept putting it off like too many people do, but I finally got her to execute one. Dying without one is nothing but trouble."

"I've met her aunt and some cousins. Did she have any immediate family?"

"No children or husband, if that's what you mean. She never married, had no direct heirs. Her will is being probated as we speak, should be wrapped up tomorrow and become public record."

"I may be out of line to ask, but who has she left her money and belongings to?"

"It's ironic, really. She'd originally left everything she had to her uncle Barrett, but, as you know, he recently died. We hadn't had a chance to update the will, but I think it will pass probate. Besides bequests to her aunt and quite a number of her cousins, her secondary beneficiary is the college where she taught, to establish scholarships for deserving horticulture students."

"What a wonderful legacy," I said. "Her uncle would be proud of her."

"He was a great guy. Anyway, thanks for coming by this evening. I'm sure that Mala is appreciating it from where she is up there." He raised his eyes to the heavens.

I said good night to some of the others and went to the lobby to call Elijah for a ride back to my hotel. Mala's student stood just outside the restaurant's entrance smoking a cigarette.

"Good evening, Dale," I said.

"Hello."

"We didn't have a chance to talk during the meeting. I'm Jessica Fletcher. I recognize you from Ms. Kapule's botany class. I stopped in there last week."

"The course on invasive plants. Yeah, I saw you there."

"Her death must have been a real shock for the class. Did she have a good rapport with her students?" I asked innocently. "I've done some teaching, and I know how difficult it is to establish a close relationship with students without crossing the line."

He shrugged. "She didn't want anybody to get close to her. Kept everyone at arm's length. She was stuck up."

"Oh? I'm sorry to hear you say that. She didn't strike me that way."

"Yeah, well, you're not a man. She knew the effect she had, flaunted it."

"She couldn't help that she was beautiful," I said. "But as your instructor, she probably wanted to maintain a professional distance."

"Well, I won't say any more. You're not supposed to speak ill of the dead."

I hesitated before saying, "You didn't like Ms. Kapule very much, did you?"

A bitter laugh escaped his lips. "Didn't *like* her? I was in love with her. And she wouldn't give me the time of day."

He took a final drag on the cigarette, ground it out with his shoe, and walked into the night.

Chapter Sixteen

E Aha Ana 'Oe?—What Are You Doing?

I asked the front desk for a wake-up call at two the following morning and set my travel alarm for two fifteen as a backup. The instructions concerning the trip up to Haleakala and the bike ride down called for me to be in the lobby by three.

My head was spinning when I climbed into bed, and I did not look forward to having to get up at that dreadful hour, but as it turned out, I was awake for most of what was left of the night and was wide-awake when the room was filled with ringing and buzzing.

I hadn't given much thought to what clothing would be appropriate for the excursion. Haleakala's summit was 10,023 feet above sea level. I knew that the air would be thinner, making breathing more difficult, and I figured it was bound to be chilly at that altitude. I hadn't brought warm clothes with me; it was, after all, sunny Hawaii. I dressed in the slacks I'd worn on the flight to Maui, a pale blue button-down shirt, and the only sweater I'd brought. Because I'd be biking down from the volcano, I wore sneakers. I also packed a small tote, managing to fill it with a waist-length tan Windbreaker, a Boston Red Sox baseball cap that I always threw in my luggage when traveling, my wallet, a couple of bottles of water, and a few toiletries that might come in handy.

I was in the lobby ten minutes early and sat on a bench waiting for the van. Evidently I was the only guest from that hotel taking the Haleakala tour that day. While I waited, the events of the evening occupied my thoughts.

Two details stood out in my mind.

Mala's lawyer had provided information about her that I'd been unaware of—that she'd benefited from a consulting deal with a company that had provided what I gathered was a substantial financial cushion. *Good for her.* Offering her impressive scientific knowledge of horticulture to a commercial concern in return for being paid made good sense. I assumed that the company for which she consulted, Douglas Fir, was involved in some form of horticulture or agriculture, perhaps seed manufacturing, landscaping, or crop manipulation to increase farmers' yields. I made a mental note to look into it further at a later date.

The second event from the evening that stayed with me was my brief encounter with Mala's would-be suitor, Dale. Although a student having a crush on a teacher is nothing new, I felt sorry for him. Dale looked to be in his mid-twenties, perhaps a little older than the average undergraduate. Maybe he'd taken time off after high school to save up money or had traveled. Mala was a beauty, no question about that. But was there more to it than simply a student's unrequited love? I was pondering that when the tour company's van pulled up. A young man hopped out, confirmed my name, and took my hand as he helped me inside, where seven others sat, three couples and an unaccompanied man, obviously from other resorts nearby.

We made one more stop to pick up another couple before going to the tour company's headquarters, where a buffet of breakfast sweets, juice, and coffee awaited us. Another young man joined our driver in giving us a safety briefing.

"There's really nothing to be afraid of," one said. "You'll be provided with special pants and jackets, a helmet, and gloves, along with a backpack. This is a freestyle bike ride. You descend at your own pace. You can stop as many times as you wish to sightsee, to have something to eat at the few restaurants along the route, and to take pictures. Please do not try to take photographs while riding. Keep both hands on the handlebars and both feet on the pedals at all times while moving. We have some forms for you to fill out, including a release. Any questions?"

A man raised his hand. "I read that there have been twelve fatalities over the years, and that the bike ride now starts lower than the volcano's summit because tour operators like you are banned from starting higher."

One of the guides laughed. "There have been a few folks who ran into bad luck," he said, "but it's rare. When you consider how many thousands of people enjoy this event, the number of folks who have had a problem is minuscule."

I wasn't sure that I bought into his philosophy to explain

away past incidents, but I understood his need to allay any fears riders might have.

Everyone filled out forms and signed the release.

"Okay," said a guide, "let's head out. We're in luck. The weather should hold, so you'll see the sun as it rises over Haleakala. As Mark Twain once said, 'Haleakala is the sublimest spectacle I ever witnessed.'"

"Did Mark Twain ride a bike down?" he was asked.

"I have no idea" was the reply. "Let's go. We don't want to miss the sunrise."

I was tempted to ask whether "sublimest" was a real word, but who was I to challenge Mark Twain?

We piled back into the van and drove off into the dark, our destination the dormant volcano, a sacred site to the Hawaiian people and the center of the controversy that had been raging since plans to infringe upon its consecrated ground were first introduced. I was seated next to the unattached gentleman, perhaps in his mid- to late forties, a dour-looking fellow with a shaved head who sat with his arms tightly folded over his chest. He'd mumbled a greeting in response to my more effusive "Hello" and didn't seem to be in the mood for conversation, which was okay with me. While most of my fellow passengers napped, I preferred to take in the scenery, as the glow of starlight cast a modicum of illumination, enabling us to see some of the things we passed. We were in farming country—the driver announced over the PA system that we were seeing protea and orchid farms. In a soft voice, in deference to those who wanted to sleep their way up the mountain, he pointed out vast groves of dark green macadamia nut trees. We then started up what the

driver said was Crater Road. "You'll notice how the temperature drops as we continue up this road, thirty miles of it with
twenty-nine switchbacks, all on a six-degree incline. When
it's seventy-five degrees down in the valley, it'll be forty-five
up on the summit. But don't worry. We have plenty of winter
coats to keep you warm while watching the sun coming up."

As we continued getting higher, a thick mist blanketed
the rolling fields on the side of the twisting road. Unable to
make out the details of the landscape, I focused on the road,
on the line of headlights and taillights bracketing our van.
While the volcano itself was the experience that everyone
lauded, the ride to reach it was also memorable. Because of
the hour, all traffic was uphill, a line of buses, vans, and cars
filled with eager sightseers bound for a unique experience.
Later, after everyone had enjoyed the sunrise, people would
be heading down the flank of the volcano, creating two-way
traffic on the narrow, twisting road while we rode bikes on
that same road.

As we climbed higher, we found ourselves passing through
clouds, and soon we were above them. To our right, the driver
pointed out, was the West Maui Volcano, older than Haleakala. It was the merger of the two volcanoes that had created
the island of Maui.

Everyone in the van, with the exception of the gentleman
seated next to me, began expressing their excitement at what
we were experiencing, and I was no exception. As we climbed
to the summit and navigated switchback after switchback on
what was billed as the steepest continuous road in the United
States, one more glorious sight after another was feast for our
eyes, suddenly coming into view, then behind us as a new

vista emerged. There were short stretches of level road, but they didn't last long. At times the ground to the side of the road sloped gently down, but other sheer drop-offs would suddenly appear close to the van, thousands of feet down, eliciting gasps from some of the passengers, all of whom were fully awake now.

"We're almost to the summit," the driver announced. "Haleakala is called 'the House of the Sun' for good reason. There's nothing more beautiful than sunrise at Haleakala."

Fifteen minutes later his claim proved to be true.

We pulled into a large parking lot where other tour company vans and their passengers had already arrived. We disembarked, drawing in the chilly air, the inside of my nose crackling in response. The clouds were all below us, filling the valleys and rolling away to the horizon. The clear air brought into sharp relief the vast sky, filled with millions of visible stars. Our guide escorted us to a railing from which we could look out over the majesty of the dormant volcano— three thousand feet deep, seven miles long, and two miles wide, a barren yet regal landscape like nothing I had ever seen before. Excited chatter surrounded us as other sunrise enthusiasts filled the spaces along the railing. I had to laugh when I heard the familiar, "Oh, Bob." I turned to see Bob and Elaine Lowell standing with another tour operator's group. They waved at me.

"Jessica, good to see you," Bob said in his by now recognizable loud and cheerful voice.

I responded, "The same here. I wasn't sure I'd find you in this crowd."

I realized as I said it that he might not be aware that

Elaine had told me about his run-in with the chambermaid and hotel security, but he laughed away that concern. "Did my sweetie here tell you about my little misunderstanding? These Hawaiians are supposed to be friendly, all that aloha stuff, but this gal I gave a hug to wasn't friendly at all. I ought to sue them. What do you think, Jessica?"

"Oh, Bob, it's over," Elaine said.

"Let's watch the sunrise," I suggested, changing the subject.

There was an "ooh" from the crowd, and all eyes focused on the horizon to our east, where the black sky was melting into a softer blue. Fewer stars were visible now, but a rainbow arced over the valley. A sliver of the sun peeked over the horizon and continued to rise, casting a red and yellow glow over the scene that would put the best of Hollywood's lighting designers and computer experts to shame. Oohs and aahs came from every witness to the event, and I realized that no matter what happened regarding Mala Kapule's death, this moment would be forever etched in my mind, truly a life-changing experience.

The guides had been right. It was cold up there above the clouds, and the coats they'd handed out as we left the van were welcome. Once the huge orange ball had become fully visible, we milled about, taking photographs and searching for the perfect adjectives to describe what we'd been witness to. But eventually the guides beckoned us.

"Time to head down to the sixty-five-hundred-foot level at the base of Haleakala National Park," one of them said. "That's where we'll give you your bikes and the appropriate clothing to make your descent more pleasant. The fun is just beginning!"

His exuberance was contagious. Coupled with the joy of having witnessed the spectacular sunrise, everyone got back into the van eager for the second part of the day's adventure.

"We use special bikes," we were told, "designed for downhill riding. They have disc brakes for that purpose, front and back, and the seats are oversized and padded. You'll have plenty of time to put on your riding clothes and take a few spins around the parking lot to become familiar with your bicycle before heading down."

We joined other tour company vans for the trip to the lower edge of Haleakala National Park, where dozens of bikes awaited us.

"These bikes are different sizes," we were told, "so each of you will have one that's the perfect size for you. Keep in mind that, because these bikes have been designed for downhill riding, they have only one gear and you'll seldom have to pedal. Always ride single file and use the front and rear brakes together. You'll be traveling almost thirty miles an hour at times, and if you use only the front brakes, you'll end up going over the handlebars. Go into curves slowly."

It occurred to me that this bike ride was going to be considerably more challenging than what I was accustomed to back home or the short rides I'd enjoyed since arriving on Maui. Had I made a mistake in signing up for it? Mike Kane had offered to drive me up to the summit the following day, an invitation I'd declined. I could still opt to forgo the bike and ride back down in the van, but that would mean giving in to unsubstantiated fears. I've always been comfortable on a bike; it's my basic means of everyday transportation. Besides, I'd conquered any fears I might have had of flying in small planes by taking flying lessons and earning my private pilot's license. Fear is to be conquered, not to be given into.

Along with the others, I was supplied with oversized, loose clothing to wear during the two-wheeled descent, including a helmet and heavy gloves. The outfit had snaps along the length of the pants and the back of the jacket to make getting into them easy.

"Okay, time to pick your bikes," a guide announced. "You're on your own schedules. Just remember to have the bikes and clothing back at our headquarters by four thirty."

Across the large parking area, Bob Lowell was perusing bicycles, as was the taciturn man with whom I'd ridden earlier in the day. Elaine hurried over to my side, a look of consternation on her face.

"Jessica, maybe you can talk Bob out of doing this. He hasn't ridden a bike since he was forty years younger and a hundred pounds lighter. I'm afraid he'll get killed."

Her husband managed to get on the largest of the available bikes. I didn't know whether there was a weight limit, but if so I assumed that he was pushing the top number.

"I really don't think he'd listen to me," I said. "Can't you convince him that it might be too dangerous?"

"I tried, but he's stubborn, always has been."

I walked to where Lowell was about to take the bike for a test run. He looked very uncomfortable on it.

"Bob," I said, "Elaine is really worried about you doing this. She says you haven't been on a bike in a long time and—"

"Wouldn't miss it for the world," he replied. "Heck, it's just a bike."

With that he started pedaling. He hadn't gotten ten feet

before he skidded into a line of riderless bikes, almost sending them sprawling and causing him to ram both feet into the ground in order to stop.

"Oh, Bob," Elaine said wearily.

He answered by giving us a thumbs-up and continued his test run, his wife trotting behind. "Get on your bike, Elaine, or you'll miss all the fun."

"There is no fool like an old fool," Elaine muttered, opting for the van that would ferry reluctant bikers down the hill.

My sour, shaved-head companion from the van stood between two bikes, one slightly larger than the other. He nodded at the smaller of the two and pushed it forward in my direction. "Looks like just the right size for you," he said.

"Yes, it does," I said, surprised he'd been so considerate. "Thank you."

He gave me a curt nod and walked the other bike to where a small table had been set up with a coffee urn and pastries. I got on my bike and tentatively began to ride in a circle around the lot. It was a sturdy bike, the oversized padded seat extremely comfortable and the handbrakes nicely positioned. I circled around a few times until I was confident I could handle it, but the lack of sleep was catching up to me and the thought of coffee was appealing.

I poured myself a cup and watched as others began the descent, including Bob Lowell, a little wobbly at first, then stronger as he sped up. Elaine Lowell sat in the van shaking her head.

"Delicious coffee," I commented to the man with the shaved head, who'd also lingered at the refreshment table.

"Kona," he said.

"I'll have to buy some Kona coffee when I get home."

He nodded and continued sipping.

I finished my cup and tossed it in the trash can. "I suppose I'd better be on my way. Looks like we're the last ones to leave."

"Looks like it." He climbed on his bike and fell in behind me as I began the sixty-five-hundred-foot trip down from Haleakala to the town of Pa'ia at its base.

I started slowly, wanting to get the feel of the road. I tested the brakes a few times and everything seemed fine, although I did detect a slight shudder when I squeezed the brake handles. Nothing serious, just a matter of getting used to it. I glanced back a few times and saw that the man with the shaved head was fifty feet behind me. Having someone within hailing distance was comforting in the event something should go wrong. Not that I expected anything to be amiss. And I knew that a van would be leaving the top soon to monitor the riders and pick up anyone who changed their mind about riding down the whole route.

The sun was shining, the wind in my face was bracing, and I realized that I was smiling at the sheer joy of it. I thought of my friends back in Cabot Cove and wished they were there to see me navigate the first switchback, although I could imagine what Seth Hazlitt would say: "Don't you think you're a little old, Jessica, to be playing daredevil?" which was what he'd said when I took up flying.

I stayed as far to the right as possible to allow cars to pass and gave wide berth to those vehicles on their way up the mountain, including an occasional truck. Drivers tooted and waved as they went by. I didn't dare take my hands off the handlebars and returned their greetings with an enthusiastic nod.

As I continued the ride my confidence grew, and I allowed myself to go faster, although not beyond where I felt in complete control. Vehicular traffic became heavier—families out for a pleasant day, tourists in rented cars making the trek to see Maui's most famous and trafficked sight.

I was pleased that I'd decided to make the trip and to bicycle down instead of being driven. The experience was exhilarating, and it had displaced what had become nonstop fixation on Mala Kapule's death. Not that those thoughts hadn't intruded from time to time, but they weren't all consuming, as they had been. On a relatively level stretch of road I glanced back to see that the man who'd left the base camp with me had now closed the gap and was only fifteen feet behind. The straight-and-level portion was quickly replaced by another switchback that curled around the mountain and skirted a steep drop-off. The man with the shaved head was suddenly abreast of me. Hadn't he heard the admonition that we were to ride in single file only? I shook my head. He didn't get the message. "Get behind me or pass," I shouted. He responded by moving close; he was now pressing against me, causing me to have to turn, which pointed me at the drop-off.

"Stop it!" I yelled as I fought to avoid going over the edge. I squeezed hard to apply both sets of brakes. The front brakes did nothing. The rear ones caught, the unequal torque sending my bike into a sideways skid. He gave me one final push with his hand and sped ahead, as I sped ahead, too—straight for a thousand-foot drop into oblivion.

Chapter Seventeen

Auē Nō Ho ʻI Ē!—Oh, My Goodness!

They say your life flashes before your eyes when you're about to die, but I was too panicked to notice. I slid across both lanes of traffic, screaming as I fought to stop the bike, now on its side, from dropping off the edge. The surface of the road tore at the biking clothes, and my head, thankfully protected by a helmet, scraped the asphalt, the sound assaulting my eardrums. The driver of a fuel oil truck coming up the mountain slammed on his brakes, its oversized wheels threatening to flatten me. It all happened in just a few seconds, yet it seemed as though it were unfolding in slow motion.

And then everything stopped. The front wheel of the bike hung over the edge of the drop-off, the pedals inches from following it. I was on my side, blinking furiously to clear the cobwebs from my brain. I stopped blinking and looked wide-eyed at my situation and position on the road.

My first thought was not to move lest any motion push the rest of the bike, and me, over the precipice. I heard footsteps as people got out of their cars and ran to aid me. A man grabbed the bike's rear wheel and yanked it, dragging me back to the middle of the road. A woman leaned over me. "Are you okay?"

"I—I don't know," I managed. "Yes, I think so."

Hands gently lifted me to a sitting position. I shook my head against a throbbing pain that encircled it. I looked down at my legs. One leg of the biking pants was torn from the knee to the hip; blood seeped through the light fabric from where the road's hard surface had scraped it.

"She needs an ambulance," I heard a man say.

"I've called nine-one-one," another replied.

"Get her off the road."

With help I struggled to my feet but had to lean against someone to keep from sagging to the ground again. Two people, one on each side, led me to a narrow strip of land between the roadway and the side of the mountain, where I sat and removed my helmet.

"What happened?" someone asked.

"I'm not sure, but I think he pushed me."

"Who pushed you?"

"The man on the bike behind me; at least he was behind me until he wasn't."

"Do you know who it was?"

"He was sitting next to me on the ride up, but I don't know his name. He wasn't particularly friendly."

But then a strange thing happened. I realized that I had seen him before. The blow to my helmeted head had jarred loose recognition. He was one of the two men I'd overheard at the luau. Once again I thought back to when I eavesdropped on their conversation.

"She's never going to give up, you know that, don't you?"

I glanced over to see two men arguing in low tones. One of them was tall with an athletic build, the other older, softer, and with a shaved head.

"Did he try talking to her?" asked the taller man.

"It's too late for talking," the other replied. "She'd better quit if she knows what's good for her. They're not going to put up with it anymore."

"She's not going to convince him to change his mind, even if she tries."

"If she scuttles this project, I swear he'll kill her."

"It'll be tough getting an ambulance up here with all the traffic," someone said, pulling me back into the present.

"Do you feel okay enough to ride down with us?" a man asked.

"I think so." I wanted to nod, but moving my head was painful.

The bike was pulled to the mountain side of the road. I was placed in the backseat of a car driven by the man who'd offered me a lift. His wife sat in front and kept asking me how I was doing. Aside from the headache, an aching back, and the bloody scrapes on my knee and hip, I was doing fine. Abject fear had morphed into anger. I was angry at what the man with the shaved head had done to me. All I could think of was finding him and making him pay. But that most basic of reactions meshed with my memories of the threatening exchange at the luau and Mala Kapule's death. Had they been talking about her? Were they involved with the committee to quash her fight against the telescope on Haleakala? My aches, pains, and scrapes somehow seemed superfluous. My experience of the lovely trip to the dormant volcano and thrilling bike ride down was now anything but pleasant. I was back to where I'd been at the start of that day, determined to get to the bottom of Mala's death—and whoever was behind it.

At first I argued against being brought to a hospital, but wisdom replaced my false sense of valor and I found myself in the emergency room at the Maui Memorial Medical Center in Wailuku, where a physician took a look at my wounds. A nurse cleaned and dressed my knee and hip, and an X-ray of my back didn't reveal any structural damage. The only concern was my headache. Had I suffered a concussion? The prevailing view was that I hadn't and that a good night's sleep and some Tylenol would do the trick. But they cautioned me to be aware of any of the symptoms they described that could indicate a concussion.

While waiting to be discharged I called Mike Kane's cell phone.

"Hello, Jessica," he said. "How was your trip up to Haleakala?"

"The trip up was wonderful," I said. "It was coming down on the bicycle that posed a problem."

"Are you all right? Are you hurt?"

I gave him a capsule recounting of what had happened.

"Terrible," he said. "Have you filed a police report?"

"No."

"You must. I'll be there in twenty minutes and take you to headquarters. You can go through the mug shots and see if you spot this *hūpō*."

"This *what*?"

"*Hūpō*. Fool."

"He's more than a fool, Mike. He's a thug, and he might be a murderer."

"I'll be there in fifteen."

"But you're working."

"If you can call it that. Dull day, no complaints from guests. Sit tight. See you in a few minutes."

While waiting for Mike to arrive, I looked around the emergency room, where other patients were being evaluated and treated. A loud moan came from an adjacent treatment bay surrounded by a white curtain. I winced in sympathy for what the person in there was suffering. The curtain parted and a nurse emerged, followed by none other than Elaine Lowell.

"Elaine," I said, getting up and sitting right back down when my own pain reminded me that my knees and back were still sore.

"Jessica? What happened to you?"

"I was about to ask you the same thing."

"Bob fell off his bike. He has a broken shoulder."

"I had an accident, too." I didn't bother going into detail about how my "accident" came about.

"I knew he was too old to ride a bike."

A bellow came from behind the curtain. "Elaine!"

"He needs me." She smiled wanly.

I followed her to the treatment bay, pausing at the curtain. Bob lay on the gurney; a pretty Asian nurse tended to him.

"Jessica Fletcher? That you?" he said, managing to raise his head.

"Yes," I said, stepping closer so he could see me.

"How come you're here?"

"It's a long story," I said.

"Bob has to have surgery on his shoulder," Elaine said.

"Stupid thing," he said. "That bike was no good. If I had a decent bike, this never would have happened. I should sue 'em."

The nurse patted his hand. "Just lie back and take it easy, Mr. Lowell. The surgeon will be here shortly and everything will be fine."

Bob grasped her hand, his eyes imploring. "How about a little hug for good luck?"

The nurse looked at Elaine and me, disengaged from him, raised her eyebrows, and ducked around the curtain.

"Oh, Bob," Elaine said.

I saw the disappointment on his face. "I'll give you a good-luck hug, Bob."

And I did, and was glad that I had.

They wheeled Bob away for surgery and I returned to the waiting area, where Mike Kane had just arrived. Seeing him walk in buoyed my spirits, and I happily hobbled from the hospital on his arm.

Once we were in the car, he handed me a package wrapped in paper towel. It was heavy.

"What is it?"

"Lani sent it to you. It's for good luck."

I rolled off the paper, and a gray rock dropped into my lap. I turned it over to see a white drawing on its smooth gray surface. It was a circle surrounding two white dots.

"That's the symbol for the goddess Uli," Mike said.

"Yes. The heavenly mother. I remember."

"Lani thought you needed a little protection, so she wanted you to have it. Although by the looks of it, Uli's already been working for you. You're lucky you're alive."

"I'm well aware of that. Please thank Lani for me. I wanted to get a gift for her, and here she's giving me a gift."

"There will be plenty of time for reciprocating, provided you stay in one piece."

"I have to stop at the tour operator to return these clothes and tell them about the bike. Could we swing by there first?"

"Sure you shouldn't go straight back to the hotel and get into bed?"

"Maybe later. Right now I need to follow up on what happened. The man who forced me off the road was in the van when it arrived to pick me up at the hotel. He must have registered."

"Okay, but fill me in on the details of what happened."

I gave him a rundown, including my delayed recognition of the man as having been at the luau the night Mala died, and recounted the brief conversation I'd overheard him have with another man.

"Were they talking about Mala?" Mike said.

"It didn't occur to me at the time," I said. "I never gave it much thought until she died. Now that one of those men tried to kill me, there can't be any other conclusion to come to."

"Let's see what they have on record at the tour operator," Mike said, speeding up.

After multiple expressions of condolences for what happened to me while on their tour—and with my assurances that I wasn't intending to sue them—I asked about the man with the shaved head. Yes, they had the reservation he'd made. "John Smith" was his name.

"John Smith?" Mike and I said in unison.

The tour operator shrugged. "We don't check on people's names," he said. "He paid in cash; it's not unusual."

"What about the hotel where you picked him up?" Mike asked.

A phone call confirmed that no person named John Smith was registered there, nor had anyone by that name reserved a spot on the Haleakala tour through the hotel. A further check of records indicated that he'd made the call from a phone not associated with the hotel but had asked to be picked up there.

"You say he deliberately forced you off the road?" I was asked.

"Yes."

"That's a first for us," the tour operator said. "All I can say is how sorry we are, and if you want another bike tour of Haleakala, it's on us."

I managed a laugh. "I'm not ready to take you up on that, but I'll keep it in mind. I left the bike on the side of the road. My apologies. I'm sure it was damaged in my fall."

"No need for apologies, Mrs. Fletcher. Please, if anything we need to apologize to you. However, I must assure you that all our bikes are checked before they leave here. We have a detailed system to ensure the safety of all our vehicles. The brakes on your bike passed our inspection—but I have to say they wouldn't now."

"You've seen the bicycle already?"

"Oh, yes, it was delivered here by one of the other tour operators. We went over it carefully and discovered a problem that wasn't there before. We believe someone must have tampered with the front brakes."

"This is taking on a whole new dimension," Mike commented as we got back in his car. "This thug who tried to run you off the road obviously works for someone who has it in for you, and the only reason I can think of is that it's connected to Ms. Kapule's murder."

"I see that you're now saying 'murder' rather than 'death.'"

"Up until now I didn't want to rush to judgment, Jessica, but as far as I'm concerned, she didn't accidently fall. Someone killed her—and has tried to kill you."

"You want me to file a report at police headquarters?"

"Absolutely, especially in light of the tour operator's comments regarding possible tampering with the brakes. You should also look through mug shots. Maybe you'll get lucky and spot this man's picture. Are you feeling up to it?"

"I'm fine, Mike. While I'm doing that, can you check on a company, Douglas Fir Engineering? It's in Oregon, back on the mainland."

"Why your interest in it?"

"Mala's attorney was at last night's meeting of the anti-telescope group. He told me she was hired as a consultant to this company in Oregon and was evidently paid a good sum of money for her work. I remember seeing an envelope from the company on Mala's desk. It might mean nothing, but I'd like to erase it off the list of things on my mental blackboard."

"Easy to do," he said.

With Mike as my escort into police headquarters, I was quickly ushered into a small conference room with a computer. Detective Tahaki was there, as well as a female uniformed officer who got me settled at the table.

"Sorry to see you again under these circumstances," Tahaki said. "Mike explained what happened."

"Thank you."

"Can we get you some coffee? Juice?" the officer asked.

"That would be lovely," I said. "You wouldn't happen to have iced tea with pineapple juice, would you?"

"I think I can come up with that," she said.

Mike left as Detective Tahaki recorded my statement about what had occurred on the bike trip down from Haleakala and said that it would be typed up for me to sign before I left. "Now," he said, "let's see if we can identify this guy who assaulted you."

He punched up a program on the computer and entered my description of my assailant. "If he's had a run-in with the law, he'll be in one of these files," he said.

With my now-favorite drink in front of me, I started the slow, tedious process of looking at face after face of men—Asian, Caucasian, a smattering of African-Americans, bearded, clean-shaven, some hardened, others not looking like anyone I would assume was a lawbreaker—a cross section of male humanity.

Mike returned while I went through the process and sat

silently as I scrolled through one page after the other, finishing one file and going on to the next. After I'd gone through them, I exhaled and shook my head. "No," I said, "I don't recognize any of these faces."

"This was just a start," Tahaki said. "We'll broaden the description and see if we can get you a hit."

While he looked for additional files for my perusal, I asked Mike whether he'd been successful in checking on Douglas Fir Engineering.

He nodded.

"And?"

"Interesting, Jessica. You'd said that you assumed it would be a company engaged in some sort of horticultural business."

"A reasonable assumption."

"Reasonable assumptions aren't always the right ones," he said. "Douglas Fir is a construction company."

"Construction? What sort of construction?"

"Well, its last major construction project was a large telescope installation in Arizona."

I'd grown sleepy looking at the photos, but I snapped wide-awake. "Douglas Fir builds large telescopes?"

"Not the scopes themselves, but they build all the supporting facilities—buildings, housing for the scientists, parking lots, that sort of thing."

"Mike," I said, "do you think that—?"

"Douglas Fir must have been in competition with Witherspoon's company for the Haleakala job," he said.

"Oh, my goodness! I hope Mala wasn't being paid to cause delays."

"If she was, she may have been trying to cost Witherspoon a fortune in hopes that he would drop out and the project would go back to bid."

Oh, no! I slumped back in my chair. Could it be that Mala's zeal for halting the construction of the telescope on Haleakala wasn't a passion to defend the rights of the Hawaiian people after all? I prayed that what this revelation suggested wasn't true. I couldn't bear to think that Mala wasn't really working to preserve Haleakala as a sacred Hawaiian site, that her motive instead was to stall it long enough for Witherspoon to give up thoughts of making a profit on the job, leaving it open for Douglas Fir Engineering to move in. I hated to think that her battle against the telescope was inspired by money rather than conviction.

The contemplation that Mala Kapule possibly wasn't everything I thought she was took all the starch out of me. I knew I couldn't rely on a day's acquaintance to judge her character entirely. But to think I might have found myself so far from the mark was disheartening.

"I really don't want to go through more mug-shot files," I told Mike and Detective Tahaki. "Can I come back at another time?"

"Sure," Tahaki said. He turned to Mike and added, "Better see your partner gets some rest."

I asked Mike to drive me back to my hotel.

"You'll be okay by yourself?" he asked as he parked in the lot. "You've been through a tough ordeal."

"I'll be all right," I said. "I'm tired, that's all. It was an early start this morning. Thanks for being here for me."

"What's a partner for?" He grinned. "I'm tied up again tomorrow at the hotel."

"That's fine," I said. "I need a more leisurely day anyway."

"I'll call you," he said.

"Good. Thanks again, Mike. And thank Lani for me, too."

It was after I'd gotten into my room, perched my stone with its image of Uli—my "protection"—on the nightstand, stripped off the clothing that reminded me of what had happened that day, and taken a hot shower that I remembered that Mala's funeral was the next morning.

So much for a leisurely day.

My stomach reminded me I was hungry. I debated calling for room service but decided against it. A bag of macadamia nuts provided by the hotel and a bottle of club soda from the minifridge took the edge off. I climbed into bed and was asleep in minutes. But in my dreams I flew miles above the dormant Haleakala on a bicycle, then suddenly fell thousands of feet into the crater, which erupted angrily and buried me in molten lava. Hardly the recipe for a restful sleep.

Chapter Eighteen

A Hui Hou—Until We Meet Again

Mala's funeral was held at Big Beach at Makena State Park on Maui's south shore, only a few miles from where she'd fallen to her death. I had hoped that Elijah Kapule would be my taxi driver, but he was probably busy helping set up the park for the event. The driver this day was a heavyset woman with a deep, raspy voice and a no-nonsense demeanor. There was no conversation while she drove, her only lapses of attention to the road when she honked and gave passing motorists what had now become a familiar Hawaiian signal, her fist raised with thumb and pinkie extended.

"*Mahalo*," I said after paying the fare.

She grunted something in return as she shoved the bills I'd handed her into the front of her red-and-white flowered blouse and pulled away. Her brusque manner was annoying, but I reminded myself that she was a glaring exception to the unfailing friendliness of the Hawaiian people, in particular those in the hospitality industry, many of whom wore buttons proclaiming LIVE THE ALOHA SPIRIT.

The beach where the park was situated was no wider than a hundred feet but appeared to be almost a mile long. Protected from the winds by a large outcropping of lava rock, it was likely one of Maui's more secluded places. But this day a large crowd had gathered for a celebration of Mala Kapule's life. Elijah had certainly been right. There wasn't a single item of solid black clothing to be seen. Instead those milling about the myriad picnic tables and barbecue grills wore a spectrum of colors befitting a rainbow, interspersed with white. This would not be a somber grieving of Mala's death. It looked more as though another luau was being prepared, and the colorful clothing better suited the festive mood. I'd opted for white slacks, a yellow-and-green flowered blouse I'd recently purchased, and a white cap with a narrow brim to shield me from the sun. I fit right in.

I stepped onto the sand. In front of me were two young women dressed in traditional hula skirts, and three musicians, two holding ukuleles, the third an electric bass attached to an amplifier tethered to an electrical outlet on a post in the ground. A four-man outrigger canoe painted with vivid slashes of red, blue, and gold rested at the shoreline, bobbing in the gentle swells of the sea. A half dozen smaller canoes flanked it, along with a few colorful surfboards standing nose down in the sand.

One of the hula dancers carrying dozens of yellow and red leis extended one to me.

"Mahalo," I said, lowering my head so that she could slip it onto my neck.

Elijah stood with several other cousins whom I'd met at Mala's house, forming an informal reception line, greeting those who came for the funeral. I took my place at the end of the queue of people waiting to see them. Up ahead I spotted Mala's former beau Carson Nihipali among the mourners.

I didn't count the number of people, but a quick, rough estimate was forty or fifty. Given that this was a Wednesday, a workday and a school day, I was pleased that so many people had come to pay their respects. Despite the fact that the more I learned about Mala, the more I realized how little I actually knew about her, I couldn't help maintaining my affection for this young woman whose uncle viewed her so proudly and whose *'ohana* admired and loved her.

One of Mala's cousins, whom I'd met at her house, crossed the sand and welcomed me. *"Aloha,"* Joshua said. "It's wonderful that you are here."

"I wouldn't have missed it."

"My brother Elijah noticed you're limping. Are you all right?"

"I had an accident on the bike ride down from Haleakala."

"Oh, no. Not too serious, I hope."

"Bumps and bruises, but nothing terminal. I'll be fine."

"Let me make it easier for you," he said taking my arm. He led me to where his aunt sat in a folding red beach chair, a glass in her hand.

"Auntie Edie, see who's here," Joshua said. "It's Mrs. Fletcher."

She looked up at me, smiled, and extended a gnarled hand. "Mala's friend Jessica," she said.

"Hello, Auntie Edie."

She nodded approvingly and fingered the lei she wore, a bright orange version of my yellow one. "You wear the *hala lei*. It is right for today."

"These leis are special," Joshua put in. "*Hala leis* are given to mark a passage, for the end of a venture or the start of a new one." He cocked his head at me. "An appropriate symbol for a funeral, don't you think?"

Auntie Edie squeezed my hand. "Mala is happy that you are here."

"I'm sure that she's happy that everyone is here to celebrate her life."

The musical trio began playing Hawaiian melodies, and Auntie Edie turned her attention to them.

Joshua, having appointed himself my informal escort, led me to a long table covered with a white cloth on which floral petals had been scattered. Along with tall, frosty pitchers of drinks, there were small framed photos of Mala, and a laptop computer set to a slideshow of family pictures in which Mala aged from infant to toddler to schoolgirl to graduate student and finally to adult. I paused to watch as the images slid sideways across the screen.

"She was beautiful," I said.

"Very beautiful," he agreed. "And generous with her cousins. She recently bought us some fancy management software for our taxi business. May I get you some pineapple iced tea?"

"I'd love some."

"We have other beverages as well, but we don't serve alcohol at funerals."

"A prudent rule," I said.

He poured me a glass.

"I've developed quite a fondness for this," I said.

"Many people do." He looked over my shoulder. "More guests are arriving. Please excuse me."

A line of cars was pulling into the small parking lot. Their passengers traipsed through the trees to get to the beach, many carrying folding chairs. Among the newcomers were Professor Abbott Luzon and his graduate assistant, Grace Latimer, attired in a black sheath under a yellow sweater. I looked for Luzon's wife, Honi, but didn't see her. Maybe she was planning to come later. Then again, based upon the angry words they'd exchanged, it wouldn't have surprised me if the Luzons often went their separate ways.

Grace was smiling as she took Luzon's arm to navigate the soft sand. I supposed it was a relief to be out from under Honi's accusations. Was she the "other woman" to whom Honi Luzon had been referring during their argument? Although Honi hadn't identified Grace by name, I had assumed Abbott's graduate assistant was the object of his wife's jealous rage. She certainly had been the object of Honi's sarcasm at the luau. Honi had displayed overt hostility toward Grace all evening.

However, after our tense meeting with Luzon, Mike Kane and I had speculated as to whether Mala herself may have entered into an intimate relationship with her colleague. I had trouble picturing Mala with Abbott Luzon, even though they had a great deal in common regarding their chosen professional path and the focus of their advanced education. For some reason, I'd had no difficulty at all imagining her with her former beau Carson Nihipali. But there's no accounting for attraction, and I reserved judgment as to whether the two professors might have been an item. After all, I may have been wrong about Mala before.

At this juncture, Mike and I were left with two motives for her murder: a crime of passion or a crime fueled by money.

Both rank high on the list of age-old reasons for homicide. But which one was it?

By the time the service was about to begin, the crowd had swelled by half and included Mala's angry but love-struck student, Dale, who stood alone in white shorts and shirt on the perimeter of the gathering, a scowl on his face. His gaze was directed at the crewman of the *Maui Ocean Star* Carson Nihipali.

Fragrant smoke from the barbecue grills filled the air as the band continued playing, and the hula dancers began to gyrate. I strolled to where a small table held a basket wrapped in a colorful scarf and topped with flowers. A woman behind the table greeted me.

"*Aloha*," she said, and asked how I knew Mala.

I explained our brief time together.

"Have you been to a Hawaiian funeral before?"

"No. This is my first."

"I saw you were interested in this basket. It's the *pu'olu*, a traditional basket woven of ti leaves. Mala's ashes are in it."

She smiled at my raised eyebrows.

"Sometimes we sprinkle the ashes in the sea, and sometimes we enclose them in a *pu'olu* like this one. Her ashes are in a biodegradable bag and will eventually be set free in the ocean."

"Somehow I'd thought Mala's ashes would be brought to the volcano, given that it was a special interest of hers."

"It would have been nice." She gently touched the basket as if caressing its contents. "Many families have done so in the past, but there has been a recent prohibition against it. Too bad. Everyone knew that Haleakala was Mala's first love."

Was it, though? I thought of what I'd recently learned about Mala's consulting contract with the Oregon construction company. Mike and I had speculated that Douglas Fir Engineering could have paid her to delay the telescope project, at least until the Witherspoon company gave up and pulled out. Had Mala's "love" for Haleakala been based on its importance and meaning to the Hawaiian people, or had her zeal to protect it been based, at least in part, on the money she was receiving? Could we ever be certain now that Mala was no longer alive to explain herself?

As I walked away from the basket holding Mala's ashes, I pondered whether Cale Witherspoon knew of her connection to the rival construction company. If so, would that have given him a motive to remove her from the picture? And who else had a motive?

Professor Luzon and Grace Latimer were approaching the table as I left, and our paths crossed.

"I'm surprised to see you here, Mrs. Fletcher," Luzon said stiffly.

"Why is it so surprising?"

"I wasn't aware that you were close to Professor Kapule."

"Don't you remember, Abbott?" Grace said. "Mrs. Fletcher was looking for her friend all night long at the luau. That friend was Mala."

"I guess I wasn't paying close attention."

"Can you believe that was the night Mala fell to her death? Oh, my goodness, Mrs. Fletcher, if you had found her, Mala might never have gone on that walk, and we wouldn't be here mourning her passing."

I didn't think Grace was mourning anyone's passing, although she certainly seemed to enjoy exaggerating a story.

Luzon adopted his best professorial expression and addressed me as if I were an inferior student: "Are you still pursuing the silly idea that Mala was murdered?"

"I don't think I'd term it silly, Professor Luzon."

"Mala was a passionate woman," he said, emphasizing *passionate* and drawing a startled glance from Grace. "If she was determined to retrieve some bit of intriguing flora under dangerous circumstances, I do not find it out of character. It fits right in with her unconventional persona."

I could almost hear Grace heave a sigh of relief.

"Hawaiian funerals are meant to celebrate the life of the deceased, not sully it," Luzon continued. "Mala accidently died in pursuit of something she cared about. To suggest that murder was behind her demise is to cheapen both her life and her death."

"I hardly think I'm sullying her reputation if I'm trying to determine who might have killed her," I said. "It's the person responsible for pushing her off that cliff whose reputation is in jeopardy."

He directed a patronizing smile at me. "Suit yourself."

Despite my best intentions, I felt the urge to argue my case.

"You know, she was a flake," Grace put in. "A nice flake, but a flake all the same. People like that take all sorts of chances. Dangerous chances."

"In the meantime, the ceremony is about to begin," Luzon said. "This discussion is over." He pulled on Grace's arm, leaving me alone with my irritation at myself for allowing him to provoke me.

While I'd been biting my tongue to keep from quarreling with Professor Luzon, the members of the group Mala had led opposing construction on Haleakala had arrived. I went to greet James Feary, Mala's attorney, feeling the need for more simpatico company as the service began.

The funeral was led by a man wearing a flowing Hawaiian shirt, slacks, sandals, and a wide-brimmed straw hat.

"Do you know who that is?" I asked Feary.

"A priest," he said, nodding.

"Was Mala a religious person?"

"Doesn't matter. The priest won't be invoking any gods you've heard of in mainstream religions. Here in Hawaii we offer up the deceased to the *akua*, all the gods. The spirit of the deceased will watch over us, especially the *kūpuna*."

"*Kūpuna?*"

"The elderly. They're the ones who are closest to getting ready to join the one who has already passed, and they're treated with special reverence. Mala's auntie Edie is the oldest of her remaining family. She'll receive the most attention from Pele, the goddess of fire."

"I have a lot to learn," I said.

"Just enjoy it." He smiled. "Allow the spirits to flow through you."

And that was what I did. The priest led the ceremony, which included music. The hula dancers performed their art as they circled the basket containing Mala's ashes. Much of what the priest said was in Hawaiian, but some was in English, which made understanding what was happening a little easier for me. The musicians were joined by three bare-chested young men wearing loincloths who played various-sized drums that ramped up the tempo and had people tapping their feet. Some danced solo, eyes closed, as though one with the spirit of the music and with other spirits that only they could see. In between musical interludes, the priest recited Hawaiian legends and called people up to read some of Mala's favorite poems. I'd never attended a funeral anything like this and found myself immersed in the joy of the event as speaker after speaker praised Mala and sent her off to a prized place in heaven.

At the end of the ceremony, the priest carried the basket holding Mala's ashes to the outrigger canoe, where four young men accepted it. They placed it in the center of the canoe, laying floral wreaths others had brought to the funeral across the bow and stern, then pushed off into the water, followed by a convoy of smaller craft. People in canoes and kayaks paddled alongside the larger boat. Two young men used the surfboards to accompany the outrigger.

Carson Nihipali had stripped off his shirt, revealing a tattoo of Mala's face on his left shoulder. He was pushing off in a kayak to accompany the little flotilla surrounding the outrigger, when Dale waded into the water. He caught the kayak by its gunwale, upending the small craft and dumping the "surfer dude," as Grace had termed him, into the sea.

"She was too good for you," Dale shouted as he tried to step around the kayak, fists ready to take on Carson. "How dare you claim her for yourself?"

Carson attempted to scramble to his feet, but a wave hit him in the chest, knocking him back. Dale splashed over to him, trying a last-minute leap onto his rival, only to catch an armful of water as Carson backpedaled away. The two men managed to stand upright, but the action of the water kept them from gaining a steady foothold, and they rose and fell as the waves pressed them toward shore.

"She didn't want me either, man," Carson yelled to Dale. His voice was hoarse. "I tried to convince her to come back to me the night she died. She turned me down. She was just wasting her time with both of us. Besides, what difference does it make now?" He ran the fingers of both hands through his hair, slicking it back from his forehead. I couldn't tell if the moisture beneath his eyes was from tears or his dunk in the sea.

Dale appeared to have received a blow. He leaned over in the water, hands on his knees, breathing heavily.

Carson caught the line of his kayak and waded to shore, dragging the lightweight craft behind him. He leaned down and swiped up his shirt from the sand without missing a step and trudged off the beach.

Witnesses to the brief confrontation turned their attention back to the little fleet of boats, which were arrayed in a circle around the outrigger.

"What's happening now?" I asked Feary.

"The ceremony of releasing Mala to the sea," he said. "At some funerals, the whole body is given over to the ocean in expectation that sharks will consume the dead."

"That sounds rather gruesome."

"Not at all," said Feary. "Any sharks that have feasted on the deceased will never again attack a human being. The human spirit that lives within them will see to that."

It was a lovely thought.

We joined a line of mourners at the shoreline as we watched the ceremonial burial at sea, listening to the chanting as the basket was released into the waters. Others in the accompanying canoes surrounded the bobbing basket with hundreds of flower blossoms of every color. Soon, the basket disappeared from our view. Mala Kapule had gone to her final resting place.

With the ceremony concluded, the celebration continued with a feast. There was chicken in lauhala leaves, roast pork, beef on skewers, poi of course, and platters of fresh vegetables and fruits, some of which I didn't recognize. I tried to sample everything without putting too much on my plate. The atmosphere was festive, a joyous send-off to Mala.

It had been four hours since I'd arrived at the park, and I was ready to leave. My knees ached, as did my back, and I felt the trace of a headache coming on. As I pondered whom to approach to call a cab, I caught sight of Dale standing to the side, watching the festivities but declining to participate. We hadn't spoken for the entire event, and I wondered what had been going through his mind when he tried to take revenge on Carson while the woman he claimed to love was buried at sea.

"Hello, Dale," I said. "You must be uncomfortable in those wet clothes."

"She's gone," he said absently.

"Yes. It was a beautiful ceremony."

He snorted. "If you don't mind the hypocrisy behind it."

"I'm not sure I understand," I said.

"Some of these people shedding tears over her death couldn't care less."

"I'm sorry to hear that," I said. "It seemed to me that the outpouring of sorrow and the celebration of her life was genuine."

"For some, perhaps."

"Who are the exceptions?" I asked, hoping my questioning wouldn't bring a halt to our conversation.

Dale looked past me to where Luzon and Grace stood talking with other attendees. "He's the worst. He would egg her on and then sit back and let her take the flack for opposing the telescope."

"Professor Luzon?"

He nodded.

"Why do you think he would do that?"

"Isn't it obvious? The more she bucked the system, the better his chances at getting the chairmanship. Luzon is nothing if not ambitious."

"I understand Mala was pretty ambitious herself."

He shrugged and glanced down at his cell phone. He tapped the screen for several moments, but I don't imagine it was working if it had been in his pocket when he tried to tackle Carson in the water.

"I wonder whether you would do me a favor," I said.

"Maybe. What favor?"

"I need a ride back to my hotel. The only number I have for a cab service is Mala's cousin Elijah." I held up the business card Elijah had given me. "I can hardly ask him to leave his family's service to drive me across the island."

"Sure, I'll drive you." He dropped his dead phone into the pocket of his shorts. "I've got nothing else to do today."

"If it wouldn't be too much trouble, I'd greatly appreciate it."

"No, no trouble."

As we walked to the parking lot he noticed my limp. "You got hurt?" he asked.

I told him about my accident biking down from Haleakala.

"Riding bikes down from the volcano is stupid."

"In my case 'foolhardy' might be a more apt term." I could have said that fighting over a dead woman at her funeral was not the smartest move he had ever made, but I resisted. I needed a ride, and it didn't pay to antagonize the driver.

Dale's car was a battered older silver two-door coupe with a few dents in the fender and scrapes along the side. "Welcome to my Maui cruiser," he said with a smirk.

"Is that a brand of car?"

"Almost. It's what we call a car that doesn't have much life left. Dented, rusted, horn doesn't work. You get the picture. Still runs, though."

I got in the passenger side. Dale took a towel from the trunk and laid it across the driver's seat, got behind the wheel, pulled a cigarette from a pack on the dashboard, and lit it, not bothering to ask whether I minded. I rolled down my window, and he did the same. The engine came to life with a loud, hesitant rumble.

"Where to?" he asked.

I gave him the name of my hotel in Kahului.

"I know it," he said. "I sometimes work as a waiter at catered events. I've worked there."

We said nothing as we drove away, Dale puffing on his cigarette until it was down to its filter. He casually tossed it out the window.

"I don't know your last name," I said.

"Mossman. My father was Jewish, my mother Hawaiian."

"You grew up here on Maui?"

"Yup. Lived here through high school until I joined the army. Did two tours in Afghanistan."

"And now you're getting your college education. Why horticulture?"

My question brought forth his first smile. "Not very macho, huh?"

"I wasn't implying that."

"My mother loved plants and flowers. She spent most of her time tending to our gardens. I guess it rubbed off on her only son."

"It's certainly a worthwhile field of study." I let a few seconds pass before saying, "You've said that you were in love with Mala Kapule."

He pressed his lips together and nodded.

"Did she—well, did she reciprocate?"

"Do you mean did we have an affair? In a manner of speaking, I suppose you could say that we did. We had a couple of dates, had to keep it hush-hush. Professors aren't supposed to go out with their students."

"But you're older than the typical student."

"I'm twenty-seven, Mrs. Fletcher. There were only five or six years between us, although to hear her tell it, we were a May-December romance." He adopted a singsong voice. "Women mature much faster than men."

"That's what she would say?"

"Yeah, but I don't think she really believed it. It was just an excuse to push me off. It may be true when you're a teenager, but by the time we're in our late twenties, early thirties, I figure we guys have caught up. Besides, a tour in the service will grow you up pretty fast."

He turned down a road leading to my hotel and stopped in front of a small food shack.

"Feel like a cold drink?" he asked.

"I—sure. That sounds good."

We took our drinks to a picnic table at the side of the establishment, a strawberry milk shake for him, a glass of POG for me. He stepped over the bench and lowered himself wearily onto its seat. It appeared to me that time and heat had dried out his white shirt and shorts. The only evidence of his dip in the ocean was his nonworking cell phone.

"I'll try burying it in a bowl of raw rice tonight," he said after unsuccessfully trying to resurrect its signal. "If that doesn't work, I'll have to get a new one."

"I don't know if you're aware that I'm working with a retired Maui homicide detective, Mike Kane, to clear up questions about how Mala died."

His surprised expression indicated that he wasn't aware of it.

"I know that the official reason for her death is an accident, but there are circumstances that might refute that finding."

"You think someone pushed her?"

"Possibly."

"Why? What makes you think that?"

"An accumulation of small things, none of which in and of themselves prove that her death wasn't an accident. But I'm determined to find out the truth, and I'm sure that someone like you would want that, too."

"Someone like me?"

"Someone who loved her."

He pressed his lips together, and I wondered whether he was holding back tears. I didn't know to what extent his personal relationship with Mala had progressed, but I sensed that whatever affection existed was more on his side than on hers.

"Dale," I said as he lit a cigarette, "I'm not interested in probing into your personal life, but since you and Mala were close, maybe you know something that will help me and Detective Kane find the answers we're seeking."

"Well, if you look anywhere, make sure you look down the hall."

"That's a little cryptic. I'm not sure I understand what you mean."

"Down the hall in the 'Ike Le'a building. You know what that means? It means 'to see clearly.' Ironic, isn't it? If ever there was a place that covered up the truth, it's his office."

"Whose office?"

"Luzon's, of course."

"Why Professor Luzon?"

"She would have been the chair of the department if he hadn't gone behind her back and bought off the administration."

"That's a serious charge," I said. "Also, I don't see how it sheds light on her death. Professor Luzon's graduate assistant, Grace Latimer, hypothesized that Mala might have been so upset at not being tapped to chair the department that she took her own life."

"That's a hoot," he said, although there was no humor in his voice.

"I agree that it's a ridiculous notion."

"He used Mala."

"In what way?"

"He led her on."

I sat back and took a sip of my drink to gather my thoughts. "Care to elaborate?" I said.

"Luzon is on the make for every good-looking young woman. Why do you think Grace hangs on his every word? He's probably promising her the same thing he promised Mala."

"Which was?"

"To leave his wife and marry her."

"How do you know that Luzon and Mala had an affair, Dale?"

"I saw what he wrote to her."

"E-mails?"

"Yeah. Mala paid me to help her do some administrative

work in her office. It wasn't much, but I would have done anything to be close to her. When she was out of the office, I took a look at the e-mail on her computer and dug around in her desk." I started to say something, but he stopped me with his upheld hand. "I know, I know. I shouldn't have done that, but I was jealous as hell, Mrs. Fletcher. Jealousy will sometimes make a guy do dumb things."

"I'm not judging you," I said. "What did the e-mails say?"

"They were from Luzon, love letters I guess you could call them, mushy notes about how much he loved her and how once his divorce came through, he'd be free to court her properly. It made me sick."

"I understand," I said. "And did she reply to his messages?"

"I don't know. She came back into the lab before I had a chance to look at her sent folder." He put his cigarette out on the ground and finished his shake. "Come on," he said, "I'll take you to your hotel. Thanks for listening. I've wanted to get it off my chest for a long time."

"I appreciate you having confidence in me," I said.

He pulled up in front of the hotel and I got out.

"Mrs. Fletcher," he said through his open window.

"Yes?"

"I really did love Mala."

Chapter Nineteen

Aia Nō Iā 'Oe—**Whatever You Want to Do**

Dale's parting words stayed with me as I crossed the lobby and headed for my room.

My reaction to him was conflicted. I admired him for serving in the military and now pursuing his college education. While he was younger than Mala, his four years in the army, including time in a war zone, had matured him beyond most of his classmates. Perhaps Mala had found his wartime experiences to be appealing. But I had to wonder whether he was exaggerating the extent to which their relationship had progressed—provided it *had* progressed beyond his infatuation with her. Too, his demeanor was disconcerting. He was consistently pessimistic, always wearing an angry expression. It's hard to warm up to someone who sees only the negative side of life. He didn't appear to be a drug or alcohol abuser, but then again, I might not recognize the symptoms; my life has brought me into contact with few addicts.

I thought back to that morning when I sat in the rear of Mala's class and observed her dismiss him when he'd tried to capture her attention. Had they had a relationship that she'd broken off? Men who've been cast aside by a lover sometimes become angry enough to physically strike out at the woman who rejected them.

These and other questions occupied my mind as I opened the door to my room to the sound of a ringing phone.

"Jessica, Mike Kane."

"Hello, Mike."

"How was the funeral?"

"It was a wonderful experience. That may sound strange, but it was so unlike funerals we have back home in Maine."

"Burial at sea, the whole ritual?"

"Yes. It was much more of a celebration of her life than a mourning of her death."

"The Hawaiian way. Jessica, I got a call from Henry Tahaki, the detective who showed you the mug shots. He said that you agreed to come back to look at more of them."

I sighed. "Yes, he's right, Mike. I did say that I'd do that."

"How about this afternoon?"

"That will be fine. I have nothing planned."

"Good. I'll pick you up in a half hour."

"Aren't you working?"

"My assistant will hold down the fort. Nothing happening here at the resort, no male guest claiming that a housekeeper is taking nips from his flask or female guest claiming that someone is up in a tree and peeking in on her."

I laughed.

"Hey! Laugh if you like, but it happened just last week.

Turned out she was right. A Peeping Tom climbed up the tree and was snapping pictures of her with his cell phone. I called the police, and they hauled him away. Seems he had a long record of peeping through windows. See you in the lobby."

During the ride to police headquarters, I gave Mike a detailed description of Mala's funeral, ending with my conversation with Dale.

"You don't sound very impressed with him," Mike said as he pulled into a parking space.

"I don't know what to think," I said. "He has such a downbeat personality. I wish I had a better handle on him."

Mike and I were seated in the same room I'd been in previously when looking at mug shots. Had I been honest, I would have admitted that I didn't have any hope of seeing the man who'd forced me off the road on my bike and almost sent me to my death. But I went along with the process because it was expected.

When Detective Tahaki greeted us, he started by handing me a folder containing a series of photographs. They were of me following the incident, sprawled on the roadway, my helmet on, then shots of me sitting with my helmet off.

"Where did you get these?" I asked.

"A man who was there shot them and thought we'd like to have them."

"That was good of him," I said, "although I hope none of them ended up on Facebook."

"Not as far as we know," Tahaki said. "He was just another public-spirited citizen. We've got lots of them on Maui."

He set up the computer containing mug shots on the

desktop. I was on my second file when my cynicism was proved wrong. There was my assailant staring at me, the same man who'd been my fellow passenger in the van going to the summit of Haleakala and who'd selected a bike for me and then used his own to attack me.

"That's him," I said.

"You sure, Mrs. Fletcher?" Tahaki asked.

"I'm positive."

He looked at me from the screen, shaved head, down-turned mouth, whiskered jowls.

"Who is he?" I asked.

"Let's print it out," the detective said and left the room.

He returned a few minutes later and handed me a sheet of paper. At the top was the same photo of the man that I'd seen in the mug shot. His name was Christian Barlow, age forty-six, divorced, two children, occupation: maritime mechanic. His rap sheet was long—arrests for assault, nonpayment of child support, possession of an unlicensed handgun; three convictions for driving while intoxicated, and car theft (charges dropped).

"Not a very savory record," I commented.

"I know the *hūpō*," Mike Kane said. "Had a run-in with him before I retired. Comes off like a tough guy, but he's really just a loser."

"Look at this," I said, pointing to more information on the sheet. "His last known employment was with Maui Ocean Star Corp. That's the company that runs the sunset cruise I went on. It's owned by Charlie Reed."

"We pulled Reed in concerning Ms. Kapule's death," Tahaki said.

"On what basis?" Mike asked.

"We considered her death an accident," the detective said, "but there was some pressure to keep the case open." He looked askance at Mike.

"Hey, I'm not official anymore."

"Your definition of 'retired' isn't my definition," Tahaki said. "Because Ms. Kapule was so active in that organization trying to kill the telescope project on Haleakala, we figured that anybody with a lot to lose was worth talking to. You know Reed. Likes to think of himself as a mover and shaker. He's head of the committee that's been fighting Ms. Kapule's efforts tooth and nail."

"I spoke with Charlie Reed at your family picnic, Mike. Remember? He told me that he'd been brought in for questioning. He wasn't happy about it."

The detective shrugged and smiled. "Men like Reed like to toss around their money and influence. I was the one who questioned him. I justified having him come in by saying that we needed him to help us come up with a possible suspect in the lady's death, you know, reaching out to community leaders and all that. He complained about having to take time off from his business but didn't make too much of a stink."

"Was he any help?" I asked.

"No. He kept saying that everyone on his committee were upstanding, law-abiding citizens, which, I should add, is undoubtedly true."

"But Barlow works for Reed," I offered. "Or he did."

Tahaki laughed. "I don't think he had Barlow in mind when he was talking about upstanding citizens. You want to file a complaint against Barlow, Mrs. Fletcher?"

"I do," I said. "After all, he almost killed me, and it was deliberate."

He picked up a phone and called in two uniformed officers, handed them Barlow's rap sheet, which had his current address, and told them to bring him in.

"No need for you to wait around," he told Mike and me. "He may have gone off island after the incident."

"I'd like to stay for a while," I said, "but maybe you'd like to leave, Mike."

"No, I'll hang in. Your officers will call when they've located Barlow?"

"They'd better."

Mike suggested that we go to a small restaurant not far from police headquarters and get something to eat while we waited. I gave Tahaki my cell phone number—he already had Mike's—and we drove to a food truck parked on the Kahului Beach Road.

"I wouldn't exactly call this a restaurant, Mike."

"You can get some of the best food on the island from these trucks."

Mike ordered a scampi and hot dog combination platter and a Coke. I was content, having eaten enough at Mala's funeral, and settled for what had become my favorite drink, pineapple iced tea.

"Glad you decided to stay a while," he said. "They'll want you to ID Barlow if he's the one who assaulted you."

"You heard the detective. They may not be able to find him today," I said.

"Let's give it an hour," he suggested. "If they haven't picked him up by then, we'll take off. They can hold him overnight based on you picking him out of the file, and you can come back tomorrow morning."

It sounded like a good suggestion, and we bided our time on a bench overlooking the harbor. Almost an hour had passed when Mike's cell phone sounded.

"Kane here . . . Great . . . We'll be there in ten minutes."

"Mr. Barlow is on his way," Mike told me as he closed the plastic foam container his food had come in and tossed it in a garbage can.

Christian Barlow sat alone in an interrogation room when we returned to headquarters. Detective Tahaki pulled aside a curtain, which allowed me to observe my attacker through a one-way mirror.

"That's him," I said.

"He put up a fight?" Mike asked.

"No," Tahaki said. "Mumbled something about his rights but other than that was a pussycat. He's a little tipsy. They found him sacked out in front of the TV at the apartment he rents."

"Will he have to have a lawyer present before you question him?" I asked.

"Negative," said the detective. "We're not charging him with anything, just asking him a few questions about what happened to you on the trip down from Haleakala. I won't mention that you're here, Mrs. Fletcher. Looking forward to seeing his expression when he finds out."

Mike Kane and I watched and listened as the detective went into the interrogation room. His arrival caused Barlow to jump up and ask why he was there.

"We've had an incident, Mr. Barlow, and want to see whether you can help us sort it out."

"What incident? I don't know nothing about any incident." His words were slurred.

"Sit down, Mr. Barlow, and take a look at these." Tahaki slid the folder containing the photographs taken by a witness to the event across the table.

Barlow eyed the folder suspiciously.

"Go on," he was urged. "Just some pictures."

Barlow opened the folder and took a photo from it.

"Ring any bells, Mr. Barlow?"

He shrugged and tossed the picture on the table. "This has got nothing to do with me."

"Look at the others."

Barlow did as he was told. After perusing the folder's contents, he sat back, a smug smile on his face. "These pictures mean nothing to me. Who's the woman? You drag me in to look at pictures of some old dame? Business must be slow around here."

Mike looked at me and raised his sizable eyebrows.

"I hope he gets life," I quipped, smiling.

"Where were you yesterday, Mr. Barlow?" Detective Tahaki asked.

"Hmmm, let's see. I was working, like I always do."

"Didn't take a day off and head up to Haleakala?"

"What, to see some dumb volcano? I got better things to do."

"You were working at Maui Ocean Star?"

"Right. That's right."

"Your boss, Mr. Reed, will testify to that?"

"Charlie? Yeah, he'll straighten you out."

"Would it surprise you that a dozen people who took the bike excursion to Haleakala will say that you were with them on the trip, and that the tour operator will testify to the same thing?"

The detective's words erased the smile from Barlow's lips. "I got nothing to say," he said. "You want to charge me with something, call my lawyer."

"You have a lawyer, Mr. Barlow?"

"No. You get one assigned to me."

Tahaki leaned closer to Barlow. "Mr. Barlow," he said, "we know that you tried to run the woman in those photos off the road on the way down from Haleakala. How would you like us to charge you with attempted murder?"

Barlow jumped up. "Attempted murder? What are you, crazy? All I did was—"

Mike Kane and I looked at each other.

"All you did was *what*, Mr. Barlow?"

"I got nothing to say."

"Maybe you'd like to say *nothing* to the woman in the photos."

The detective waved at the mirror.

Barlow's eyes widened before he twisted in his chair and turned away. "She's there?" he said, pointing a thumb over his shoulder.

"Right next door. She's watching as we speak," Detective Tahaki said. "Mrs. Jessica Fletcher, the woman you tried to kill."

"Oh, no, I didn't try to kill nobody," Barlow said. "Hey, if she's there, she's alive, huh? I never tried to kill nobody."

"Then why did you try to run her off the road?" Tahaki asked.

"It was an accident. I—I lost control of my bike."

"It was *not* an accident," I said to Mike. "He deliberately caused me to fall, and I almost went over the edge."

Tahaki echoed what I'd said to Mike. "Mrs. Fletcher says you pushed her. If her bike had skidded a few inches more, she would have tumbled to her death. That would have been murder. As it is, it's attempted murder."

Barlow's previous bravado melted. He looked toward the mirror through bloodshot, watery eyes, extended his hand, and raised his voice, "I'm sorry for your troubles, lady. Really I am."

"You don't have to shout. She can hear you just fine."

Barlow hung his head.

"Who told you to do it?" Tahaki asked.

"Nobody."

The detective let Barlow's answer hang in the air for several moments, saying nothing. Barlow coughed and added, "Charlie was upset, that's all."

"Good going, Henry," Mike muttered.

I raised my brows at him.

"If you let some silence follow a perp's answer, he usually adds more information. I taught him that technique." Mike winked at me.

"Is Charlie Reed your boss?" Tahaki asked.

Barlow solemnly nodded.

"Is that a yes? Speak up!"

"Yeah."

"How upset was he?"

"Pretty damned upset," was Barlow's reply. "Pardon my French," he said, glancing at the mirror.

"He was upset that Mrs. Fletcher was looking into how Mala Kapule died?"

"I don't know nothing about that," Barlow said quickly.

"Then what was he upset about?"

"You never know with Charlie. He's got a temper. Man, has he got a temper."

"Did Charlie Reed tell you to try to injure Mrs. Fletcher?"

Barlow shook his head. "No, nothing like that, only I knew he was upset with her, so I figured that maybe I'd help him out. He said that she—meaning that lady next door—that she should leave Maui and go home to wherever it is she lives." He looked at the mirror again and shrugged. "Sorry, ma'am."

"Go on, Mr. Barlow," Tahaki said.

"Charlie, he's always threatening to can me, so I figured that if I put a scare into the lady here he'd get off my case. All I meant to do was give her a little scare."

"You did a lot more than that, Mr. Barlow. You almost killed her."

He hung his head and slowly shook it. "It was a dumb thing I did, and I know it. Sometimes I do dumb things."

"Thinking that you could go up to Haleakala with a dozen people, run Mrs. Fletcher off the road, and walk away without anybody being able to identify you was one of those dumb things, Barlow," Tahaki said.

Silence filled the room.

"I really am sorry, ma'am," Barlow said softly; then he shouted at the mirror. "I swear I'm sorry, and I'm glad you're okay."

"I appreciate that, Mr. Barlow," I said, although I knew he couldn't hear me.

"So what's going to happen to me?"

"That's up to Mrs. Fletcher," Detective Tahaki said, standing. "I'll go ask her."

"I need to think about it," I said when Tahaki opened the door of the room where Mike and I had observed the questioning.

"Fair enough, Mrs. Fletcher. We'll hold Mr. Barlow while you decide whether or not to press charges."

"Good job, Henry," Mike said to his colleague, swatting him on the shoulder.

"Hey, brah, I learned from the best."

Mike and I left the room and went outside.

"He's a jerk," Mike said.

"And, as he admits, a dumb one," I said.

"What I don't get is how he knew you were going to be on that trip."

"I wondered about that myself. There was a jewelry and craft show in the lobby of the hotel when I made my reservation. There were a lot of people milling around, but now that I think about it, I remember a heavyset man who was hiding his face behind a newspaper."

"He must have been following you. So now what are you going to do about him?"

"If Charlie Reed had instructed him to accost me, I'd feel differently. I'd press charges against both of them. But you know what, Mike? I really don't see anything to be gained by bringing charges against Mr. Barlow. Hopefully this experience will be enough to make him think twice about what he does with his life."

"I wouldn't count on it, Jessica."

"Call it positive thinking," I said. "I need a good dose of positive thinking."

Chapter Twenty

Maikaʻi No Au—I Am Fine

"Can I drop you anywhere?" Mike asked as we stood outside police headquarters.

I looked from the parking lot up the road to the hospital where I'd been treated, and where Bob Lowell was a patient following his shoulder surgery.

"As long as I'm here," I said, "I might as well stop in and see someone I've met since coming to Maui."

"Who's that?"

I explained having met the Lowells at the luau, and Bob's mishap while biking down from Haleakala. "He's a bit of a character," I said, "but a decent sort. I'm sure he'd enjoy a visit."

"Lani asked me to invite you to dinner. Are you available?"

"Oh, please thank her, Mike, but I think I'll have a bite at my hotel and make it an early night."

"Just give a yell if you need anything," Mike said.

"Count on it. Thanks for everything you've done."

"It's been my pleasure. Glad you were able to ID the guy. Now we just have to get you to press charges."

"I'll have to give that some serious thought."

"You do that." He wished me a restful evening, got in his car, and drove away.

Bob Lowell was in a private room on the top floor of the hospital. After receiving a visitor's pass from the lobby desk, I rode the elevator to his floor and checked room numbers, eventually coming across his wife as she came out of his room.

"Hello, Elaine," I said. "How's Bob?"

"Oh, Jessica! How good of you to stop by. He's doing fine."

"Just wanted to check up on the patient. After all, we share a common adventure, falling off our bikes."

"He'll be delighted to see you."

Lowell was sitting up in his hospital bed when I entered the room.

"Look who came to see you, Bob," Elaine said.

"Hey, what a great surprise," he said. "Came to check on whether I died?"

"No, I came to see how your shoulder was."

"Pretty darn good. Hurts, but the little green-and-yellow pills take the edge off the pain send me into la-la land. I kind of like it there."

I heard a soft "Oh, Bob" behind me.

"How are *your* war wounds?" he asked.

"Healing nicely," I said, and took a bedside chair.

"Seen any of the others from the luau?" he asked.

"Yes, I have. You?"

"No. That professor and his wife and girlfriend were a strange couple of ducks, weren't they? Or should I say trio of ducks?"

"Girlfriend?"

"Yeah, the cute blonde. What was her name?"

"Grace," his wife supplied.

"She's Professor Luzon's graduate assistant," I added.

He laughed, then winced at a spasm of pain it generated. "They didn't fool me, Jessica. Graduate assistant my—oops, got to watch my language with two pretty ladies in the room."

"You said that they were strange," I said. "In what way?"

"Oh, I don't know, the way he and his wife didn't get along." He struggled to sit up straighter and became conspiratorial. "You know what I think?" He looked at the door as if he expected someone to be eavesdropping.

"What?"

"I think the professor and his cute blonde are having one torrid affair. Heck, that's why his wife is such a sourpuss. She knows what's going on. Why do you think she wasn't with her darling hubby when we had drinks?"

"You had drinks with Professor Luzon?"

"Sure did. Elaine, she hit the sack the minute we got back from the luau, but I wasn't ready to call it a night. I watched a little TV, then went into the hotel bar, and there they were, the professor and— What's her name?"

"Grace," Elaine said.

"Right, Grace. When I walked in, there they were, real

cuddly-like. They didn't seem pleased to see me, but heck, I didn't let that bother me. I sat right down with them, offered to buy them a drink. He's the snooty type, the professor. Of course, I could see that his wife wasn't with him, so I asked about her, kind of give him a subtle reminder about his marriage vows."

"What did he say?" I asked, amused, thinking that nothing about Bob Lowell was subtle.

"He says she wasn't feeling well, the usual excuse. They didn't stay long once I arrived. After I had my drink, I went out back to the patio that overlooks where the luau took place. It was late."

"What time was it?" I asked.

"Had to be after one. The place was already cleaned up, tables and chairs hauled away. Anyway, I saw 'em standing under a palm tree." He became conspiratorial again. "They were playing kissy-face."

Elaine said, "You can't be sure of that."

"Of course I can. I may be getting older, but the eyes work just fine."

"How long will you have to be in the hospital?" I asked.

"He's getting out tomorrow," said Elaine. "We're flying home the day after."

"I'm sure you'll be glad to be leaving."

"Not me," Bob said. "I like it here, all those cute little hula-dancing girls."

"Oh, Bob," said Elaine.

It was my cue to leave.

I found a taxi waiting at the curb and got in, gave the driver the name of my hotel, and sat back and relaxed. We'd gone only a few miles when the smell of smoke wafted through the cab's open windows.

"There must be a fire," I said.

"Those are the sugarcane fields," the driver said. "They're starting to burn them."

"They burn the fields?" I said.

"Yes, ma'am, every two years. The stalks get too high and produce less sugar, so they burn the field to the ground and start a new crop. Usually the wind blows north to south and the smoke goes to where the sugar refinery workers live, but the wind has shifted today. We'll be out of it in a few minutes."

I closed my window and my mind wandered in many directions, including the conversation Mike and I had had with one refinery worker, Mr. Mohink, Koko's father. While I still hadn't had an opportunity to talk with the boy again, I couldn't shake the feeling that he knew something about Mala's death and was perhaps afraid to reveal what it was.

My instincts in such things have held me in pretty good stead over the years, although they've also led me astray at times. My frustration comes when I'm unable to confirm whether they are valid or not. Hopefully that wouldn't be the case when I packed my bags and headed home to Cabot Cove from Maui.

Chapter Twenty-one

Uahi!—Smoke!

I'd just stepped out of the shower the next morning when the phone rang. I debated whether to wrap myself in a towel and answer or to let the hotel's automatic answering service take it. I would have opted for the latter except that the phone kept ringing. Whoever was calling evidently had asked the hotel operator to keep putting the call through and not to activate the answering system.

"Hello?" I said, struggling to keep the towel in place.

"Jessica, it's Mike Kane."

"Hello, Mike."

"Catching you at a bad time?"

"That's all right. What's up?"

"I'll keep this short. You know the Mohink kid, Kona or Koko or whatever his name is? He's missing."

"Oh, no! His family must be frantic."

"His father reported it to headquarters. A search party is

being assembled. I've volunteered to coordinate it with the police."

"Where are you now?"

"I'm heading for the college campus. That's where the search effort is being staged: law enforcement, fire department, volunteers from the community. I won't have time to pick you up."

"Don't worry about me. I'll find a way to get there."

"No need for you to come. I'm sure the kid will show up soon."

"I'll see you at the college," I said. As he started to hang up, I added, "Oh, Mike, remember what his father told us, that his son likes to hide in the sugarcane fields."

"Gotcha, Jessica. See you later."

As I rushed through my morning ablutions to get ready to leave, I kept thinking about that little boy with the big glasses. I had been convinced that he knew something that would help us get to the bottom of Mala's death, and I had wanted to see if I could coax that information from him. But whether he could help resolve my questions was irrelevant now. We had to find him. We had to return him safely to his family. His well-being was my only concern.

I skipped breakfast and went directly to the lobby, where I asked that a taxi be called. The cab that pulled up less than five minutes later was driven by Mala's cousin Elijah.

He greeted me as I climbed into the backseat. "Hello, Mrs. Fletcher."

"Hello, Elijah. I'm going to the college campus."

"On a beautiful day like today, I thought you might be using a bicycle."

"I need to get there as quickly as possible."

"Sure thing. Is there a problem?"

"A boy is missing."

"Oh, yes. I heard about that. It came through our dispatcher, and it was on TV. They say they'll be running a picture of him soon."

"I know the child," I said. "My colleague Mike Kane is coordinating the search for him. Do you still have those granola bars, Elijah? I didn't have time for breakfast."

I chose one from the cardboard container he handed me and started fishing in my purse for money.

"Oh, no. My treat. Mala would be angry with me if I took money from her famous friend."

"Famous?"

"I heard. Everyone says you are a very important writer."

"Let's just say that I write and manage to make a living at it. But thank you."

As we approached the campus, wisps of smoke were visible in the sky just to its south.

"Is that a sugarcane field being burned?" I asked.

"Yes, ma'am. A necessary evil to be sure that the next crop will be a good one. No need to worry. The wind will carry the smoke away from the college."

My concerns weren't about being impacted by the smoke. I thought of Koko and his pleasure in exploring the cane fields, and I hoped that he hadn't decided to play hide-and-seek in the one that was going up in flames.

Surely Mike was right. Koko would be found quickly and returned to the safety of his father's arms. But that was my optimistic side talking. I remembered what Mohink had said about the boy's mother having died, and that his grandmother was helping to raise him. Judging from the father's age, his wife must have been a relatively young woman when she passed away. Had it happened recently enough that Koko missed his mother, or had she died when he was just an infant? Either way, the loss of a wife and mother was tragic, and having a child that young to bring up was no easy task for his father.

The campus was bustling with people as we pulled up in front of the administration building. I paid Elijah—I wouldn't hear of not paying the fare—and walked swiftly to where the center of the action seemed to be. I spotted Mike Kane issuing orders to small groups of people, some in uniform, most in civilian clothing, who broke away once they'd received their instructions. He'd been joined by Detective Henry Tahaki. Mike motioned for me to join them.

"Plenty of help to find the boy," I said.

"Nothing like a kid in jeopardy to bring out the best in people," Tahaki said.

We looked up at a helicopter passing overhead.

"Air One," Mike said. "We've got two of them involved in the search."

I stood silently by as Mike dispatched another group of people to where they should look for Koko. During a brief lull, I asked Mike, "When did he disappear?"

"The father reported it at five this morning. From what I'm told, he'd driven to work and his mother called to say the boy was gone. He thinks Koko might have been hiding in the backseat of his car—he found the child's glasses under a blanket—and ran off into the sugar field when Mohink went indoors to work."

"And so many people have already volunteered?"

"Word gets out fast. The media was immediately informed, along with every other means of communication."

"Is there any chance that he was abducted?" I asked, hoping for a negative answer.

"We have to keep that possibility in mind," Mike said.

"Where is his father?" I asked.

"Around here someplace."

The large cane field now ablaze was directly to the south of the campus. One of the helicopters hovered over it, the downdraft from its rotors sending the smoke in angry swirls that looked like a special effect from a computer-generated motion picture.

Mike was approached by two doctors who'd arrived in a mobile field hospital. They were accompanied by EMTs.

"Anything new, Detective?" one of the doctors asked.

"No, but we're pulling out all the stops," Mike said.

"We talked with the father," the second physician said. "He says the boy has asthma." He looked in the direction of the burning cane field and added, "Hope he doesn't get a nose full of that smoke."

The thought of Koko being trapped in that smoke sent a chill up my spine. But surely he wouldn't remain if he knew that a field had been set on fire. Unless he was disoriented or injured or . . .

Again my thoughts turned to the possibility that he had been forcibly taken from his home. I admit to having trouble believing that anyone would harm a child, but unfortunately there are people in the world who are capable of all manner of evil deeds.

Warren Mohink approached Mike and me, accompanied by a uniformed officer. Two reporters followed. I recognized Joe Luckey, the young man with whom I'd spoken at Cale Witherspoon's press conference. Mohink nodded at me and shook Mike's hand.

"Look. I can't just stand around doing nothing," Mohink said, his jaw working. He swiped a hand across his mouth. "Anything new?"

"Not yet," Mike replied. "We've established a search grid and have dispatched teams to those areas. We've already searched along the Wailea Coastal Walk and are double-checking again. Have you been in touch with the plant where you work?"

"Yeah," Mohink said.

"I assume your cane fields are among those being burned."

"Sure."

"Some of the search teams are covering the closest fields, but they'll have trouble because of the fires and smoke," Mike said. "We haven't sent a team yet to the one over there." He pointed south. "You mentioned that your son likes to play in the fields. Any special areas within them that he's been known to visit?"

He sighed and shook his head. "You think you know your kid and then this happens. I have no idea where he goes when he's playing in the fields. I just give him a yell and he usually comes running back. But sometimes—"

"Did anything happen recently that might have set him off, like an argument at home or a fight with a friend?"

Mohink shook his head. "I can't think of anything. We

were here at the college yesterday. There was a puppet show put on by the horticulture school about plants and flowers, kind of a silly thing, but Koko really wanted to see it. He'd learned about it from a friend and begged me to take him. I even took the day off just so we could come here."

Mohink was interrupted by a volunteer who pulled Mike away to answer a question.

"A puppet show?" I said to Koko's father. "Did anything take place during the show that might have scared him? Children that age are so easily frightened by things they see or hear that don't even register with adults."

"Koko is—well, I think I told you before. He's got a vivid imagination. He freaked out right after the show."

"Freaked out? In what way?"

"What about the kid's mother?" Joe Luckey interjected.

Mohink glared at him. "His mother's dead," he growled.

"Sorry," Luckey said. "I didn't know."

"Has he run away before?" the other reporter asked.

I held up a hand and said, "Gentlemen, you'll have to excuse us. Mr. Mohink needs his privacy right now." I led him away from the reporters and spoke in a low voice so they couldn't overhear. "What do you think caused Koko to 'freak out,' as you say? What set him off?"

"Who the heck knows? He's such a crazy kid. One minute he was happy as a clam. He loved the puppet show and we were on our way to get him an ice cream cone. When we got near the stand, he looks at the people in line, grabs my leg, and starts whimpering."

"Was there someone in line he knew, that *you* knew?"

He pressed his lips together in exasperation. "I wasn't

looking. He said he wanted to go home, so that's what we did."

"What about after you'd returned home?" I asked.

Mohink ran one hand through his hair. I saw that his fingers were trembling. "He went in his room, and I did some work in my home office. He wouldn't talk much at dinner. He can be moody at times. He's a sensitive kid, *too* sensitive for his own good. Afterward he went back into his room and stayed there playing with his toys until bedtime."

Mike rejoined us with a stack of photocopies of the picture Mohink had provided of Koko. "These are ready for distribution. The local TV channels are running them, and I have people driving around the area handing them out to stores."

"What can I do?" Mohink asked.

Mike handed him a pile of pictures. "Why don't you see if anybody here needs one?"

Mohink went off to help pass out the copies, with Joe Luckey and the other reporter following, pads and pens at the ready.

I informed Mike about the father-and-son outing the previous day.

"What would upset him so much that he'd go from being a happy little kid at a puppet show to grabbing his father's leg and begging to go home?"

"He must have seen someone or something that frightened him."

"I'd love to know who was in that ice cream line," Mike said.

"Maybe if—no, make that *when*—he's found, we can try to get him to tell us."

The morning wore on as search parties came back to check in following the scouring of their coverage areas, only to be sent out again with maps of new areas to explore. The helicopters continued to circle overhead and an array of fire department vehicles and police cars were parked haphazardly throughout the staging area. Two trucks selling ice cream and pretzels had learned of the gathering crowd and arrived to feed those in need of snacks and drinks.

As I looked for familiar faces, I saw Cale Witherspoon cross the parking lot. With him were six other men, including Charlie Reed, owner of the *Maui Ocean Star*, and Mala Kapule's former boyfriend Carson Nihipali. For someone who'd only recently arrived on Maui, I already knew a surprising number of people. I thought of the morning I'd met Mala and her comment that Maui was a small island and that everyone knew everyone else. I was starting to become a believer.

"Hello, Mr. Reed," I called out.

He stopped, peered at me as though trying to force recognition, smiled, and approached.

"You're here to help find the boy?" I asked.

"Of course," he said. "There's nothing worse than a youngster in danger."

"I certainly agree," I said. "Hello, Carson."

"Mrs. Fletcher," he said.

"Cale Witherspoon has brought some of his employees to aid in the search," Reed said. "He's also got some heavy equipment in case it's needed."

"That's good of you, Mr. Witherspoon," I said.

"It's the least I can do," he proclaimed. "Any word on the boy?"

"Not that I know of."

I wondered whether Witherspoon was aware of Mala's financial arrangement with his Oregon competitor, Douglas Fir Engineering. If I had to guess, I'd say it wasn't likely. Surely he would have pointed to it publicly, charging her with a conflict of interest. It was clear to me as I stood talking to the two men that they were closely aligned in their campaign to override the objections of Mala and her group. She'd been up against some heavy hitters.

Reed looked in the direction of the burning sugarcane field. "The wind's shifting. Looks like it could end up coming in this direction."

"Who's in charge?" Witherspoon demanded.

"Detective Kane," I said.

"Who's he?"

"A retired cop," Reed said dismissively. "Over there. The big guy at the mike."

Someone from the college had supplied a microphone and amplifier for Mike to use.

"Listen up," he said. "We need volunteers to work with the fire department to go into that burning cane field just to the south of us. About a third of it isn't on fire yet, but it'll be hot and smoky."

Carson Nihipali joined a group of men who'd gathered around Mike, including a half dozen uniformed firefighters. "What are we standing around for?" Carson yelled. "Let's go find the kid."

Witherspoon ordered the men he'd brought with him to join the others as they piled into vehicles and headed south.

"Why would the kid go into a burning field?" Witherspoon mused aloud.

"For some reason he enjoys playing games in the sugarcane fields," I answered. "At least according to his father."

"Seems like a dumb thing for a kid to do," said Witherspoon.

"He's just a little boy."

"Well, his father needs to teach him better."

There was nothing to gain by debating it with him or pointing out that children have their own reasons for doing what they do, so I walked to Mike, who was busy gathering volunteers and assigning them to search areas on the grid he'd drawn over a map of Maui. The search effort had become large and well organized, thanks to Mike and others, but it was dependent upon the theory that Koko ran away and hid somewhere on Maui.

But what if leaving hadn't been his choice? What if he'd been abducted by someone with nefarious motives? A child molester perhaps. Or a murderer trying to cover his tracks. If that were the case, he could be hidden away with little or no chance of the police, firefighters, and volunteers ever finding him—*at least soon enough.*

The crowd swelled with each passing minute. The police had done a good job of getting out the word about Koko's disappearance, and the outpouring of volunteer help was both inspiring and gratifying. There were families, teenagers, single men and women, waiting to be assigned search areas. A few people had brought their dogs on the chance that they might prove useful. The Maui PD had also dispatched a canine unit, which had been sent to the immediate area near the Mohink house after Koko's father had provided them with an item of his son's clothing for the dogs to sniff.

And there was Mala's auntie Edie, who'd arrived a few moments ago, leaning on the arms of two young cousins I'd met at Mala's house. I went to her.

"How are you?" I asked.

She smiled sweetly at me and said, "I am fine, but I heard about the little lost boy."

"Yes," I said, "everyone is so concerned."

"A child is sacred," she said. "If anyone has harmed him, that person will be punished."

"We're hoping that he just ran away and will be found," I said, not wanting to feed into the possibility that he'd been snatched.

One of the cousins brought the old woman a folding chair and Auntie Edie lowered her body onto the flimsy seat. She reached beneath her green-and-white shawl and held up a piece of round, charcoal-colored rock. I leaned closer to see what was on it. Within a white circle were two large, round white eyes. The older woman seemed transfixed as she stared at the lava rock, her lips moving as she silently spoke to an unseen person.

The cousin said to me, "She's invoking the spirit of Uli, Mrs. Fletcher, our mother of creation. She's asking Uli to provide her calming and peaceful energy to all those searching for the lost boy and to smooth out the problem of his disappearance and bring him home to his family."

I wanted to say something in response but didn't want to

disturb Auntie Edie and her meditation. Whatever would help bring back Koko alive and well—whether I believed in this sacred Hawaiian goddess or not—was worth pursuing.

"Mrs. Fletcher. You seem to be everywhere."

I turned at the sound of my name to see Professor Abbott Luzon and his wife, Honi. The professor was dressed in a sport jacket and bow tie, his wife in a flowing yellow sundress, oversized sunglasses, and a tan hat with a large, floppy brim.

"Mr. and Mrs. Luzon," I said. "Are you part of the search party?"

"Abbott gave a lecture earlier this morning," Honi said, "or we would have been out here sooner. Any news about the missing boy?"

"Not yet, I'm afraid. But with all these resources looking for him, I'm sure he'll turn up."

"Children often do perplexing things," Luzon said.

"Spoken by a man who has no children," Honi said with an audible sigh. She addressed me. "They have no idea where he might have run away to?"

"Not at the moment," I said.

"Is it possible he might have been kidnapped?"

"Kidnapped?" Luzon said. "Who would do such a thing? Is his father rich?"

Honi ignored his question. "I understand you're investigating the circumstances surrounding Mala Kapule's death, Mrs. Fletcher. Did I hear that right? Anything new on that front?"

Her query startled me back to that issue. With all the focus on Koko Mohink's disappearance, I'd forgotten for the moment that Mala's death remained unresolved.

"I don't believe so," I said.

"Smells like the wind has shifted," Luzon commented.

I turned from them, peered south, and raised my nose to the air. Sure enough, the smoke was moving in our direction, and the odor of the burning cane was getting stronger. When I turned back, I spotted Grace Latimer, Luzon's graduate assistant and, according to Bob Lowell, his mistress. She stood apart from the crowd, arms crossed, taking in the spectacle unfolding on the campus. I thought she might join me and the Luzons, but instead she walked in the opposite direction and disappeared into the crowd.

Luzon turned his attention to Auntie Edie praying over the lava rock with its two white eyes staring up at her, the symbol of Uli, the Hawaiian goddess of creation and a dozen other mystical powers. I, too, watched her as her brow furrowed, her lips moving silently, her long fingers making signs over the rock. Luzon indicated his amusement with raised eyebrows and a thin smile.

"Do you know Mala's aunt?" I asked him.

"I introduced myself at the funeral," he said curtly. "What's she doing, praying to some god about the missing child?"

"Something like that," I said, not successful at masking my pique at his snide, condescending tone.

Honi had slipped away while I was speaking with her husband and was headed for the entrance to the horticulture building. As soon as she disappeared inside, Grace Latimer stepped to the professor's side.

"Hello, Grace," I said.

"Hello, Mrs. Fletcher." She said to Luzon, "Hadn't we better get to work on the proposal?"

"Yes, I suppose we should." He seemed suddenly aware that his wife was no longer with us. "Did you see where Honi went?" he asked me.

"I saw her go into that building," I said.

"We can get to it later," Luzon told Grace.

With that, he placed his hand on her elbow and guided her away from me.

The aroma of smoke, both sweet and acrid, continued to reach my nostrils, and I wondered whether the shift in the wind would cause the staging area to have to be relocated. I went to Mike to ask.

"I've just been discussing that possibility," he said, holding up his head like a weathervane twisting in the wind. "The direction of the smoke seems to be changing every few minutes." He leaned closer to me and added, "This is dragging on too long, Jessica. The chances of finding him become less likely with every passing minute."

His grim analysis caused my heart to sink. He was right, of course. I'd learned from the police briefings and seminars I'd attended over the years that unless a missing child was found quickly, certainly no longer than forty-eight hours from the time of the disappearance, the possibility of a happy ending decreased dramatically. It had been only seven hours since Koko's father had discovered him missing, but the minutes seemed like hours. *Where are you, Koko?* I silently asked myself. *Where have you gone?*

Auntie Edie suddenly looked up from her stone and smiled. She nodded as she raised her eyes to the sky. Then she tucked the stone under her shawl and called for the young cousins to help her from her seat. As they made their way out of the staging area, the sound of honking horns could be heard in the distance.

I looked around for the source of the din. A convoy of three or four cars and trucks came roaring onto the campus led by Carson Nihipali's red pickup truck. As it came to an abrupt halt, Carson, shirtless, the sun reflecting off his burnished shoulders, the tattoo of Mala's face glistening, stood up in the truck's open bed. It took a second before everyone realized what he held in his arms.

A cheer went up. "It's the boy!" a chorus of voices said, joined by triumphant shouts and relieved laughter. "It's him! It's him!"

The boy was limp in Carson's arms, and the joy everyone felt was tempered by the fear that he was injured, or worse. One of the EMTs raced to the side of the truck, and Carson handed Koko down to him. The EMT ran with his precious bundle to the mobile field hospital, where the doctors took Koko from him and entered the vehicle.

Warren Mohink, alerted that his son had been found, pushed his way through the crowd that had surrounded the hospital on wheels and tried to climb inside.

"The doctors are with him right now, sir," the EMT said, using his arm to bar the door.

"But that's my son in there."

"We'll let you on in a moment. The doctors are examining him now," the EMT said. "They have to make sure there are no serious injuries. Please stay outside."

"No! I want to see my son," Mohink shouted. As he did, one of the doctors emerged from the trailer.

"I'm his father," Mohink said. "Is Koko all right?"

The doctor grinned. "Yes, he's all right," he said. "He's shaken up, and he's inhaled a lot of smoke from the cane field, but he'll be okay. Just give him, and us, some time. You can come in and see him in a few minutes."

Like everyone else, I was overcome with joy. Mike looked at me, grinned broadly, and gave me the Hawaiian victory sign, hand in the air, pinkie and thumb extended, and I returned it.

I walked up to Warren Mohink, who was pacing in front of the medical truck. "I am so happy for you."

"Silly kid," he said. "Had us all worried to death." He had tears in his eyes.

"What matters is that he's been found," I said.

A few minutes later Koko's father was allowed to enter the mobile unit, and ten minutes after that he stepped from it with his son in his arms. The sight of them was met with applause and whoops of relief. Koko squinted against the bright sunlight, his arms around his father's neck. Although his face had been washed, it was still smudged from the ashes in the field, and his hair was tangled. I took note that he was not wearing his thick glasses. But his father reached into his shirt pocket and retrieved the pair he had found in the backseat of his car. Koko raised his head and put them on. He looked at us and the shy smile that crossed his small face was contagious.

Mohink was on the receiving end of questions from the press on the scene, which now included television and radio reporters as well as Joe Luckey. I imagined that Koko's father would have preferred simply to get in his car with his son and go home, but he politely answered the questions. Mike and a young man brought the amplifier and microphone to where Mohink stood. "Maybe if you make a statement," Mike suggested, "they'll back off and let you leave. I know the crowd would love hearing from you."

Mohink thanked the onlookers for all they'd done to find his son. "His grandmother's going to want to hug each and every one of you." Koko, too, rose to the occasion. He scanned the crowd, a smile on his face, his eyes darting back and forth behind the thick lenses of his glasses, taking in every face, and giggling when his father said, "This little guy has given us all heartburn, but looks like he'll have to be welcomed home with a huge dish of his favorite ice cream, Kauai Pie, with fudge and vanilla crunch cake."

Mohink looked at Koko. "How's that sound, buddy?"

"Yummy, yummy." Koko ran his tongue over his lips, bringing gales of laughter from the crowd.

Mohink seemed to be enjoying the spotlight, too. Having generated a laugh, he proceeded to tell a few humorous anecdotes about his son. As he did, Professor Luzon reappeared, without Grace Latimer on his arm. In her place was his wife, Honi, in dark glasses beneath her floppy hat. She stood slightly beside her husband and peered around him, almost as though using him as a shield. I heard her say, "Come on, Abbott, let's get out of here."

Luzon turned to leave. As he did, a gust of wind took Honi's hat into the air. She squealed and reached to catch it. Koko, who had seemed happy basking in the crowd's adoration, suddenly let out a cry and hugged Mohink tight, his face buried in his father's neck.

"What's happening?" someone said.

Honi Luzon grabbed her husband's sleeve and pulled on it. But before they could leave, Koko looked up through his tears and, seeing her again, shut his eyes and cried. Mohink's confused expression mirrored everyone else's.

I tapped Mike Kane on the shoulder. "Someone should stop her from leaving," I said.

"Who?"

"Mrs. Luzon," I said, indicating the couple as they walked quickly in the direction of the horticulture building. "Koko recognized her and got frightened."

Detective Tahaki overheard what I'd said to Mike.

"What's going on?" he asked.

"You might want to talk to that blond lady over there holding her hat," Mike said.

"About what?"

"About why the boy is so scared of her."

"And about what she knows of Mala Kapule's death," I added.

Chapter Twenty-two

Haʻ Ina Mai Ka Puana—The Story Is Told

W arren Mohink sat on a wooden bench and held Koko in his arms. The boy had calmed down, although there was still a vestige of fear in his expression.

"Is he okay?" I asked.

"Yeah, I think so," Mohink said. "What upset you, son?"

Koko drew in deep breaths and struggled not to cry again.

"Was it that blond woman you saw?" I asked.

He averted his eyes as he nodded.

"What about her?" his father asked. When Koko didn't respond, he said to me, "You know, I've seen that woman before."

"You have?" Mike Kane asked.

"Yeah. She came to the house asking about the woman who fell off the cliff. She said she was a friend of hers and wondered what we knew about the accident."

Mike and I looked at each other.

"And now that I think of it, she could have been in the ice cream line after the puppet show. I wouldn't swear to it, but—"

"Koko, did you see that lady waiting in line for ice cream yesterday?" I asked.

My question elicited another nod from him.

"I think he's answered enough questions," Koko's father said. "He's been through an ordeal and I'd like to take him home."

"Sounds like a sensible idea," Mike said. "A squad car will take you back. The cops are going to want to interview you and the boy, so there still may be a lot of questions once he's had a chance to calm down."

"You mean once *I've* had a chance to calm down," Mohink said, managing what passed for a smile.

Mike motioned for some uniformed officers to join us and suggested that they escort the father and son home. As they walked away, Mike said to me, "What's this business about Mrs. Luzon?"

"I'm not sure, Mike, except that Koko reacted in fear when he saw her. And his father says she might have been the one in the ice cream line who made him 'freak out,' as he described it."

Mike looked in the direction of the horticulture building, his face wrinkled in thought.

"Do you think that the kid saw her with Ms. Kapule the night she died?"

"I think it's possible, Mike. Look, I don't know anything for certain, but it's worth questioning her."

"Let's go," he said.

We entered the building. The corridor was empty. No Mr. and Mrs. Luzon, no Detective Tahaki.

"Let's try the professor's office," I suggested.

I knocked. When no one replied, I turned the knob anyway. Luzon was standing by the window. Honi sat in a chair as far away from her husband as the room's dimensions allowed. Detective Tahaki perched on the edge of Luzon's desk.

"Henry?" Mike said. "Okay if we come in?"

"Fine with me," Tahaki said. "We were just having a little chat."

Mike and I stepped through the door and closed it behind us.

"They have no right being here," Luzon said, facing us. "Get out!"

"I don't know about that," Tahaki said. "They're private investigators, investigating a murder." He winked at me.

"Private, my foot. Besides, what does that have to do with us?" Luzon asked, but he didn't insist that we leave.

I decided to be direct. "Mrs. Luzon, you saw the reaction of little Koko Mohink when he saw you in the crowd. He was pretty frightened. Apparently, he saw you yesterday and had the same reaction. In fact, I'm guessing it was his fear of you that spurred him to run away today."

"And I'm guessing that he's obviously a very disturbed child," she countered, her mouth set in a hard line, arms crossed defiantly on her chest. "I've never seen him before. And to think we were going to help the search parties find him. Now I'm glad we didn't volunteer. He's just a spoiled brat."

"Let me tell you something, Mrs. Fletcher," her husband put in. "If I were you, I'd mind my own business. Just because you're a famous writer doesn't give you the right to question us."

"Maybe you'd rather have *me* ask the questions," Mike said.

"You?" Honi laughed. "I read the papers. You aren't even a policeman anymore. You're retired."

"But *I'm* not," said Tahaki.

Honi sputtered something in response but fell silent.

"This is a violation of our rights," Luzon said. "Come on, Honi, we're leaving. They have no legal right to hold us here. We've come here voluntarily, but now it's time to go."

"Technically, you're correct," Detective Tahaki said. "But it might be to your benefit to hear what Mrs. Fletcher and Detective Kane, retired or not, have to say. If we don't get to ask our questions here, it'll be someplace else. Right now, based upon the boy's reaction, you're considered persons of interest in the death of Mala Kapule."

I added, embellishing the truth a little, "And based upon what the boy has *said*."

Luzon grabbed his briefcase from next to his desk and took steps toward the door.

"Oh, give it up, Abbott," his wife said. "Be a man for a change."

Luzon glared at her.

She laughed. "Look at you, the great professor of horticulture, and now the chairman of the department. Those credentials mean nothing to me."

With that she got to her feet and approached him. "You are a lying, slimy excuse for a human being. One mistress wasn't enough for you. Last year it was Janet. The year before that—what was her name?—oh, yes, Paula, lovely, empty-headed Paula. This year it's Grace. But one at a time isn't sufficient for you, is it, Abbott? There had to be Mala, too."

Luzon backed away and addressed us. "She's crazy," he said, extending his hands palms up. "She sees affairs behind every bush, doesn't trust me and never has." He spun around to face her again. "Keep your mouth shut, Honi, and come with me."

She slapped away his outstretched hand.

"You want the truth?" Honi said. "I'll give you the truth. Remember the night of the luau, Mrs. Fletcher? When it was over, my husband said he had to go back to his office to work, some lie about a last-minute project that had to get done. He assumed I was going home, but something didn't smell right to me. I knew he'd been having an affair with his precious Grace and figured he'd be seeing her. I pretended to leave, but I stuck around. You didn't know that, Abbott, did you? Sure enough, he didn't head for the college. He goes strolling up the Wailea Walk like it's noon instead of midnight. I followed you, you know. Oh, yes, I was right there thirty feet behind you. I was ready to give you and Grace a piece of my mind. Imagine my surprise; it wasn't Grace at all. It was your supposed rival for the chairmanship. Was that how you got her to agree not to oppose you? I stayed a distance away, but not so far that I couldn't see you put your arm around her. It was disgusting."

"Never happened," Luzon said.

"You must have been very angry," Mike said.

Honi snorted. "A gross understatement," she said, reminding me of Grace's response when I'd commented on how expensive it must be to live on Maui. "Wouldn't you be angry if you found your wife in a similar situation?"

Mike ignored the question and said, "You confronted them?"

A crooked grin crossed Honi's face. "Oh, I intended to, but—"

We waited for her to finish.

"But what?" I asked.

"Tell them, Abbott," his wife said. "Tell them what you did."

"Shut up, Honi!"

"I will not shut up," she snapped. "Tell them what happened— or I will!"

Luzon said nothing. His hands were balled into fists at his sides, and he visibly shook.

"Let's cut to the chase," Detective Tahaki said. "Were one of you, or both, present when Ms. Kapule fell to her death?"

Honi had resumed her chair. "Yes," she said, raising her chin as if daring her husband to contradict her. "Wouldn't you say so, Abbott?"

"No! Honi, you're only making it worse."

"And where were you exactly, Mrs. Luzon?" Mike asked.

Honi waved her arms. "Near enough."

"Near enough for what?"

"To see his latest lover."

"You're crazy, Honi. You couldn't see anything. It was dark."

"There was a moon. I could see just fine."

"You're making it up."

Mike said, "What say we take a little trip to find out what Mrs. Luzon could or could not see?"

"Trip?" Luzon said. "To where?"

"Back to where the incident took place. Mrs. Luzon can walk us through what happened that night."

"Absolutely not," said Luzon.

"I think that's a good idea," Honi said, standing again. "I'm ready."

"And I'm leaving," Luzon said.

"Not so fast," Tahaki said. "You and your wife have information about the death of Mala Kapule. It's an open case, and I have the authority to take you into custody for questioning as material witnesses. It'd be a lot easier for both of you if you cooperate with what Detective Kane has suggested—go to the scene and reconstruct what happened based upon your observations."

We all watched Luzon as he struggled with a reply.

"Your choice," Tahaki told him. "It's either that or we can continue this conversation at headquarters."

Tahaki didn't wait for a response. He pulled his cell phone from his pocket and called for two uniformed officers and an SUV. The call completed, he opened the office door and said, "Time to go."

In Wailea, the five of us trooped across the field where the luau had taken place to reach the coastal trail. I remembered that day clearly, stopping by Mala's class, meeting her and having coffee. She had impressed me with her knowledge and poise and her dedication to follow what she believed was the honorable course, to defend the sacred site of Haleakala from further development. Was I so far off the mark in my assessment of her? Had she compromised her values for the sake of money? Had she been having an affair with her challenger for the chairmanship? And could Grace possibly have been right? If I had found her that night, would Mala still be alive?

Mike and I led the way, with the Luzons next and Detective Tahaki behind them. The uniformed police brought up the rear of our little expedition.

When we reached the spot where Mala had fallen, I looked in the direction of the Mohink house for a sign of Warren and Koko, but saw nothing.

Although Tahaki was the officer in charge and had arranged for us to be there, Mike took the helm.

"Okay, Mrs. Luzon," he said, "here we are. You said that you saw your husband in an embrace with Ms. Kapule. Exactly where were they?"

"Where you're standing," Honi replied. "No, a few feet in that direction, closer to the edge."

Mike changed his position. "Here?"

"Yes, there," Honi confirmed.

"And you?" Mike asked. "Where were you?"

Honi looked back along the path. "Over there," she said, pointing to where the trail curved around a wall thirty feet away. The opposite side of the path was lined with bushes.

"Please show Mrs. Fletcher exactly where you were standing." Mike suggested. He turned to me and said, "We need to know what she could see from that vantage point."

Honi and I walked back along the path to the place

where she said she'd hidden. She chuckled. "This is like an episode of *Law and Order*, reenacting the crime."

"Do you find it amusing?" I asked.

"Very."

Mike ordered Luzon to stand just off the path.

By now the professor had adopted a cynical, almost amused posture at what was going on. "Of course, sir," he said, emphasizing "sir."

From where Honi and I stood, her husband was partially visible, our view marred by the branch of a tree that arched over the path.

"Now, Mrs. Luzon," Mike said, "tell us what you observed."

Mike and Tahaki stood on the path, their attention moving from one spouse to the other. Luzon remained on the soft ground, staring off at the horizon. The water below was choppy and a brisk breeze provided relief from the hot sun. A gust of wind pressed the overhanging branch down, obscuring my view of the men.

Honi looked at me as though wanting permission to speak.

"Are you certain of what you saw?" I asked.

"I saw—I saw Abbott push Mala over the edge," she said in a surprisingly strong voice heard by everyone.

Luzon guffawed. "See?" he said, "I told you she was crazy. Why would I do that?"

"Because you were having an affair with her," Honi said.

"I never had an affair with her."

"Well, not for lack of trying, right, Abbott?"

I interrupted their bickering. "Are you saying that your wife is a liar?"

"That's right. A bald-faced liar. I can't even see you now, Honi. That tree branch is in the way."

"But I was able to see you," his wife shouted. "You weren't looking, and I moved closer." She demonstrated by stepping into the path and hugging the wall, edging closer to the men.

I walked past her, taking my place next to the detectives.

Luzon turned to face us, but as the three of us stared at him, the cumulative effect seemed to strip him of his bravado. He put his hands in his pockets and slowly shook his head. "Okay," he said, "Mala fell while we were here together. But I didn't push her. We had an argument."

"An argument over what?" I asked.

"What she was trying to do. She threatened to report my affair with a student."

"Grace?" I asked.

Luzon nodded.

"Grace!" Honi said under her breath.

Luzon ignored her. "Mala said she was going to go to the administration," he continued. "They'd already told me that I had the post. I knew they were ready to make the public announcement. She wanted to derail my promotion, wanted to be chair of the department herself. Mala had a mean streak in her; believe me. She wasn't all sweetness and light. I tried to reason with her, but she just laughed away anything I said. She wanted me to take myself out of the running for the chairmanship and recommend her instead. I refused. That's when she—well, that's when she took a few steps back and the edge gave way and she lost her balance. I saw her arms fly up in the air. She shouted something, but there were these birds. I couldn't hear what she said."

"What happened next?"

"She grabbed for a bush, but the branch broke. I'm ashamed to say I didn't reach out to try to save her. I was afraid I'd go over the edge, too. Afterward, I was in shock. She was gone. It was an accident, pure and simple. I never touched her, never pushed her. I swear it."

I was certain that my thoughts mirrored what Mike and Tahaki were thinking, that there was no evidence to prove that Luzon had been instrumental in Mala's death, that he'd ever laid a hand on her. It was his word against his wife's. The defense would paint Honi as a bitter, angry woman whose husband had cheated on her multiple times and who was out for revenge. They would both go free.

"What did you do after she fell?" I asked.

"I panicked," he said. "I left."

"You didn't try to help her?"

"I didn't think anyone could survive that fall."

"If you were innocent, why didn't you call the police?"

"I wasn't thinking clearly. I just wanted to get away."

"You didn't see your wife?"

"No, I never saw her."

"I hid behind the bush until he was gone," Honi said.

"You never tried to determine if Mala was still alive?" I asked.

"No," Luzon said.

"I did," Honi called out.

Mike turned to her. "What did you do, Mrs. Luzon?"

She slowly approached.

"I came here where she had gone over the edge and pulled myself onto this rock." She climbed up to the spot where Mike had looked down the cliff the morning after Mala had been found. "I saw her body on the rocks below."

"How long did you stay?"

"I don't know, a few minutes, maybe longer. I looked around to see whether anyone else had witnessed what I'd seen. It was dark. No one could see anything. That's when I left. I went home and was in bed when Abbott arrived an hour later." She hopped down from the rock and dusted her hands.

"Where had you gone?" Mike asked Luzon.

"I didn't want to go home yet. I went to the bar to get a drink."

And met up with Grace, I thought, remembering Bob Lowell's story about seeing them together. "Mrs. Luzon, did you ever consider going to the police to report what you'd seen?" I asked.

"I considered it," she said, "but I decided not to. Frankly, I wasn't sorry that Mala had died, and I wasn't about to send my husband, as despicable as he is, to prison while I ended up struggling for the rest of my life."

"Did your husband know that you'd witnessed what you claim happened?" I asked.

"'*Claim* happened'? Are you suggesting that I'm lying?"

"Did he know?" I repeated.

"He knew—because I told him. He denied having pushed her, of course, but I thought perhaps it would be useful to hold it over his head. I had the ridiculous notion that it would straighten him out, that it would curb his infidelity. It didn't, of course. Ask Grace Latimer." She snarled as she said Grace's name.

"Be careful, Honi," Luzon said.

"Why should she be careful, Professor?" I asked. "Is it because this has just been an elaborate story the two of you concocted to protect each other, to cover up a murder?" I turned toward Honi. "*You* pushed Mala over the edge, didn't you, Mrs. Luzon? You thought Abbott and Mala were having an affair, but they weren't. Mala had higher standards than to have an affair with your husband."

"Higher standards! You think that superannuated surfer dude she hung around with was an example of higher standards?" Luzon said.

"I wondered where Grace learned that term. That's what she called Mala's friend."

"Grace again!" Honi muttered. She shook her head. "Can't believe it. It's never enough."

"Honi, be quiet. Our lawyer will take it from here," Luzon said angrily. "You think you're so smart, Mrs. Fletcher, but it's all speculation. You have no proof."

"Ah, but we do, Professor. There was someone who saw Honi push Mala over the cliff. A little boy who lives over there." I pointed to Koko's house. "And, Honi, you knew that there was a witness. In fact, you came to the house to find him, but when Koko saw you, he hid in his room, crying, and refused to come out. And when he saw you again yesterday, he was so scared, he was afraid to stay home, and hid in his father's car."

"I can't believe it's still Grace," Honi ground out.

"Honi, that's enough." Her husband put out an arm toward her. "We'll be fine."

Honi turned to her husband and let out what could only be described as a growl. "Fine! You think that we can be fine as long as Grace is still around? I should have killed her, too. This is for Grace," she shouted as she shoved her husband in the chest. Luzon stumbled backward, arms reaching out to grab something, anything. Tahaki, Mike, and I rushed forward, but before we could reach him the soft earth beneath Luzon's feet gave way. He bellowed as he fell, tumbling down headfirst, sending a flock of francolins screeching into the brilliant blue Hawaiian sky.

Chapter Twenty-three

***Aloha*—Hawaiian Greeting That Can Mean "Good-bye"**

Did Abbott Luzon's serial infidelities drive his wife to kill Mala Kapule in the mistaken belief that she was yet another of his lovers? He must have recognized some culpability on his part when he agreed to help Honi cover up her actions by accusing each other of the crime.

And was the professor guilty of deliberately sabotaging his colleague's chances for the chairmanship as Dale had suggested? Was that what Mala accused him of the night she died? If so, he paid dearly for his underhanded actions. And if he hadn't tried to damage Mala's reputation—well, he suffered a severe penalty for his adulterous conduct, compliments of the heels of Honi's hands.

I was convinced early on that if Mala had been killed by someone, it had its genesis in the controversy over the building of the solar telescope on Haleakala, that magnificent

274

landscape that plays such an important role in Maui's culture and belief system. As it turned out, more basic human motives were involved.

I must admit that certain aspects of Mala's life tainted my perception of this young woman whom I had admired so much both before and after arriving on Maui. But was I allowing circumstantial evidence to influence me? Dale had thought she and the professor were having an affair, but he'd seen only one side of their correspondence. According to Luzon, Mala was using his unfaithfulness to blackmail him in order to secure the post of chair of the department for herself. We'll never know the truth because neither party is alive.

And was the money Mala received from the Oregon construction company used to delay the lucrative Haleakala contract only for the purpose of allowing Douglas Fir Engineering to push Cale Witherspoon's firm out of the way? Had her efforts to throw roadblocks in Witherspoon's way been to benefit herself and not the Hawaiian people who opposed the project? And was Christian Barlow telling the truth when he said it was his idea alone to drive me off the side of the road leading down from Haleakala? I hoped so, because I'd decided not to press charges against him.

Unanswered questions leave me frustrated. I love a clean resolution, which certainly wasn't the case with the cast of characters surrounding Mala Kapule.

There was, of course, one certainty, and that was that Honi Luzon had killed Mala and had pushed her husband to his death, both times in front of witnesses, even if the witness to the first murder was too young to testify. It was hard to feel sorry for Honi. She was such an unpleasant woman. But had she always been so? Her husband had subjected her to years of mental abuse thanks to his unchecked libido. Never having experienced such a situation, I could only speculate about how deleterious an effect it would have on her—have on any woman, for that matter.

"Will she be charged with murder?" I asked Mike Kane after dinner at his house that evening.

His wife, Lani, had insisted that I join them, and I was happy to oblige. After the upsetting events of the day, it was comforting to be with a normal functioning family. I arrived with several of my books to inscribe to Mike and Lani, and found what I hoped was the perfect gift for her, a small mounted photograph of sunrise over Haleakala by the same photographer whose work I had bought for myself. Lani was delighted, or at least she said she was.

"You know, I've never been up there at sunrise," she said. "Mike, now that you're retired, you'll have to take me."

"I will as long as you promise not to ride down on a bicycle."

We all laughed.

"My guess is that Honi will go away for a long time," Mike said when we got around to the events of the day. "Her defense lawyers might plead temporary insanity, you know, having been pushed over the edge by him." Mike smiled. "'Pushed over the edge.' Sounds like I'm making a joke. I'm not."

"I didn't take it that way," I said, "but insanity pleas seldom succeed, and how could she claim *temporary* insanity twice?"

"She snapped; that's for sure. Maybe a jury will see it that way and cut her some slack."

Before Mike drove me to my hotel, Lani draped a lei around my neck that she'd made just for me. "So you'll always remember us and Maui."

"I don't see how I can forget."

I would see Mike Kane one more time before returning to Cabot Cove. We were scheduled on Saturday to teach one more class to young Maui police officers. After a wonderful night's sleep, I arrived at the college early and sat outside the horticulture building basking in the sunshine and pristine air and watching the parade of people passing by. One of them was Grace Latimer.

"Good morning, Grace," I said.

She stopped, turned, and said, "Oh, hello, Mrs. Fletcher. I didn't expect to see you again."

"It'll be the last time," I said. "I'm teaching a final class this morning with Detective Kane."

She said nothing.

"Grace," I said, "I'm sorry for what's happened to Mala and Professor Luzon. I know that you were close to him and—"

A torrent of tears interrupted what I was saying.

She embarrassedly looked around as she pulled tissues from her pocket and dabbed at her eyes.

"We were in love," she said.

"You and Professor Luzon?"

"Yes. He was going to marry me once he divorced his wife, and we were going to start a company together. I can't believe that he's gone, that that dreadful woman he was married to pushed him off a cliff. Mala, too. She'd threatened him with exposing our relationship so that she could become chair of the department."

"That's what Professor Luzon told you," I said.

"Yes. He told me everything. There were no secrets between us."

"May I offer you a piece of advice?" I said.

She looked quizzically at me.

"First," I said, "I wouldn't believe everything Professor Luzon claimed. But more important, Grace, you're an intelligent, attractive young woman with a fine future ahead of you. Becoming involved with a married man is never a smart thing and almost always leads to heartbreak. I know that his death represents a loss for you, but it also frees you to find a better path in your life."

What had been a pathetically sad, tearstained face morphed into an angry expression.

"You don't understand," she said. "You're too old to feel the way Abbott made me feel, that I was the most important person in his life, his first true love."

"Perhaps you're right," I said as Mike Kane came around the corner and waved as he approached. "I wish you everything good in your life, Grace."

She walked away as Mike arrived.

"The professor's graduate assistant?" he said.

"Yes," I said. "She's very young, and very foolish." I brightened. "Ready to impart more wisdom to a class of future Mike Kanes?"

* * *

I never had a chance to touch base again with the people I'd met while on Maui—Charlie Reed; Elijah Kapule; Auntie Edie; Cale Witherspoon; Carson Nihipali; Dale Mossman; and especially Koko, the precious little boy who'd run away, afraid of the lady he'd seen on the cliff where someone had died. I just hoped that he would eventually put it out of his young mind. How successful he would be depended a great deal on his father.

I flew home the next day, stopping in Boston and transferring to a small plane flown by Jed Richardson, our local airport manager, who delivered me to Cabot Cove. Seth Hazlitt was waiting.

"*Aloha*," I said as I settled into the passenger seat of Seth's car.

"Speaking Hawaiian now, I see," he said.

"That's about the extent of my knowledge." I said, laughing.

"Good trip?"

"Mostly."

"Shame what happened to Mala Kapule. Barrett would be devastated."

"Yes, it was a tragedy, Seth, but not the only one."

"Oh?"

"It's a long story, my friend. Give me a few days at home and I'll be happy to tell you the whole unfortunate tale."

"And I'll look forward to hearing it, Jessica. Do you need to stop at the market on your way home?"

"Only if they have pineapple iced tea, which I have a hunch they may not. No, Seth, I'm ready to go home."

*   *   *

I kept in touch with Mike Kane and his family. He told me that the telescope project was going forward, although there was an ongoing battle between competing construction companies. It certainly wasn't my battle, although I admit to rooting against the arrogant Cale Witherspoon.

I'd given Bob and Elaine Lowell my e-mail address and received what seemed like a daily message from the ebullient Bob. But then one arrived from his wife. Bob had been jitter-bugging enthusiastically with a young woman at a party when he collapsed, the victim of a massive heart attack. The news saddened me. Although he wasn't the sort of fellow I aspired to spend lots of time with, he was a good and decent man who loved life and all that it offered. I sent my condolences.

The photograph I purchased of the sea turtle, or *honu*, is proudly displayed in my home office, reminding me of the Pacific Ocean and the beautiful island of Maui. I hoped that the telescope being erected on Haleakala wouldn't in any way spoil its remarkable beauty and meaning to the people of Hawaii.

For me, the trip to Maui had been eye-opening, to say the least. I wished it had gone as planned: teaching courses to young Maui police recruits and using my downtime to relax and explore the island, its rich customs, and its loving people. But although I may have missed some of its more typical attractions, I think I experienced much more than the average tourist. And whenever I worry that things are not going quite right, I pick up my lava stone inscribed with a circle and two dots, and I imagine that the goddess Uli is watching out for me.